Smooth As Whiskey

LYRA PARISH

OFFICIAL PLAYLIST

Cruel Summer - Taylor Swift
Whiskey Glasses - Morgan Wallen
Too Sweet - Hozier
Down Bad - Taylor Swift
Lose Control - Teddy Swims
Curiosity - Bryce Savage
High - Stephen Sanchez
Tennessee Whiskey - Chris Stapleton
Beautiful Things - Benson Boone
Last Night - Morgan Wallen
invisible string - Taylor Swift
What My World Spins Around - Jordan Davis
Better Together - Jack Johnson

LISTEN TO THIS PLAYLIST:
https://bit.ly/smoothaswhiskeyplaylist

MEET THE VALENTINES

Beckett Valentine
Kinsley Valentine
Harrison Valentine
Remington Valentine
Colt Valentine
Fenix Valentine
Emmett Valentine
London Valentine
Sterling Valentine
Vera Valentine

in order from oldest to youngest

**Each book in the Valentine Texas Series
is a stand-alone with rom-com vibes and
a Happily Ever After.**

To the book girlies who still wish upon stars.
Next time you get two.
It's just how the wish distribution system works.

Wishing it is half the battle.

AND ISN'T IT JUST SO PRETTY TO THINK
ALL ALONG THERE WAS SOME
INVISIBLE STRING TYING YOU TO ME?

—*TAYLOR SWIFT*
INVISIBLE STRING

CHAPTER ONE

CASH

"You may now kiss your bride."

My best friend Beckett wraps his arm around his beautiful wife, Summer, and their lips desperately crash together. Love and happiness radiate from them.

I smile and glance at Remi Valentine, Beckett's *younger* sister, and our eyes lock. She wears a lilac bridesmaid dress that clings to her body like a second skin and holds a bouquet of bright-colored wildflowers close to her chest. Her long brown hair frames her pretty face, and she smiles in awe for her big brother.

She's fucking mesmerizing.

We're lost in the moment, in the *could be*. The air hangs heavy with unspoken words, and Remi's breath hitches in response.

What I'd do to kiss her like this, to claim her as mine in front of a hundred people without consequence.

As we stare at one another, the world around us slows to a crawl, and it's just us, suspended in time, making wishes that can't and won't come true. Weddings remind me of what I can't have—*her*.

The intensity threatens to consume us both, so I force my attention away from Remi and return it to the newlyweds.

When Beckett and Summer release their embrace, the guests stand and erupt into thunderous applause.

"Ladies and gentlemen, I'm pleased to officially introduce you to Mr. and Mrs. Beckett Valentine."

On cue, the exit music plays, and Summer and Beckett glide down the makeshift aisle adorned with silk material and rose petals. As they pass, confetti showers them like a gentle rain. They laugh, steal another kiss, and the wedding party follows behind them.

Once the group is out of sight, I speak directly into the microphone still attached to my lapel. All heads turn toward me. "Hi, everyone. The Valentines would like to invite you for finger foods, adult beverages, and dancing in the barn. There will be cake too. The lit trail will guide the way," I say, pointing in that direction.

As I look around and notice the happy couples, regret takes hold.

I blame my obsession with becoming one of the best equestrian vets in Texas. Many warned me this would happen if I continued to chase success, and they were right. I'm 33 years old, going on 34, and single but *somehow* also taken. It's complicated, but I gave my heart away nearly seven years ago.

I scan the crowd, and as I do, I find Christine, the woman I invited to be my plus-one for the occasion. She waves her hand to grab my attention. A herd of people surround her as she steps to the trail's edge, and she points toward the barn. I can't hear what she says between the music and the chatter, but I get the gist—she'll meet me there—so I give her a thumbs-up.

I remove my microphone and hand it to Grace Valentine. She married Beckett's brother, Harrison, and organized the wedding. Tonight, she's the one in charge and calls all the shots.

"How's everything going?" I ask as she glances down at her long checklist.

"As planned, how I like it. You did great, as always," Grace says with a smile. I officiated for her and Harrison last month. "Have fun with your date."

She glances up at me with confusion but doesn't continue. They were roommates for almost six months.

Somehow, I knew she'd notice.

"Yeah, thanks," I say as she moves to complete the next task on her list. She speaks into a handheld radio as she rounds the large house.

When I arrived with Christine, all heads turned. I expect rumors about my *new girlfriend* will spread around town before the rooster crows tomorrow, which is perfect. I've always heard the saying that when you play stupid games, you win stupid prizes, and I'm okay with that. I'll do whatever it takes to get what I want, even if that means creating false narratives.

After the group photos, the wedding party goes their separate ways. As Beckett and Summer walk onto the back porch, I smile and greet them. It's the first time I've caught them alone since the rehearsal dinner a few days ago. When I'm within reach, Beckett pulls me into a brotherly hug.

"Congratulations," I say, with my arm wrapped around him. We forged our friendship in the fires of childhood and created a bond that's as thick as blood. Tonight, I stood beside him, not just as his best friend, but as the officiant of his union with the love of his life—Ms. Summer Jones. Excuse me, *Mrs. Summer Valentine*.

"Thank you for everything." Beckett's voice quivers with gratitude, his happiness is palpable as country music drifts in the distance through the late spring air. The party started fifteen minutes ago, but I can tell it's gonna be a rowdy one.

"It's an honor," I admit as we let go of one another.

He's entered a new era of adulthood that includes a

spouse, and eventually kids, and too many animals. Beckett is proof that our lives are changing and we're growing older.

When did we become adults?

"You're both living your dreams," I say proudly, pulling Summer into a heartfelt hug. My best friend has crushed on her since we were teenagers. Nothing makes me happier than seeing them like this.

"Thanks, Cash," she says, her voice filled with genuine appreciation as she squeezes me. "You're pro-level at being an officiant."

"I'm well-practiced," I admit as we release our embrace.

This is my twenty-fifth wedding to officiate. I became ordained as a fucking joke in college, and years later, the joke is on me. Now, I'm always marrying people and never the one saying "I do". Ironic.

"Make sure to enjoy the night," I remind them. "You only get married once."

Summer giggles. "That better be the case."

"I'm never letting you go, SumSum," Beckett says, capturing her lips. Summer playfully swats at him for calling her the nickname he often uses to tease her.

They're so damn happy that it's contagious.

I can only imagine what it's like to have everything—the perfect job, great friends, and a relationship worth risking it all for. It's the trifecta that I've chased for years, that I'm still chasing.

The photographer snaps candid photos of us laughing. The flashes nearly blind me, but I'm a good sport and pretend like she's not there. It will be a fun memory to look back on when we're old and gray.

When Beckett and Summer's parents steal their attention, I step away, giving them space, and look out at the pasture. Training horses graze in the distance as the sun sets below the horizon. I check my watch, knowing this shindig will only last a few hours.

As I turn my head, I see Remi enter the bed and breakfast. I should go to the reception and find Christine, but instead, I tuck my hands into my suit pockets and move inside the farmhouse like I'm chasing the white rabbit. It's reckless, considering most know how that went for Alice in Wonderland.

Her heels click against the hardwood floor, and she stops walking when the screen door closes. When I round the corner, she stands with her arms over her chest at the bottom of the stairs that lead to the top floor. Remi's blue eyes claw into me, taking hold, pinning me in place.

"Are you following me?" Her eyes flick down my body, then back up to my mouth as she eye fucks me. She did the same during the ceremony, and I nearly forgot what I was saying.

I smirk. "No."

"*Liar*," she whispers, stepping closer. "Shouldn't you be with your date?"

I gently reach for her elbow, brushing my thumb against her soft skin. "Is that *jealousy* I sense?"

I love that she wants to keep me to herself, even if she doesn't admit it.

She lets out a humph and presses her pouty red lips together like a pure fucking temptation.

"You didn't answer the question," I mutter, wishing I could worship her how she deserves, how she craves.

I study her, never able to get enough of how damn gorgeous she is with her cute button nose and freckles that sprinkle across her cheeks. I've spent hours swimming in her deep blue eyes, the ones that see straight through me.

"Reverse the roles. Had I invited an attractive man to be attached to my side, how would you feel?" she asks.

I couldn't handle it. However, when it comes to her, my stance has never changed.

"We're friends, and she knows I'm unavailable. *Everyone* knows I'm unavailable," I say truthfully, not wanting her to agonize. "I brought her as a conversation starter and because she was bored. Trust me, Rem."

She moves toward me, removing the space between us. "You're the *only* person I *ever* let call me that."

I place my hand on her cheek, brushing my thumb across her bottom lip, wanting to cross the line.

"Fuck," I hiss, knowing I can't kiss her. To be clear, I fucking *want* to. I always want to.

"We agreed we wouldn't do this," I whisper against her mouth as she nearly begs me to make the first move.

"You're right," she says like she's fighting the urge.

We're at a stalemate knowing that if we open Pandora's box again, we'll never close it.

We last kissed at her brother Harrison's wedding a month ago. That night, we couldn't keep our eyes off each other, and it came to a headway in her old bedroom. Things got out of hand; we were desperate and messy, and I nearly fucked her on her childhood bed as everyone drank sparkling champagne in her parents' backyard. We called it quits before we went too far.

Just because we're not fooling around doesn't mean she's not my guilty pleasure. She is.

We're right back to where we were, listening to heartfelt vows, knowing we could have that together but can't pursue it. The thought wounds me.

"I'm sorry," I whisper, studying her. I shove my hands into my pockets and create space. The brain fog she puts me in slightly fades.

"It's the right call," she says, understanding I'm a forbidden fruit. Beckett has always told his sisters that I was off-limits. Remi was a boundary I never intended to cross.

Now that I'm back in Valentine, I've returned to the same place I was seven years ago—wedged tightly between giving myself to a woman I could spend the rest of my life with and carrying the guilt of losing my best friend. Either way, I'm fucked. In this scenario, I don't win.

"Did you decide on my offer?" she finally asks.

"Becoming roommates is a bad idea," I admit. It's difficult to deny her when she looks at me like that. She controls our destiny, and I happily allow her to play puppet master, but living together is too risky. We'd grow too comfortable secretly playing house, and it'd become messy. At some point, pretending would be impossible for me. Would it be for her?

"We'll make rules. You need a place. I need a roommate to help me finish out my lease. We work two different schedules, so it's not like we'd be home at the same time. It's the perfect situation."

"For disaster." I cross my arms over my chest, knowing better.

The silence draws on, but I can read her mind. And because she's a stubborn Valentine, she will push the topic. It's in their nature.

"Harrison is paying half my rent because he stole Grace from me. Beckett is the only one who needs convincing, and I've already put a bug in his ear about this, so who knows, he could become receptive. Miracles happen daily."

"It's unrealistic. You and I are hardly friends publicly," I remind her, testing her just a tad to see where she really stands.

"That's for appearances." She grabs my hand, pulling me back to her. "I want to see you more."

"Maybe I'll tell everyone our truth so we can stop playing games."

She wraps her arms around me, peppering soft kisses against my neck. "We can't. But what happens behind closed doors can stay there."

I constantly crave her closeness.

"You're *my* Valentine, Rem," I whisper, wanting her to

understand this isn't a game or a summer fling. When we're together, it's overpowering, intoxicating.

Our relationship is a secret that she'll carry to the grave if that's what it takes to continue seeing me.

"I've missed you," she admits.

It's been weeks since I saw Remi. Her asking me to move in replays in my mind like a hazy dream that I've relived over and over. We were in her old bedroom, she nearly begged me. I couldn't answer and told her I needed time.

"I've missed you, too." I rest my hands on her shoulders, threading my fingers through her silky hair, holding her against me.

She inhales me and sighs. Her phone vibrates, and she pulls it from a pocket in her dress. With hesitation, she backs away from me. "I've gotta go. Have fun with your date. I'll start my search for another roommate."

"Rem," I say. "It's a *big* decision that shouldn't be taken lightly."

"I understand. I just thought we could have time together. It was stupid. Let's forget it," Remi says, taking the stairs to the top floor of the B&B. When she glances over her shoulder—watching me watch her—I wish she understood she's the *only* woman I've *ever* wanted. I'd do anything for her.

"Promise me you'll consider it."

"I will," I say.

I *have*.

Moving in with her would be a dream come true, but it's a selfish decision. I need a sign, something to tell me to move forward because if it doesn't work out, I'll lose *everything*.

If Beckett and her other brothers—Harrison, Colton, Emmett, and Sterling—learn the truth, they will hunt me down. They're overprotective wolves who run in a pack and will attack.

I watch her until she's out of sight, then leave the bed and breakfast.

As I suck in fresh air, I stare at the Zodiacal lights, wishing things were different.

Could they be?

As I take the gravel road to the barn, my boots kick up dust. It's a longer route, but I need time to clear my mind because it's a tangled mess. Being around Remi does that to me. She's poison in my veins, and I'm without an antidote.

Laughter and music drift from the structure, and when I enter through the oversized entryway, I catch glimpses of so many happy people. There isn't a face without a smile.

The Heartbreakers, London Valentine's band, plays *The Way You Look Tonight.* Beckett and Summer are in the center of the room, dancing.

Moments like this remind me why I returned to Valentine.

And damn, it's really good to be home.

CHAPTER TWO

REMI

I go upstairs to the room I used before the ceremony to change shoes so my feet don't kill me tomorrow. I close the door and press my back against the cool wood. With my eyes closed, I wish for my heart to stop pounding so hard.

Being with Cash may be wrong, but like a moth to a flame, we fly directly toward the thing that will destroy us—each other.

I almost lost control.

I almost kissed him again.

I don't know what we're doing anymore and haven't since he tumbled back into my life four and a half months ago. When Cash moved back to Valentine, I knew I wouldn't be able to avoid him. I couldn't. I still can't.

We'd fallen back to where we were when he left the first time. It felt like seconds had passed, not nearly seven years. Now we're older, and the world has made us harder, but the electricity still streams between us, keeping us hostage and tethered to one another. It's a bond that can't be broken; I've tried. The current of him constantly pulls me under. Now I'm stuck wishing we could be together, knowing and understanding we can't.

Or can we?

If Cash and I dated and broke up, it would ruin his friendship with Beckett, especially if he did the breaking. My brother would *never* forgive him for hurting me.

I knew that when *I* pursued Cash all those years ago. It's why the secrets of our past should stay hidden and out of sight. I've already come to terms with this man being the end of me.

Once my heart rate settles, I run my fingers through my long hair, reapply my lipstick, and walk to the barn. The stars are out and the crickets chirp while music drifts in the breeze.

A meteor skims across the sky leaving a trail of glitter and green smoke in its wake. I make a wish upon a star, desperately hoping it comes true.

When I enter the barn through the back, I glance around, loving how Grace decorated the place with rustic lanterns and colorful bouquets of wildflowers.

I spot Haley Shaw at the front of the wine line and go to her. She's one of my best friends and the co-founder of our single girls club. We're sharing the presidency and are the only members in town.

"There you are," she says, finally noticing me beside her. "I texted you twenty minutes ago. Where have ya been?"

I smile. "Sorry, I needed a breather."

"Ah." She nods her head toward Cash and his date. "Because of that?"

The bartender fills two plastic cups with Chardonnay, and we grab them. I'm tempted to chug it, but the last thing I need is a hangover.

"Who is she?" she whispers.

I shrug. "Not sure."

Moments later, my twin brother Colt stands beside me, sipping a beer. "I didn't know Cash knew Christine."

No reaction is best.

"So, her name is Christine. That's good information to have," Haley says, butting into our conversation.

"She's the tenant in my rent house outside of town. I told you she moved in two weeks ago, sis."

"More good info to have," Haley adds.

"Oh yeah, I forgot." I realize I'm staring.

I've been a hermit lately and isolated more than not, but I've also worked the night shift at the B&B. I'm on no one's schedule but my own. When I'm crawling into bed, most are waking up to start their days. I'm living in my vampire era.

"You *want* to know more about her," he mutters, smirking. My twin brother thinks he knows it all.

"Why would I care?"

Cash said they were friends, and I believe him. That man would never lie to me and I know that to be true.

My eyes move from Christine to him smiling at her. She's beautiful with olive skin and a short, sophisticated bob. They're two attractive humans who are close in age, and their relationship is believable. She would never be mistaken as his younger sister.

Cash looks incredible in that black suit and tie. His dark brown hair sits in messy waves, and his hazel eyes sparkle under the glowing light. Sometimes, they look blue, and other times, they look green or gray. I used to joke that they'd change colors with his mood.

He leans in and whispers something in her ear, and a pang of jealousy courses through me. Even if it's fake, it should be me standing close to him, but as usual, my insecurities get in the way.

The rumors about them will spread, and hopefully, it will buy *us* some time. No one will wonder about our status if we're seen together if Cash is openly with someone else. I can slide right back into the best friend's younger sister role that I've always played.

I know the truth though.

We're in one another's orbit just as we were that summer we spent together, but this time, it's different. This is our retrograde, our second chance, and it's almost like we're traveling back in time to fix what we broke—each other.

I'm no longer a naive twenty-year-old with a stupid crush on an older man. I've been through some shit and had a job that nearly destroyed the essence of who I was. I've lost and found myself again, twice. This time, I'll do the hard things that younger me wouldn't consider. This time will be different.

I double down on the big lie. "I heard they were into one another," I say, totally okay with adding fuel to the fire. Sometimes, I regret not being honest. Could the truth set us free?

"That's *great*," he sarcastically says as Harrison waves him over. "Anyway, have fun tonight."

"You, too," I tell him, happy that conversation is over. As he walks away, I notice how buff he has gotten from renovating houses.

Haley and I are left to ourselves. "Did Cash ever tell you his answer about moving in?"

"I doubt he'll take my offer. It's too bad he'd have made the perfect roommate."

She gives me a sad look. "Yeah, hm. I don't understand that man. But I guess it's probably best. Your brothers would've shit a brick."

I shrug. "I can live with whoever I want."

And I want it to be him.

"No, you can't," she laughs. "My brother isn't as scary as yours, and I know Hayden would never allow it."

"You have no idea how lucky you are that you only have to

deal with one terror," I tell her, then spot Grace walking toward us.

"I think I do," Haley says as we smile at Grace.

Taken looks amazing on Grace. She's practically glowing and has been since she married Harrison. They were childhood besties, and everyone thought they'd end up as a couple until my brother proposed to another woman. It was drama.

She approaches us wearing a pretty pink dress tied tight at her waist. It accentuates her curvy figure.

"You're not welcome here," I joke with a grin. "This is the singles' corner."

The two of us became fast friends when we lived together, and now that she moved out of our condo last month, I barely see her.

She playfully rolls her eyes.

The overhead lights lower, and when London sings the first line of *The Way You Look Tonight*, several large disco balls spin and paint the crowd with silver reflections.

"Who is he with?" Grace whispers. She doesn't have to be specific. I know who she's referring to.

She nearly caught us together one night and if she wouldn't have come home, we would've had sex. Our clothes were spread on the floor of the condo because I hadn't expected her to come home.

She's kept my secrets, just as she kept my brother's. I trust her and know she wouldn't do anything to ruin this for me. In a way, I think she understands what it's like to want someone so fucking bad and not have them. It's the foundation of her and Harrison.

"His date," Haley answers because I am too busy staring at Cash. I'd forgotten the question.

When I glance at Haley, she's staring toward the opposite side of the room where my brother Emmett is.

Grace's attention turns to Haley. "Wait."

Haley has been obsessed with Emmet after their meet-cute last month. She had a flat in her Bronco and he stopped to help her.

"Don't ask. You'll never escape the conversation," I say. To be honest, I think Emmett will break her heart. He's quiet, but a total fuck boy thirst trap. I'm unsure what's going on in his world or if the woman hanging on his arm is his girlfriend. I've told Haley I'll gather information so we'll know if he's available or not. The least I can do is help, even if I think she can do better.

Haley chuckles. "She's right. We'll have to plan a coffee chat soon and catch up since you've been so ocupado."

Grace shrugs. She's barely come up for air after marrying Harrison. "What can I say? Gotta lot of years of denial to make up for."

Harrison grabs the microphone and taps it. "Wow, it seems like we were together not too long ago."

Many of the same people who celebrated their prenuptials are here to congratulate Beckett and Summer, too.

Harrison clears his throat. "So, I wanted to give this speech about all the embarrassing things my brother has done over the years, but *my wife*, the only voice of reason I listen to…"

Grace places her hands over her mouth and yells. "That's right, baby!"

Everyone laughs.

"Well, she said it was a stupid idea. So, I'll say this. Beckett, my brother, one of my best friends in the whole world, I'm so happy that you were able to marry the love of your life and didn't end up like a hermit who collects horses like we all thought." He meets Summer's eyes and laughs and the crowd joins in. "I'm glad you found someone who won't put up with your shit and isn't afraid to call you out."

Grace clears her throat, and Harrison roars with laughter.

His best friend is the only one who can reel him in. We've all tried.

"Right." He raises his glass. "I'm so happy to welcome you to the family, Summer. You're my favorite sister-in-law. And if Beckett ever hurts you, me and the rest of my brothers will kick his ass for you."

My older sister, Kinsley, yells. "Me too!"

"Love y'all. Truly happy for you."

The room roars with applause, and I watch Cash cross the room. When he glances up at me, I tuck my lips into my mouth, trying not to smile. When he shoots me a wink, I turn my head. He's playing with fire as Harrison hands him the microphone. Confidence oozes off of him, and he smirks.

"Damn, *Valentine*. You're looking gorgeous tonight," he says, meeting my gaze. I know he's talking *to* me. It's our little secret, a nickname he uses just for me. However, everyone in the room believes he's referring to the townsfolk. Valentine, Texas, was founded by my family over a century ago.

Cash clears his throat. "What can I say about these two who were always meant to be together? Like my other brother Harrison, I thought deeply about what I would say about Beckett in front of a room of people. The stories I could tell, the shenanigans we used to get into, wow. That's not appropriate for our parents to hear though." He waves at my folks, who adore him. "Beckett is like a brother, my longest friend, who deserves true happiness and love like this. For as long as I can remember, Summer was always the brightness in his sky, but she was also off-limits. He agonized over it because it's difficult to want to be with someone who's best friends with one of your siblings. There's always risk involved with that."

His eyes meet mine, and I'm glad the room is dark. That way, no one can see the blush that hits my cheeks as I read between the lines. Cash makes butterflies swarm me.

"But everyone knows, the Valentines don't ever play by the

rules, especially when it comes to love. It's obvious when two people are meant to be together, and when I look at *you*, there are no doubts about it."

I swallow hard. He's fierce as he plays with fire.

"Summer and Beckett, I'm so happy for you and thrilled that you were able to find yourselves in one another. You make me believe love exists and that maybe I'll have a chance, especially after one of the biggest assholes in the state found their someone." He chuckles. "Love y'all. I wish you a life full of happiness and laughter and horses. Congratulations! And Summer, if Beckett ever needs an ass-kicking, I'll add my name to the list, too. Cheers."

I finish my wine and clap when he's finished. Kinsley steps forward.

"Wow. What a hard act to follow, but you know what they say: always save the best for last. Unlike the two gentlemen before me, I didn't have to think about what I would say today. Summer once told me that she wouldn't hook up with Beckett if she were the last woman on earth and it was up to her to rescue the human race."

I glance at my brother, and he actually looks offended but then laughs.

"Oh, wait, she said she would if we taped his mouth closed."

Summer howls with laughter, and so does everyone else in the barn, even Beckett. He wraps his arm around her and kisses her.

"However, I always knew that they would be together, and I'd like to take full credit for the manifesting and matchmaking I did to make it happen. With all jokes aside, I want to say that I love you both so much, and I love seeing you over the moon. I've always wanted the absolute best for my big brother, and the same goes for my best friend. If anyone is still asking themselves if Beckett and Summer are perfect for one another...the answer is yes. I know when two people are made to be together." My sister glances at Cash who stands to the side of her then she looks at me. "And you are."

Then Cash and I lock on to one another from across the room. The silent conversation begs me closer to him, but I keep my feet planted.

Kinsley was clearly talking about us.

I know it. He knows it. And so does she.

Pulling my gaze from his isn't something I can always do when I'm under his spell, but somehow I manage.

Kinsley laughs. "Anyway. Congratulations. Now, please make me an aunt sooner rather than later," she says with a smile.

My sister's personality is a tight braid of charisma, spice, and woo-woo. She's great at public speaking and commands a room in ways I never could.

I'm the Wednesday Addams of the Valentine family, and everyone knows it. I think that comparison started after Cash left and a piece of me died. Being an introvert, I loved it, and lately I've been leaning into it as I've entered my no fucks to give era.

My eyes slide back over to Cash's, and he gives me a smoldering smile, the one that melts panties.

I wish he'd stop.

"Now, can everyone lift their glasses and celebrate the happy couple? I love y'all."

"Remi," Haley whispers, elbowing me as Cash raises his glass toward me. "Your glass."

"Oh, right," I say, snapping out of my daze for the hundredth time tonight.

Summer gets up and hugs Kinsley. When they shed tears, I put the empty cup to my mouth wishing I had one more sip. I need a refill.

They make me feel like a robot with their emotions or

maybe I really am dead inside. I almost laugh as Grace and Haley follow me to the bar.

As we wait in line, Cash approaches. I look at him like he's got a third eye because we always avoid one another in public settings.

"Hi," he says, his voice lowering as he leads me away from everyone. "Do you have that key?"

I hold back my smile. "You changed your mind?"

"I hadn't made a decision earlier," he says. "I have now."

I pull it from my dress pocket. I kept it on my person, secretly hoping he'd ask me for it even if I thought he wouldn't. He reaches forward, and I place it in his palm. "Move-in date is June first."

"One week. Perfect," Cash says, his gaze lingers then he walks away.

I keep my expression neutral because I don't know who's watching our interaction, then I meet Kinsley's eyes and she smirks before raising her glass upward. An acknowledgment of us, maybe even approval.

Me and Cash's relationship is complicated. We're two tornados creating a path of destruction as we dance because no one saw us coming.

Except Kinsley.

I'm positive my sister knows.

Who else does?

CHAPTER THREE

CASH

I hold the spare key in my hand like it's a golden ticket. Kinsley's words, her knowing when two people should be together as she glanced between Remi and me felt like a sign.

She knows, and it was the nudge I needed.

I drop the key into my pocket and cross the room to Christine. She's laughing with one of the ranch hands named Dustin so I give her space. When he finally walks away, I meet up with her and grin.

"There you are," she says.

"Sorry about that. Got caught up back there." A new song begins, and she sways to the beat. "Would you like to dance?"

"I thought you'd *never* ask," she says, and we move to the middle of the barn.

I place a hand on Christine's hip and we two-step in a clockwise pattern. There are so many wandering eyes. I even catch my girl staring from across the way.

"Is Dustin single?" Christine asks.

I chuckle. "I'm not sure. I thought you weren't interested in dating."

She snickers. "Mainly I'm not interested in dating you. I don't date men who are smarter than me. Ever."

I burst into laughter. "Why?"

"Because all of my exes were."

"Ah. Well, hate to break it to you, but some of the smartest men I've ever met were cowboys. Hard ones, too. The kind who still do week-long cattle drives during branding season. I wouldn't underestimate any of them. They might have shitty grammar but they're smart as a whip."

She smiles at Dustin across the room. "There's just something about him that I like."

"You should go for it."

Beckett and Summer dance close to us.

"Who's this?" Beckett asks. I can tell he's had a lot to drink, but Summer is stone-cold sober. Sometimes, when Beckett drinks, he gets loud; it's a dead giveaway he's heading straight to Wastedville. When that happens, we get the asshole version of him or the prankster.

"This is Christine," I say, and he holds out his hand to shake hers. "She's new to town. Moved into Colt's house a few weeks ago."

"Hi, Christine. Nice to meet ya. This is my wife, Summer. Hope my best friend is showing you a good time and treatin' you well," Beckett offers.

Summer smiles and gives her a nod before glancing at me.

Christine laughs. "Lovely to meet you both. Beautiful wedding. I've had a great time so far. Congratulations on the marriage. You're perfect together."

"Glad to hear it. And thanks," Beckett says, grinning at Summer. His dad cuts into their dance and steals his bride. Beckett finds his way to the beer garden. When the song ends, Christine excuses herself, and I join my best friend.

"This is amazing," he says. His smile doesn't falter.

"It is. I think it's proof dreams can come true."

When we're handed beers, we stand off to the side. Beckett's focused on Summer, who's now dancing with Harrison, who's spinning her around.

He glances at me. "You know, you should think about moving in with Remi."

I nearly choke on my beer. "Excuse me?"

"She could use a roommate and someone around who's empathetic," he says.

"We work two different schedules."

He meets my eyes and we hold a silent conversation. It feels like a push.

"This is a joke," I say, not believing it. I laugh, unable to hold it in. I asked for a sign and tonight I got two.

"Harrison is paying half the rent until Remi finds a replacement, and I know she's not searching. He needs to save money for a house. He has husband responsibilities now."

"Damn," I say, believing I might have the best luck in the world. However, it shouldn't be this easy, not considering I already have the key burning a hole in my pocket. So, I try to play it cool.

"I'm not convinced she'll go for it."

I find Remi across the room chatting with Haley. A smile plays on her lips as she glances at me.

"I'm gonna talk to her for you," Beckett says. "Right *now*."

"Beckett," I whisper, not wanting him to draw any unnecessary attention. When he's confrontational like this, it never ends well. But it's too late, though; he's already across the barn, giving zero fucks as he approaches her. I keep my feet planted, refusing to touch this with a ten-foot pole, but she does look shocked when he gets close.

If there's one thing I've learned about Remi, she can handle herself—especially when it comes to her brothers.

Beckett places a hand on her shoulder. He says something, and her eyes dart toward me. She's as confused as me. Remi's mouth opens, and she shakes her head. Beckett turns and points in my direction, and Remi huffs, making her way across to me.

She grabs my arm and leads me outside. The music leaks from the barn as she moves me around the back, giving us much needed privacy.

"I thought he was about to confront me about us. Shit," she whispers. "I didn't expect him to say that."

"I didn't either," I tell her. "I guess whatever you said to Beckett the other day *worked*."

She smirks, taking a step forward, pushing my back against the cool metal. "I'm supposed to convince you to move in with me right now. My brother's orders."

I grab her hip, tilting my head at her as sparks fly. "Hmm. I think you've had too much to drink. We know how tipsy Remi is."

My eyes darken as I stare at her.

"She gives no fucks," Remi states as I lick my lips, needing to kiss her.

"Convince me then."

The moonlight is bright enough for me to see her staring up at me with a sparkle in her eye.

"Hmm. Maybe I'll beg," she says, grabbing my tie with her fist.

"Don't tempt me with a good *fucking* time, *Valentine*," I mutter.

The sweet scent of her perfume encapsulates me. We should've built an unscalable wall with our boundaries because, after a few drinks, they're gone.

Before we're lost in the moment, she opens her mouth to speak. "We—"

"What are you doing?" Harrison barks with his arms crossed over his chest. He glares at me as Remi takes a step back. I straighten my stance, shoving my hands into my pockets, then I adjust my tie.

I give Harrison a cold look as a dangerous expression meets his face. He saw us, and there's no denying it.

"Considering Beckett volunteered his best friend to be my roommate, we're discussing it," Remi snaps, giving him her fierce attitude. "Don't you have someone else to haunt?"

"Being your what?" Harrison's brows furrow. "Absolutely not. Beckett is drunk out of his mind right now, and you're taking advantage of that. Both of you are."

She turns her entire body toward her brother and pokes her finger into his upper chest. "You *don't* control me, especially after everything I've done for you. This benefits you, too."

"This is not fucking happening," he says in a threatening tone.

Remi stares him down. "Back off, Harrison. My life doesn't concern you, okay? I'm a *big* girl with big girl responsibilities and problems."

He glares at me. There's anger behind his gaze, a silent threat that's heard loud and clear.

Grace comes outside and slides her arm into Harrison's and pulls him toward her. His jaw relaxes as she tears him out of his blind rage.

"What are y'all doing out here?" Grace asks.

"We were chatting about how Cash is becoming my roommate. Beckett's idea," Remi explains with a sweet smile.

Everyone believes she's a delicate flower, but I have her thorns memorized. I love them.

Grace nods and immediately supports it. "That's *perfect* for both of you. Maybe you can spy on Remi for us and share who she's been sneaking around with."

Remi's mouth quirks up. *We* are a joke between them, something they giggle about.

Harrison's nostrils flare with anger.

"The summer months are typically the busiest, so I expect to be living at the office. Doubt I'll be home much anyway," I explain, but I don't think Harrison gives two fucks about that.

"See, it's nothing to be concerned about. And Beckett said you needed to save for a house," Remi says. Her entire demeanor changes, and she's not backing down.

"Exactly," Grace tells him. "Don't be stupid, Harri."

I need to deescalate this situation. "I have to get back to my date."

I walk past them and make my way inside the barn. Christine is now laughing and dancing with Colt while Beckett sits in the front, holding Summer on his lap. They're lost in one another.

Harrison comes up from behind me, placing his hand on my shoulder. "Mess with my little sister, and I'll kick your ass."

I shove his hand off of me and turn to him. "You better check yourself before you wreck yourself. I think you forgot who the fuck you were talking to."

I'm five years older than Harrison. He always followed Beckett and me around when we were teenagers. I've treated him like my little brother, and I'd kick his ass like he was if it's needed.

"Harrison!" Remi says. "Stop. I swear. I'm going to tell Dad."

She's a daddy's girl and could get Harrison in more trouble than he can handle. Before it gets too rowdy, Grace takes Harrison by the hand and leads him away. She glances over her shoulder and whispers, "I'm sorry."

Remi stands next to me, inhaling deeply. Neither of us says a word. I meet her eyes, knowing I'd risk it all for her, but then I force myself away. Right now, we need space. What we did was reckless.

If I'm ever asked about Remi, I won't deny it. Most are too chickenshit for confrontation.

I wait at the edge of the dance floor for Christine, and when the song ends, she finds me. She's all smiles, and I can tell she's having a good time. I'm happy to see it.

"There you are," she says, looking at her watch. "I hate to do this, but I have to leave soon. I have an online meeting with my manager at five in the morning. Stupid time zones."

"No problem," I say as she loops her arm with mine. "Did you get his number?"

"I did," she says, giddy. "Did you take care of what you needed to handle?"

"I did," I say, and I'm beginning to wonder if we're not so transparent. "Actually, what did you mean by that?"

She leans in and whispers in my ear. "You and Remi. That's your secret girlfriend, right?"

I meet her eyes and don't say a word.

She grins. "I knew it. It's written across your forehead."

My brows furrow.

"It's *obvious*."

The lights in the barn brighten, and Beckett and Summer stand behind a chocolate and vanilla-tiered cake. On top is a figurine of them, along with a miniature bed-and-breakfast and a training barn. It's perfectly them.

The photographer stands to the side and snaps a photo of them laughing. They pose next to the cakes and cut tiny slices to feed to one another.

Before Summer, Beckett was miserable and angry at life. Kinda like I am right now.

"Would you like some cake?" I ask Christine.

"No, thanks."

I smile. "Great, we can head out if you're ready."

As I turn to leave, I walk past Remi, and her gaze lingers a second too long. It nearly holds me hostage and pulls me under like quicksand. The way she commands me with a single look is insanity. *Fuck*, it's almost too much as she reaches out and brushes her fingers against mine when I pass.

I don't want to let go as her simple touch steals my breath away.

When I step outside, I realize I'm tense.

"Are you okay?" Christine asks.

"Yeah," I say looking up at the stars, waiting for one to fall so I can make a wish. It doesn't happen.

We walk to my truck, and when we're close, I open the door for her. She climbs in and we leave. As I head toward the country road, the bed and breakfast glows golden in the dark.

The gravel road slightly curves, and I glance at the clinic I built on the Horseshoe Creek Ranch. Beckett and I made an agreement, and I'm leasing five acres of property for one hundred years. It's an agreement that will expire long after we're gone, an offer he made to bring me back home.

I've told him a contract won't keep me here and if I'm meant to leave, I will. It was the risk he took, one that may hover in his mind for a lifetime.

Some days I can't believe that the state-of-the-art facilities are mine. The stables are a dream come true; one I busted my ass for. I've dedicated fifteen years of my life to my profession, but it's also why I'm in my current predicament.

Christine yawns and it steals my attention. "Waking up early for these meetings makes me feel like a grandma. I'm exhausted by eight."

I laugh. "You're right. These days I'm crashing before the sun goes down."

Her house is a few miles outside of town. It's a cute two-bedroom I would've rented from Colt, but he found a tenant right after he posted the listing. Rental property doesn't stay available for long in the area.

"How's Smooches?" I ask. We met when she brought her poodle in for yearly shots. On a different night, she was at Boot Scooting and joined me at the bar. I explained I was seeing someone, and she told me I wasn't her type. We became friends.

"Smooches is great. All day long, she goes in and out of the doggy door. It's like she can't make up her mind."

"That's hilarious."

She grins. "I feel bad for making you leave your best friend's wedding early."

"Nah, don't be. We didn't miss much—the bouquet and garter toss. I'm good on those. In my opinion, it's the most annoying part of a reception."

"Agreed," she says as I pull into her driveway.

"And I have to be up at sunrise, too."

She unbuckles and clicks the side button of her phone to check the time. It's nearly nine. "Are you working on a Sunday?"

I shake my head. "I have a weekly coffee date with an old friend."

"Gotcha. Well, thanks for the invite. That was a lot of fun. Let's have a drink soon."

"Sure, I'd like that," I tell her.

She grabs the door handle, giving me a wave as she climbs out of the truck. With the headlights pointed toward her porch, I wait until she's inside before driving away.

I'm tempted to text Remi, knowing she's still at the wedding, but I don't. We hardly text or call one another, not after she ghosted me years ago.

As I drive out of city limits, I think about moving in with Remi in seven days.

How many days would it take for all boundaries to fall?

Our relationship started nearly seven years ago. Maybe history is repeating itself and this is our second chance at love.

Fuck, I hope it is.

CHAPTER FOUR

REMI

ONE WEEK LATER

My mattress dipping on the side wakes me. I roll over, my eyes fluttering open, and Cash sits on the edge of the bed. The sun shines through the window behind him, and I make out the outline of his baseball hat. It's bright in here, and I'm still half asleep.

It's like I'm imagining him, and if I reach out, he'll disappear. His hazel eyes meet mine, and his lips transform into a sexy grin. The dimples in his cheeks show, and I can't help but smile. He's the best part of waking up.

After losing him once, I treasure these special moments more. I never thought we'd be back here after he left. I'd only hoped our secret love story wasn't over.

"Good mid-morning, my Valentine," he says, his voice as smooth as whiskey. He hands me a large coffee. "For you."

"Are you real?" I ask, sitting up, wondering if I'm still dreaming. I've been counting down to today since I gave him that key last weekend. I remove the lid and blow on it, noticing the color. "Black like my soul."

He chuckles. "You're fucking adorable."

I need to wake up. "What time is it?"

Cash clicks the button on the side of his phone. "Ten. Sorry, you probably didn't get much sleep after your night shift."

"No, I don't mind. I got a solid four hours," I say, yawning, wishing I could pour this caffeine into an IV and insert it into my veins. "I gotta prepare for Beckett and Summer's party at seven."

"Ahh, yes," he says. "Were you threatened with your life if you didn't show up?"

I nod, meeting his gaze, and I love how that smirk plays on his lips. He looks exhausted and stressed though.

"How have you been?" I ask.

"Making it," he says. "Melody, my summer intern, arrived this morning. Gave her a walk-through."

"Yeah? That will be great for you."

"I think so. She graduated and is licensed, so I might hire her full-time if she makes it past a month."

I smile, take a sip of coffee, and watch him over the rim. "Yikes. I hope it works out."

"I'm a hard-ass. But, anyway, I've missed you," he admits.

We haven't seen, texted, or spoken to each other since Beckett's wedding. We're on two different working schedules. Finding a time to be together without getting caught is already tricky enough, but this makes it more challenging. Plus we haven't crossed any lines since Harrison's wedding where I nearly begged for him.

We lost control.

He reaches forward, tucking hair behind my ear, and I grab his wrist. He smells like leather and soap.

Goosebumps trail up and down my arm, and he notices what his touch does to me, what it's always done to me.

"We need house rules," I say.

"You're right."

"I'm not the same person," I explain. "Sometimes I think about all those summers ago and—"

"It feels like a dream?" He meets my gaze.

"Yeah. How'd you know?"

"It's relatable." Cash looks down at his calloused hands. "There are times I have regrets."

"About us?" That was an admission I wasn't expecting.

He glances at me. "Hell no. Regrets about leaving you."

"Please don't do that," I say. "We agreed to be together for a summer. We stuck to the plan and continued forward with our lives."

"True," he states. "But what did we lose in the process? If one path is chosen, another isn't traveled. I often think about the life that we could've had, Rem. The life we gave up."

"Cash," I say his name and it lingers in the air as guilt surrounds us.

I mourned that life for years, wondering if I'd ever experience an intense emotional connection with anyone other than Cash.

Spoiler alert: I haven't, even though I've desperately tried.

I get lost in the past, replaying old memories. I didn't want him to choose me because I was too risky to be with. I still am.

SEVEN YEARS AGO

It was a Saturday morning in the middle of May. I had two weeks before I graduated from college with a degree in computer science, and I was home studying for midterms. I'd grabbed the keys to one of the ranch hand trucks and drove downtown to continue memorizing definitions at Grinding Beans.

After I entered, I ordered the largest cup of black coffee. I picked it up and walked to my favorite table, but stopped when I saw him sitting in my chair.

Our eyes met, and his brows creased. So, I made a face before finding somewhere else to study. With my back facing him, I pulled out a notebook and a piece of paper and opened my laptop. After my earbuds were in, he moved and sat directly in front of me.

I stared at him. "What do you want?"

"Remi? I barely recognized you."

"That's what happens when you haven't seen someone since they were a kid. It's called growing up," I said, my gaze sliding down to his plump lips. He smiled, and it nearly stole my breath. Time had been good to him, and he aged perfectly. Cash was muscular with a tan.

"I guess so," he said, studying me.

"How long has it been since you've visited home?" I asked.

"Eight years," he admitted. "Too long, but school and internships had me occupied."

"Are you back for good?" I asked.

"For the summer. I'll leave for a job at an animal hospital in Houston. My contract starts in September."

The attraction that swirled between us was undeniable. For the first time, Cash hadn't looked at me like a kid, but like a grown woman.

"Congratulations," I said. "Bet your parents are proud."

"Very." The moment lingered too long. "Well, I hope to see you around over the next few months," he told me.

His words hung heavy in the air. I hoped the same.

"Give me your number," I said.

He licked his lips, grabbed the pen from my hand, and wrote it at the top of my notebook paper. "Call me anytime, Valentine."

"I will," I said more confidently than I should.

"I hope you do."

Then I watched him walk away and sat intoxicated by his mere presence.

I'd always imagined what I'd say to my brother's best friend when I was old enough to know better. It wasn't that.

I realized then maybe I had a chance of being with the man I'd always wanted. Even if it were only for a summer.

. . .

HE CLEARS HIS THROAT, and I realize I was lost in my thoughts.

"What's on your mind?" he asks.

I laugh. "I was thinking about the first time we ran into one another after you graduated."

"Ah, yeah. At the coffee shop." He shakes his head but grins, showing those cute-as-hell dimples. "I should've known you were trouble then."

"You *knew*," I say with a brow raised.

"I'm not sure I did," he admits. "But I have no damn regrets."

Everything changed between us that summer.

I actively pursued him, wanting him to see me as the nearly twenty-one-year-old woman I was, not his best friend's little sister.

I was never on his radar, but he was an unavoidable blip on mine.

We sit in the room's stillness, and neither of us speaks. Not touching him is hard, and while I want rules, following them will be difficult.

"I don't want to be a summer fling again," I say. "Not this time."

He studies me. "You were *never* a fling, Rem."

"I want more than a fuck buddy, Cash. They're a dime a dozen in Alpine."

We meet each other's gaze, and I sip my coffee.

"And I want to tell everyone about us and not hide like we're afraid of what we have."

His words cut like a knife.

"There's too much at risk," I say knowing he could lose his clinic if he upset Beckett. I also know what would happen if we didn't work out. I don't want to break him or be broken. The undeniable attraction and need for one another will have us base-jumping without parachutes. We won't survive.

Not only is Cash's longest friendship at risk but so is his livelihood, and everything he's worked for. I am not worth that. I will not let him give it all up for me.

The silence draws on for a few seconds as I blow on the steamy liquid. Beckett texted me this morning at six because that's when he naturally wakes up. I read it with one eye open before falling asleep again.

"Oh, I thought I should warn you that Beckett texted me. He said us becoming roommates was a horrible idea but I could do whatever I wanted and apologized for pushing me to speak to you. So, he left the decision up to me and you," I say.

"Well shit," he says. "That wasn't on my bingo card this morning."

"Let me remind you that I'm a grown-ass woman who can live with and date *whoever* she wants. Even *you*, Cash."

"I'm aware of that, Rem. Are *you*?" His eyes pin me in place.

I take several gulps of coffee, and it warms my throat. "My lease expires in ninety days. So, we'll be roomies until then. If you still want to do this."

"Ninety days, okay. You realize that puts us at the same timeline we had before? June 1st to August 31st."

My mouth slightly parts. "Weird coincidence."

"So, what happens afterward?"

I look him square in the eye. "I don't know. Maybe we'll get each other out of our systems for good or realize we can't live without the other. It gives us an out with no hard feelings if this isn't working."

Cash gives me a sad look, then holds out his hand, and I shake it. "Deal."

His hazel eyes darken when shadows cast over the sunlight beaming across the floor. "And to the outside world, what are we?"

"We're roommates." I shrug, lifting my coffee to my mouth. "Now that you have Christine."

"Ah, yeah, I was asked about her this morning at Grinding Beans," he says, watching me.

I inhale, not liking the idea. Call me possessive, but it makes me hella jealous.

"She knows about us," he says.

"What?" This is news to me.

"I told her I had a girlfriend, and she guessed it was you."

I swallow hard, butterflies fluttering. "How do people know?"

"I haven't figured it out yet," he says. "But the truth is, I'm taken, Valentine, whether you're ready to admit that right now or in ninety days."

His admission has me in a choke hold, and it refuses to let go. No matter how much I try to deny it, this man does something to me. "I'm not seeing anyone, Cash. Maybe I'll bring Eric back from the dead."

It's the code name I used for Cash to my family. He was an online boyfriend who lived in a different state. They'd asked for pictures of him, and I'd show them pics of one of my horse camp leaders' photos because he was *gorgeous*.

"Eric." He chuckles, knowing. "Almost forgot about him."

I grab his hand and squeeze. "We have three months to figure it out."

"It's more than enough time for you to wake up and realize what you've got, Rem," he says. His phone vibrates, and he looks at it. "Shit."

"What's up?"

"Beckett wants to have lunch."

"Protect your face," I say, smirking. "When will you start moving things?"

"If I survive? Tomorrow." He stands, turning to me. "Want to ride with me to Summer and Beckett's later?"

"You think that's a good idea?" I ask.

He chuckles. "We're roommates. It comes with the territory, right?"

"You're already starting shit," I say, shaking my head. "We can't go from zero to a hundred because we're living together."

"Just give everyone that scowl they're so scared of."

I snort. "Too bad it doesn't work on you."

"Oh, it does. I just fucking love it," Cash admits. "Have a great day, Valentine. Pick you up in a few hours?"

"Let me think about it," I say, knowing we have to be smarter after Harrison lost his shit. I don't need him starting fights with Cash. Out of my five brothers, he's the loose cannon. "Thanks for the coffee, roomie."

"Any time."

After he leaves, I put the lid back on the top of my cup and set it on the side table next to the bed. I desperately hope that at the end of ninety days, living together wasn't the missing ingredient in a recipe for disaster.

If I've ever needed a crystal ball, it's *now*. Maybe I'll ask my sister Kinsley to do a tarot reading.

I briefly think about it and immediately change my mind because it's always overly specific and *never* great.

This time when I'm with Cash, I'd rather not know if I'm doomed.

CHAPTER FIVE

CASH

Once I'm inside my truck, I reply to Beckett.

CASH

Where ya wanna meet?

His text bubble appears.

BECKETT

the deli around 11.

CASH

Sounds good.

I have thirty minutes to prepare myself for his lousy attitude now that I know I'll get it, considering he contacted Remi early this morning. After the alcohol wore off, I'm sure he had a moment of clarity and a shitty hangover.

The warning is appreciated.

Needing to waste time, I drive to Main Street Books, which Hayden Shaw's family owns. We've been friends almost as long as Beckett and I have been. He's engaged to Kinsley, and now they're living their second chance.

Lucky bastard.

As I walk into the building, sweet scents of freshly baked chocolate chip cookies float through the space. He comes from the storage room carrying a large stack of novels and sets them on the counter. I snag a cookie and smile.

"How's shit been?" he asks.

"Okay. Been working a lot. How 'bout you?"

He shrugs. "I'm doing the same, especially now that my dad retired. Running the store and writing as much as possible."

Hayden has a book releasing early next year.

"You seem happy," I tell him. It's obvious how in love he is with Kinsley. They dated in high school and afterward Hayden moved away. Last year, he returned and rekindled their relationship.

"I've never been happier. Oh, we decided on our wedding date—September twenty-eighth. Invitations are going out next week. Are you busy?"

I chuckle. "Go ahead and ask."

A smile meets his lips. "Will you be available to officiate?"

"Absolutely," I say, shaking his hand, and he pulls me into a brotherly hug. "I'd be honored."

"Thank you! I think you might become a Valentine tradition," he says. "Might put Pastor Mike out of business."

A laugh escapes me. "Only for the *heathens*."

Hayden smiles and places the books on the rolling cart and pushes it forward. I follow him to where he sets up a display.

"Kins will be happy when I tell her. You going to be at Beckett's tonight?"

"You think I have a choice?"

"Fuck no," he says. "So, you and Christine?"

I shake my head. "No. We're *just* friends."

"Ah." He meets my eyes, and I can tell he wants to say more. "It makes me wonder who you're seeing."

"I'm married to my job," I admit, not wanting to talk about this.

He smirks. "Right. You're transparent, Cash. See right through you."

My expression doesn't change. "Why don't you come out and say what you mean?"

Maybe I'm being too direct.

"I don't have to," he tells me. "But, how about you don't fuck it up?"

"What are we talking about exactly?" I ask.

He slides the last book into place and turns to me. "You're not as sneaky as you think, my man. Also, I don't care who you date. Let me make that clear. No lines in the sand here, okay? Do what makes you happy and forget about everyone else."

I nod, and my phone buzzes. "I gotta go. Beckett is close."

"Doesn't he have a party to get ready for?" Hayden checks his watch.

I hadn't thought about that. "Actually, yeah."

"Mmm." Hayden shakes his head. "They seem scary, but they get over it. I got shit, too, but at some point, you don't care anymore. Eventually, you'll be willing to fight for it, for her."

"Thanks," I tell him, holding out my hand. She has to fight for it, too, and I know she's not there yet.

He takes my hand with a firm grip and a warm smile. "I'm rooting for you."

I check the time. "Let's get together soon. Gotta go."

Hayden kept me in check when we both lived in Houston. I told him truths I know he hasn't forgotten, but I trust him.

Instead of driving to the deli, I walk the five blocks. When I enter, Beckett and *Remi* sit at a table in the corner, and he laughs at something. Seeing her here is a pleasant surprise.

Her gaze meets mine, and my world gently spins when a small smile touches her lips. Those blue eyes peer straight through me.

She gets up and sits next to Beckett as I slide into the booth. I glance between them.

"Hey Cash."

"Remington. I didn't realize you were gonna be here," I say, keeping my tone flat and my face expressionless.

Her brow quirks up, and I know why she decided to sit before me instead of beside me. It's easier to steal glances.

"Oh, I invited her," Beckett says, picking up his mug and drinking.

"I can leave," she slaps back. She's so damn good at this.

"It doesn't matter to me," I say.

"We already ordered," Beckett tells me. "I was starving."

The server smiles. "Need a menu?"

"Nah, I want black coffee, scrambled eggs with cheese, extra crispy bacon, hashbrowns, and toast."

"Got it, sugar," she says, winking. Less than a minute later, she sets the mug on the table's edge before walking away. Nothing has changed in the deli, not the tables or the wood panel walls.

"So, what were you saying?" Beckett asks Remi. "You mentioned getting back together with Eric? That douche?"

"He wasn't a douche," she says, sipping some water.

Beckett shakes his head. "Whatever. You were destroyed the last time you dated him. I don't support this."

This conversation doesn't sit well with me, knowing she was

hurt by me. I have no idea what happened after I left because she wouldn't speak to me.

My brows furrow as I stare at her.

"I don't know what you're talking about," she tells him.

Beckett turns his body toward her. "You want to discuss this right now?"

She sighs. "You're annoying."

"I don't like him," Beckett says. "I'm glad he never came around. I'd have fucked him up."

"That goes for anyone I've ever tried to date. I turn twenty-eight in three weeks. When are you going to stop?" She's seething.

He glances at me. "Never."

"What happened with this Eric guy?" I ask, blowing on my coffee.

"He broke up with her after one summer, and it took Remi *years* to get over it."

"Beckett," she growls. "It's none of *his* business."

I smirk. "Sure it is. Anyway, continue."

"I don't want to see my sister like that ever again. After that vacation they took to Florida, I was worried her heart would never recover. She became a shell of herself."

I had no idea, and the scowl on my face is evident. Beckett has the same expression.

"Shut up and stop talking about me like I'm not sitting here," she snaps. "And if you don't, I'll go home. My past relationships aren't either of your concerns."

"Don't let any man change you," I firmly state.

Me included.

This conversation is fucking torture. The happiness I felt when I walked in is gone.

Beckett doesn't respond to her and focuses on me. "Now that you'll be roommates, you can keep a lookout. Help me watch her since she's so elusive. And if Eric shows up at your condo, you have my permission to fuck him up," he says.

Rage settles behind his gaze, and Remi and I will discuss this the next time we're alone because Beckett wouldn't exaggerate.

"You do realize we won't see one another much," I say as my food slides in front of me.

"Forget this conversation," Remi says to me. "Please."

"Yeah, I don't think I can do that," I admit, wishing I could. Remi not sharing this hurts.

Moving in with her will allow me to have the hard conversations we've avoided. Ninety days, it's the time we're given, and it's now or never.

I clear my throat, glancing at his hand and noticing his wedding ring. I'm still getting used to this. After Hayden gets married, my guy friend group will be gone. I missed a lot, and for what? *Money?*

"When are you moving in?" Beckett asks.

"Tomorrow," I say as the server refills my coffee.

Silence lingers. "So, tell me about Christine. Kinsley said she was great."

I smile, knowing what he's doing, trying to see where I stand in the relationship department without asking.

"Oh, she's a nice woman. *Smart.* She's only here until September, though, because she's working on a special project at the Permian basin."

It's the area's oil and natural gas fields. Since I returned in January, the number of outsiders who've moved to Valentine and the Fort Davis area has tripled.

"Well, that's a shame," Beckett says. "You two looked great together."

"Totally," Remi adds, and I glance at her.

"Yeah, she's cute, but we're just having *fun.*" I grin.

It's not a lie, but the statement is so general he'll fill in the gaps. It could mean drinking coffee together or having sex.

Over the years, I've mastered avoiding Beckett's questions about my love life, even if he's just checking on me. He knows I'm married to my job, even if it runs much deeper than that.

However, I still choose my words wisely.

Once Remi realizes we're meant to be together, I'll tell him myself. She has to be the one to initiate this, though. For once, she has to choose me.

"What about you and Samantha?" he asks.

Remi tilts her head. "Oh, who's that?"

"Someone I dated in Houston," I tell her, and her eyes narrow.

We both have secrets.

"You were into her. Honestly, I thought she was the one."

He has no idea what he's talking about, but I see jealousy spread across Remi's face as her cheeks heat.

"Yeah, it was too bad," I say, wanting her to understand that she could've lost me for good. "I asked Samantha to move here and work at the clinic, but she said she couldn't live in the middle of nowhere."

Remi coughs, and Beckett turns to her as she clears her throat. I'm two seconds from performing the Heimlich.

She chugs water. "Sorry, it went down wrong."

We chat about the weather and how busy they are at the training facility with lessons.

"Oh, did you hear about Sterling? He's becoming a farrier," Beckett proudly says. Sterling is the youngest Valentine brother and graduated high school a year ago. He's worked with Beckett and Harrison at the training barn since.

A wide grin fills my face. "Really? That's incredible."

"I didn't know that," Remi says.

"Last week, he said he'd been accepted into the program. With all the wedding stuff, it slipped my mind. He's leaving at the beginning of September and will be gone for two months. Dad is proud."

"Wow, yeah, this is great. I'll have to congratulate him. Sterling will be so good at this," Remi says.

"Right? Now I'll have a farrier and a vet on call." Beckett laughs. "It's good to be me."

"Sure is," I say.

We finish eating, and Beckett pays for everyone. I ask for a coffee to go.

When we're outside, Beckett turns to us. "This was fun. We should do this again."

"Thanks. I'd like that," I say.

Remi hugs him.

As Beckett walks to his truck, he hollers over his shoulder. "I'll see you both tonight at seven. Don't be late. Summer might lose her shit. Her patience level has been in the negatives lately."

"I'll be on time," I confirm and wave to him. He drives off, and I turn to Remi.

"Did you walk?"

"Yep," she says.

"Great. I parked at the bookstore."

Remi falls in line beside me. We say nothing as we stroll to the end of the block and then cross the street.

"About what Beckett said—"

"We have a lot to discuss." I glance over at her.

She nods. "We do."

"But not right now," I tell her. "Tomorrow."

"Okay," she says. "Tonight, I'm riding with Haley to Summer's shindig."

I smile at her. "Sure."

I've always allowed her to call the shots, lead the way, and do whatever makes her comfortable.

"I don't like this awkwardness," she says.

"I don't either. We need to discuss a lot, and we will again, but I want to talk to you without interruptions."

The sun hangs high in the sky, and warm, dry air surrounds

us. Soon, it will be summer, and it will be too hot to be outside midday without sweating.

Her brows furrow. "Even Samantha?"

"If you want," I confirm. "No questions are off-limits to you, Rem. You know that."

CHAPTER SIX

REMI

I give him a nod, and he walks me to the front door of our place. His biceps nearly burst out of the sleeves of his dark brown polo, and I want to be wrapped in his strong arms, pressed against his body. It's his closeness that I crave.

When I finally meet his eyes, the world closes in, or maybe it's the walls I've built to hide us. Cash is my bad habit, and damn, I don't know if I'll ever be able to break it.

"Do you think this is a mistake?" I search his face, waiting for his expression to change.

It doesn't.

He's confident as a ghost of a smile touches his kissable lips.

"Fucking never," he whispers. "You've never been a mistake of mine and never will be."

I lick my lips and glance away from him before I do something I shouldn't.

"See you later," he says, almost as if it physically hurts him to put space between us.

"Yeah." I turn and unlock the door. I walk inside, and my heart threatens to flutter out of my chest. I stand on my tiptoes and look out the peephole, and he walks down the sidewalk toward the bookstore.

I look around the condo I've lived in alone for the past month. Before that, Grace was here, stress-cleaning with a toothbrush because she was too afraid to admit how she felt about Harrison.

Is that my problem, too?

Am I so blinded by this man, by my wants, that I can't see reality?

I've witnessed love do that to people.

Has it finally gotten to me?

Shit.

AFTER LUNCH, I needed a nap, but I did finish my laundry and clean up some. My phone dings, and I roll over to silence it. I was getting up.

HALEY

I'm outside. Coming in.

I SEND her a thumbs-up emoji and slide out of bed, heading toward the front door. I swing it open as Haley approaches. She's dressed in tight jeans, a yellow shirt that shows her midriff, and enough cleavage to make anyone curious. Her dark brown hair and tan skin make her look like a goddess.

"Ready?" she asks with a brow popped, wearing a judgy expression.

I glance down at what I have on. "Didn't they say outdoor, fire pit fun?"

"Yes, that was the dress code. But there's no way I'm showing up to one of your family events looking like a trash panda."

I snicker. "Or maybe it's because you'll know Emmett will be there."

"For sure," she says, flipping her hair over her shoulder. "You're dressed like you have no one to impress, and we both know that's not true."

Before I can protest, Haley walks past me, leading me to my room. She flicks on the light and enters my closet. Hangers scoot across the rod, and seconds later, she moves toward me. "This is what you're wearing tonight."

My brows raise. "Kinsley gave me that."

It's a white mini sundress that cuts low in the back. She hands me a pair of wedges.

"Too bad, I was about to say you've found your style. Put it on, then let's go."

I give her a look. "You're forcing me?"

"Yes," she says, reaching forward and tugging my hair out of the ponytail holder. "When you walk in and he looks at you like you're the only woman who's *ever* existed in his world, you can thank me."

"Who?" I ask, playing dumb, knowing he already looks at me that way.

She lifts a brow. "You don't have to admit anything is happening between you and Cash because I can tell. I read way too many romance novels. There are signs."

"Whatever," I say, trying not to smile, but she catches me.

She reminds me of Kinsley, but Haley has always been like a sister. "Now go change. Spray some perfume. Add some lipstick. You have two minutes; if we show up late, I'm telling Summer it's *your* fault."

"Fine," I say.

"Not a minute longer," she orders before leaving me to myself.

I shimmy out of my clothes and slide on the dress and wedges, and I stand in front of the full-length mirror. "Damn, she was right."

I put on my favorite mauve lipstick and some mascara. When Haley texts me it's time to go, I grab my phone and meet her in the Bronco.

"That's more like it," she says, backing out of my driveway. We drive straight to the Horseshoe Creek Ranch.

"I'm nervous. Are you?" Haley turns the radio down.

"Not really," I admit, knowing my night will be full of stolen glances and silent conversations, but that's always the case when I'm in the same room as Cash.

Haley soars down the old country road, hugging the curves. I glance at the time, knowing we won't be late.

"Did you find out if Emmett is seeing anyone?" she asks.

"He's not. I asked him directly," I say.

"Do you think my crush on your little brother is weird?"

"Not really." Emmett is three years younger than us. "He's a heartbreaker, Hal."

"I'm not searching for a husband."

"Ahh." I glance out the window. "Do you ever feel like real life is stranger than fiction?"

"No. The other day I read a detailed sex scene that included a gigantic demon dick with tentacles," she explains. "Nothing in real life can beat it."

"Text me the link to that book. That's what good friends do."

Haley snickers. "I will because you have to experience it. And damn, was it an experience."

Considering her family owns the only bookstore in town, she reads several books weekly, typically romances. I read a lot, too, and enjoy completing puzzles.

All I'm missing is a house full of cats and learning how to

crochet, and I'll officially be old. However, I've lived in my single-girl era for years, so I should be used to it by now.

She sighs. "Emmett is so elusive. It's almost like years have passed since I saw him last. Now he's everywhere at once."

"You never paid attention until now. He's always been around."

I know that look.

"It's like I woke up and finally *saw* him," she says. "He's gorgeous even if he's a thirst trap."

"Do what makes you happy."

"I will. I hope you do, too," she says, glancing at me and flicking on her blinker. Haley slows and turns onto the newly-made second entrance to the private section of the Horseshoe Creek Ranch.

The gravel path leads to the two-story house with a wraparound porch that Summer and Beckett built. Construction started last year, and they moved in thirty days ago, but this is the first time friends and family have visited.

The driveway is full of vehicles, and I think we might be the final guests to arrive. Haley parks next to Cash's truck, and I think about the discussion the two of us still need to have. Awkwardness lingered between us earlier, and I didn't like it.

We're both great at pretending the other doesn't exist, but that's not reality. When we're in the same room, he's the center of my attention, even from a distance.

She turns to me. "Good luck tonight. You look hot."

"You too," I tell her.

We exit the vehicle, and country music echoes in the distance. Haley and I walk toward the backyard. Strings of patio lights hang above and illuminate the area. There's a food table, and people sit near the firepit in bright-colored Adirondack chairs. When I scan the space, my eyes land directly on Cash.

His brow perks up so slightly that I almost miss it. This dress was a good call.

Emmett rounds the corner wearing his cowboy hat with dirt on his jeans. He smiles at me, and his eyes slide to Haley.

"Hey, little brother," I say, stopping him before he can escape.

"Hi," he says. "What's been going on?"

"Working with Summer," I tell him. "And you?"

He shrugs. "Same old shit, cattle wrangling. I've been practicing my saddle-making, though. Just wish I had more time for it."

"And that's why you should join the training facility," Harrison says, butting into our conversation. "We'd have let you off early for a family event."

"If you keep it up, I'm telling Dad," I say because Emmett works on our parents' ranch.

Harrison has been trying to steal him for a year, but Emmett is loyal, for now, until Harrison and Beckett make him an offer he can't refuse.

Harrison's eyes narrow at me. "If I were you, little Valentine, I wouldn't mess with me."

I burst into laughter. "You realize that Grace and I have a girl code, right?"

"I don't even know what that means." He glances over his shoulder. "Gracie!"

My brother waves her over, and when she's close, he places his arm over her, pulling her to him. It's undeniable how adorable they are together, but they've always been like this.

"Remi mentioned a code or something," he says. "Is that true, and also, what the fuck does that mean?"

Grace chuckles. "Oh, you told him?"

I tilt my head at Harrison. "See."

"You're both messing with me."

Emmett turns to Haley. "Want to get a drink?"

"Sure," she says, and they walk away. Their arms brush together.

I return my attention to Harrison. "The girl code means if

you do anything that destroys my life, Grace won't make little Harri happy."

His brows crease. "*What?*"

Grace shrugs. "Summer is on it, too. You and Beckett should choose your actions wisely."

Harrison grabs her hand. It's a threat, one she gives with a smile.

As I let them hash it out, I stroll over to my parents sitting by the fire. I lean over, hug my mom, and then my dad. "Nice seeing y'all here. Do you know what this get-together is about?"

"No idea." Mom glances at her phone. "Summer said they'll get started in about ten minutes. Would you get me something to drink?"

"Sure," I say. "What about you, Dad?"

"That'd be good," he tells me with a smile.

I move to the snack table and reach for a cup, and someone stands close beside me.

It's Cash.

I don't have to confirm because his cologne gives him away. He doesn't acknowledge me even though his presence sets my body on fire. It's unbelievable how it still happens after all this time.

After I grab two cups of punch, I walk away with a galloping heart.

I turn to steal another peek and stumble forward, crashing directly into a human wall. The red liquid spills on the mint green shirt of a man of steel. He's covered.

"Oh my goodness, I'm so sorry," I say, meeting his blue-green eyes and seeing the messy blond hair on his head. When he smiles, my mouth slightly parts.

"Hello, beautiful," he says in a velvety British accent.

"Um. Hi. Please let me get you a napkin or something." My cheeks heat with embarrassment.

"Did any spill on you?" he asks, creating space between us.

"No," I whisper. "A miracle, to be honest."

He chuckles and removes the button-up shirt, revealing a white tee that hugs him tightly. I'm staring, and he catches me.

"It's not an issue. But I think you might owe me," he says, holding up the shirt that made his eyes pop.

"Are you openly flirting with me?" The breeze blows, and I inhale the hint of sandalwood on his skin.

"*Maybe*. I'm Archie. Are you always so blunt?"

"Yes," I admit. "How do you know Beckett and Summer?"

"Mrs. Carol is my grandmother, and she forced me to be here *to make friends in town* since I'm staying for the summer." He points to where she's chatting with Beckett. She runs the romance book club with my mother and Mrs. Shaw.

"That explains it. I'm Remi."

"Remi," Mom says, pulling my attention away.

"Sorry," I say. "I better get some more punch."

"Lead the way." He nods and falls in line beside me, his shirt held loosely in his fist. "Why are you here?"

"Beckett is my older brother," I explain, grabbing two new cups.

"Ah, yes. Uncomfortably firm handshake," Archie says with a chuckle as I return to the punch.

"Yeah, that's him." I notice the red liquid on his jeans. "I'm really sorry about that."

He grabs a cookie. "No worries."

"Hope to see you around," I say, walking away from him. When I turn my head, I catch sight of Cash, whose jaw is tightly locked. I move back to my parents and hand over the drinks. "Apologies."

Before I can escape, my mom gently grabs my hand and tugs me toward her. "Were you introduced to Archie?"

"Introduced is pushing it, but we met," I tell her.

"And?"

"Mom. Don't play matchmaker," I whisper. "I'm seeing someone."

"Who?" She's confused.

"*Eric.*"

My mom makes a face. Everyone knew how upset I was when Cash left, but they had no idea it was him I was so desperately missing.

My broken heart was in pieces for far too long. It was deeper than an internet crush, and I have an invisible scar to prove it. It was the first time I understood what it was like to be loved and be in love.

"Why are you entertaining Eric?" she asks.

"Because we had something special," I tell her.

No one understands.

"Give Archie a chance. He's adorable and polite. He used to play professional rugby and retired earlier this month. I had tea with him yesterday," she says. "You two have *a lot* in common."

Archie meets my eyes. He holds his glass up to me, a tiny toast, and smiles before speaking to his grandmother.

"Mmhmm," my mom says. "Sparks are flying."

"Please stop," I tell her, noticing the sun dipping close to the horizon. Soon, it will be a golden hour, my favorite time of day.

"It's time to get started," Summer says to Beckett, pulling him away.

"Okay, I have to do a quick head count. No one move," Beckett yells as his eyes scan the backyard.

Summer grins with her hand on her hip as he continues counting us like cattle. He shoots her a wink.

After Beckett gives a thumbs up, she steps up to the microphone. "Hi, y'all! So glad you could make it. We're right on time."

Beckett holds a basket full of stark white envelopes and hands them out.

"Don't open it yet," Summer instructs, looking around. "Hold them up in the air when you've got one."

They're acting weird, but I lift my envelope above my head.

"Everyone has one?" Beckett asks.

The small crowd of friends and family nods.

"Great. On the count of three, I'd like to do this together. Okay? Not a second sooner," she says. "One. Two."

Beckett and Summer look at one another. My brother grabs her hand and they kiss.

"Three."

The only thing that pulls me away from them is my mother screaming, followed by wails from Summer's mom.

My brows furrow as I open my envelope and pull out an ultrasound photograph.

Get ready to meet Baby Valentine.

I gasp, my hand reaches for my heart. My mom and dad rush toward Summer and Beckett. Her parents do the same.

Happiness radiates through me when I realize I'll be an aunt, and Beckett and Summer are having a baby. I hold the photo and am overcome with emotion. They found each other after all that time, and now they're starting a family.

As our parents and grandparents surround them, I fall to the back of the crowd. Cash steps beside me.

"Did you know?" I ask. The two of them share everything, almost.

"I suspected," he says. "But no, can't believe they kept it a secret."

"The Valentines are good at keeping secrets," I say.

"Hmm." He glances over at me. "Who were you speaking to?"

"It's Mrs. Carol's grandson, Archie. I just met him."

He takes a sip of his drink. "You two hit it off."

My mouth turns into a firm line. "Jealous?"

"Absofuckinglutely," he hisses. "I didn't like how he looked at you or how you—"

Haley walks over and interrupts the conversation, which is probably for the best, considering that if he had continued, he might've regretted what he said.

"Did you know?" she asks, paying Cash no attention as he stands close like my bodyguard.

"No," I say, shaking my head. "And I've seen Summer nearly every day for the past month because we've been alternating schedules while training the new hires."

"Wow, she's a vault," Haley mutters.

"Apparently. It makes me wonder what trash she has on Kinsley."

As my sister's name leaves my mouth, Kinsley rushes to her best friend. She and Summer cry together.

"One day, that will be us," Haley says.

"I don't know if tears will come."

She chuckles. "Same."

Cash's cell rings and he walks away to answer. The awkwardness between us cuts like a knife.

"Who was that guy you were talking to?"

"Archie. He's Mrs. Carol's grandson, the man they've decided to hook me up with."

"Really? Well, maybe you could use this to your advantage." Haley wears a devious smile.

"What do you mean?"

Sometimes Haley can be the literal devil.

"Nothing like a little friendly competition to get the testosterone pumping," she says.

"You're evil," I tell her.

"And you're single. Let them fight over you. Winner takes all."

"I don't want any drama."

Moments later, Haley and I congratulate Summer and

Beckett. A large crowd waits to chat with them, so we don't take up much of their time, but I hug my brother, and squeeze him tight.

He finally has everything he ever wanted—the job of his dreams, the wife of his fantasies, and the baby he always wished for.

I hug Summer and give my congratulations. Beckett steps away and quickly returns. "Remi, I think you should go on a date with Archie."

"I...uh."

Eyes are on us. "You two have so much in common."

Archie gives me his boyish grin. Glancing around, I notice how many are watching us.

"I'm seeing someone," I say loud enough for the small crowd to hear.

"Eric doesn't count," Beckett says.

He turns to Cash, who's standing off to his side. "What about you? Don't you think my Remi needs to take some risks in life?"

I meet Cash's gaze, and he forces a smile but his eyes are cold. His hands are as tied as mine.

"I think she should do whatever she wants," he says firmly, his jaw locked tight.

My mother and Archie's grandmother join in, and the next thing I know, a group of people peer pressure me into going out with this man.

CHAPTER SEVEN

CASH

After the baby announcement party, everyone leaves, and I see Remi chatting with that British fuck.

"Thanks for coming," Beckett says, squeezing my shoulder.

I'm no longer in a good mood.

"I wouldn't miss something like this," I admit, reflecting on tonight's events. "You shouldn't force your sister to go out with people."

He chuckles. "You wouldn't understand."

"Explain it to me, then," I urge. We're too old for that shit. I'm aggravated that he took it that far.

Beckett sighs as we stand out by my truck. "After Eric, Remi didn't date anyone for years. He destroyed her."

I remember the time we escaped to Florida after she turned twenty-one. We left town at different times, hopped on a plane, and were gone for seven days. We took hundreds of photos, swam in the ocean under the moonlight, and made love until the sun rose.

Beckett shoves his hands in his pockets. "I think he used her for sex, considering she hadn't been with anybody until him."

"What?" I ask.

"Yeah, he took her virginity. I thought you knew that," Beckett says. "Fucking *bastard.*"

This admission has my heart beating erratically. Had Remi lied about being a virgin? And why the fuck would she do that?

He continues, and I can barely pay attention to him as I search through all the old memories and conversations we had. She'd told me she'd been with someone, but I also know Eric never existed.

"Now that she's back with him, I'll do whatever I can to help end that toxic relationship. I don't know shit about him, but I never want to see my sister like that again. She needs a nice guy. Someone who won't use her."

Frustration is written on his face. Beckett has been on a rampage about Eric since Remi brought it up this morning at lunch.

I need her to explain what the fuck happened because I don't have all the puzzles pieces. I hurt her, and that's crystal clear. It frustrates me that I'd nearly—how did Beckett word it?— *destroyed her.*

"I hear you, but she seemed uncomfortable," I tell him, not wanting him to ignore the unnecessary pressure he put on her. It wasn't okay, and I won't sit back and allow that to happen again.

"Remi needs to be pushed in the right direction because she hasn't moved on from Eric. It's why I need you to keep an eye on her."

"I won't spy on your sister."

He laughs. "Well, I heard Summer is changing Remi's schedule starting July first so you'll see her a lot more next month."

I keep my excitement to myself. "I don't care. She can do what she wants, like I said before."

Remi walks around the house with Archie beside her. The two of them laugh at something, and I'm instantly jealous.

Beckett glances over his shoulder, seeing them. He has no idea how destructive this is for me.

Remi glances up at me before turning her attention back to him.

"They're good together," Beckett says. "Carol said he'd move here if he had a reason to."

"That's interesting," I say, trying to seem amused, but I'm not. Fuck him.

"You good?" he asks.

"Yeah, fine. I'm exhausted. Had a long day yesterday and was up at the crack of dawn. Been working a lot, and I don't see that slowing down."

I don't want to learn anything else about him.

She walks him to the old truck of Carol's he's driving. Remi holds out her hand, and he smiles and takes it. After he leaves, the taillights fade in the dusty distance as he turns onto the main country road.

She waits in front of Haley's Bronco that's next to my truck. The bright screen becomes a beacon in the night, lighting her pretty face.

"So, you move in tomorrow?" Beckett asks.

"Yes," I say. "I already told my parents, and I think they were excited to get the house back to themselves."

Beckett chuckles. "I'm sure they are."

I glance away from him.

"Please promise me that you'll tell me if she's not okay."

When I meet his eyes, I know he has his sister's best interest in mind. "I will."

"I have your word?" His brows raise.

This could get messy, and it's how things get twisted. I'd prefer not to be in a position like this, but if Remi was not okay, I'd tell him. It's not a lie.

"You have my word. Anyway, congrats again. So happy for you."

It's an unbreakable promise, something I hold with the utmost regard.

"Thanks," he says. "Let's hang out again soon."

"Deal," I tell him with a wave as I continue to my truck. Beckett heads back to his house.

I glance over at Remi. She pushes off of Haley's SUV and strolls toward me.

"Are you going out with him?"

She stands in front of me, keeping enough space in case there are any wandering eyes.

"Is that *jealousy* I sense?" she asks. It's the same question I asked when she saw me with Christine at Beckett's wedding.

When I look at her and smell the sweetness of her skin, I worry that I'll wake from a dream and she'll fade away.

"You didn't answer," she mutters.

"You know it is," I hiss. "You know I can't see you with another man."

She glances around and it's only us. "Will you take me home?"

"Yes," I tell her, unlocking the passenger door of my truck, and she climbs in. I move to the driver's seat, and the tension cuts through the air.

We open our mouths to say something, knowing there won't be anyone who overhears us.

"You first," I say.

"I explained to him that I have a boyfriend, that *if* I ever have coffee with him, which I won't, it would be as friends only. I'm unavailable."

"And let me guess, he said that would be fine," I say, cranking the engine.

We drive away.

"Well, yeah."

"That's how this works. Men say *we'll be friends* until you're not." I stop at the end of the driveway.

"What's the difference with Christine?" she asks.

I suck in a sharp breath. "The difference is I know I want you and no one else. Also unrelated, but I never had ulterior motives when it came to you, Rem. I didn't use you," I say, recalling what Beckett said.

Her brows furrow. "I know that. What sparked this?"

"Beckett." I sigh. I turn onto the country road, heading toward downtown Valentine.

Silence slices through the air as we drive to her place, soon *ours*.

"Is he who you want? If it is, I'll accept it with no questions asked."

"Wow, you're *big* jealous," she says, shaking her head. Remi reaches over and grabs my hand. "You have no reason to be, okay? Do you trust me?"

"I don't trust him."

"Wasn't my question," she says.

"Yes, I trust you," I confirm.

"Okay, then trust me."

I'm lost in my thoughts, in the possibility of her even pretending to go out with someone else. The thought nearly drives me mad. She unlocks her phone and types something. If I had to guess, she texts Haley or Lexi. It could be Summer or Kinsley, too.

Ten minutes later, we're turning onto Main. The streetlamps light the way to the other side of town. I pull into the condo and turn off my lights.

She unbuckles. "Will you come in?"

"Do you want me to?" I ask.

"I won't be able to sleep until we hash out this wedge sliding between us. Also, Summer gave me tomorrow off to help you move in."

A smile touches my lips. "You know I hired movers to deliver everything."

"I know. It's just more time I get to spend with you." She reaches for the door handle and pushes it open.

When she steps on the cement, she turns and looks at me. "Are you going to make me beg?"

"Shit," I say, knowing I can't deny her when she's like this. When Remi knows what she wants, and it happens to be me, it's my damn kryptonite.

She glances over her shoulder, ensuring I follow her as she unlocks the condo. Any other time I've come here with her late at night, I've snuck in through her window like we're teenagers, afraid of getting caught.

Valentine is a small town. Someone is always around, and no one minds their business.

Once I'm inside, she turns and presses me against the door. My hands land on her hips, and we walk the edge of a line we shouldn't cross yet.

"I'm not kissing you until we talk." I force myself to grab hold of the situation.

"That's smart," she says.

"You look gorgeous," I whisper.

Her lips quirk upward on the edges. "I wore this for you."

"I know," I tell her, taking a few steps forward, placing my hand on her cheek as her fingers hook into the belt loops of my Wranglers. "Rem, who took your virginity?"

"What?" she stiffens, and her eyes widen.

My jaw clenches tight. "Please tell me."

"Does it matter?"

"Yes, it matters. Are you kidding me?"

Her reaction gives validity to what Beckett said tonight, and I *hate* the thought.

She moves toward the kitchen, opens a cabinet, and pulls out a bottle of Crown Royal Apple. She unscrews the top and presses it to her plump lips, taking two big gulps and offers it to me.

"No, thank you," I tell her as she walks past me and flicks on a table lamp. She kicks off her wedges and pats the cushion next to her as she sits on the couch. She takes two more gulps of liquid courage. She might need the whole damn bottle to finish this conversation.

"Do we have to talk about this?" she asks when I sit next to her.

"Yes. I need the truth."

"*You*," she whispers. "I gave you my virginity."

"What?" It crushes my soul and I don't know what to say. "Why didn't you tell me? I could've *hurt* you."

"You didn't," she admits. "You were so gentle and kind, and honestly, I think back to that night with a goddamn smile on my face, so don't make it out to be like it was some cruel night of virginity snatching. It wasn't."

"Rem," I whisper, recalling the first time we hooked up. We took it slow because she admitted she was inexperienced. "You lied to me."

"I'm really fucking sorry. In the moment, I was embarrassed. I didn't want you to think less of me or treat me with kid gloves. I promised myself I was going to tell you, but then you left and it didn't matter anymore." She pauses. "I don't know what Beckett told you, but don't believe a word of it until you've heard my side, okay? That's all I ask. He doesn't know half of what I've been through. No one does."

I pick up the bottle of Crown and take several large gulps. I'm too on edge. "Will you tell me?"

She glances away from me. "Just shitty relationships. No one ever treated me like you did, and I've been searching for your replacement for nearly seven years. After dating and dumping handfuls of men, I gave up, realizing I was still..." Remi briefly pauses. "In love with you," she says.

When our gaze locks, Remi leans forward, sliding her lips against mine. My fingers thread through her hair, and our tongues twist together.

"We weren't supposed to do that," I say.

"You're my best-kept secret, Cash," she says.

My heart lurches forward. I don't want to be a secret, but she already knows that.

"He said Eric destroyed you," I mutter.

"I was destroyed after you left. That's not a lie."

I give her all the time and space she needs to share her truth. It tastes bitter going down. "I'm sorry."

"It was of my own doing. I wanted to replace you and couldn't. I wanted to erase you from ever existing because you'd been places no one had. You were everywhere inside me physically, mentally, and emotionally, haunting me every damn day. I thought I'd be able to handle it. I barely did."

"Why—."

"Didn't I tell you?" She finishes my sentence. "So you could do what exactly? Come back and rescue your damsel in distress? Before we started fooling around, we agreed it'd be temporary. I wouldn't go back on my word. I wouldn't be the woman that you gave it all up for. And I still won't."

The revelations make my world spin.

"I knew you'd eventually come back to me. And you did."

"Rem, the guilt is almost too much."

"Please don't do that to yourself," she says. "I'm fine now. It taught me a difficult lesson about loving and losing."

"A lesson that shouldn't have been learned."

"We can't take that back."

I pick up the bottle. "Why did you ignore my texts and calls over the years?"

"Because I didn't want you to leave Houston for me. Now look at you, you're at the top, Cash. Your dreams came true."

"They didn't," I say. She doesn't realize how damn in love

with her I am, and how a life without her is far from a dream. It's a fucking nightmare. "I wish I'd known, I would've—"

I shake my head, not able to finish.

"I can't believe this," I say, leaning my head back on the cushion. If Beckett knew the truth about this, I'd have his fist in my face.

"I didn't want you to think I was a twenty-one-year-old *loser* for not having sex yet. I was waiting for the right person, someone I trusted who wouldn't be a creep. I'd heard too many horror stories, and no one my age ever did it for me. I wanted it to be you, Cash, and it was. And it was so damn beautiful."

"I don't know what to say." I lean back on the couch. "This is a lot."

She smiles. "You made it more special than you know. It was mind-blowing, the type of sex a person only has in movies. I always thought about how I would tell you."

I shake my head. "I'm sorry you didn't trust me."

"Cash, no. It had nothing to do with trusting you, I promise. I trusted you with my life. I still do. I was insecure about my body and my experience."

"I never judged you, Rem. I respect your decision if that's what made you feel comfortable, but it hurts. I just would've done things differently."

"I'm so damn sorry I hurt you." She swallows hard. "I didn't want my virginity to be the center of your attention. I didn't want a big deal or for you to act weird. That night was the first time I was touched, the first time I came, and I had you buried deep inside of me. It was incredible, I *promise*. I'm so sorry," she says. "I deeply cherish that moment with you. I just hope you can forgive me one day."

"Okay," I whisper. "I forgive you now, Valentine. So when Beckett shares something new about Eric, he's talking about me?"

"Yes," she admits with a sigh. "I guess he paid more attention than I thought. Had I realized that, I wouldn't have revived Eric. It's what I deserve for trying to be clever. My family's memory is impeccable."

"Maybe it's time you break up with him," I say. "Beckett is convinced you and Eric are toxic together."

She reaches for the booze and sits back, drinking it. "You were the opposite of a red flag, okay? But I do think Eric has to go. There's a lot of baggage."

"Does Beckett have it right, though? Were we toxic for one another?" I think about the question, too.

"No. I don't think *we* were. I think I was toxic with myself after you. Unfortunately, my brothers will blame everyone except me. A lot of it was my stubbornness and wanting to be alone. I should've called and told you how much I missed you."

I open my arms, and Remi crawls into my lap. I hold her tight against me, inhaling the sweet scent of her shampoo. "I would've come back had I known."

"You had things to take care of. You're here now. What will we do differently?"

"What will you do differently? I ask, loving having her close, something I've wanted since the last time we were together.

"I'm a risk," she whispers. "You can still lose it all because of me, and I don't like that. But I'm trying."

Remi creates space between us, placing her palm on my face as she studies me, smiling. "I told Archie I was dating someone and he asked if it were you."

I tilt my head at her. "What did you tell him?"

"Yes," she says. "And that it would be in his best interest not to fuck this up for me. Then I set him up with Haley."

"Clever girl," I tell her, mentally adding another person to our confirmed list.

Remi moves forward and brushes her nose against mine. "I don't want any drama. I have enough to figure out without anyone else being involved."

"I don't either," I admit, searching her face.

"Cash, I can't be the reason why you lose your clinic and best friend. If we do this, I don't think we can tell anyone." She presses her forehead against mine.

I meet her eyes. "One day you'll be ready, and I'll be waiting."

"I know."

"Good news is for the next three months I'm yours, Valentine."

And after that I hope it's forever.

CHAPTER EIGHT

REMI

I want to kiss him again, taste the sweet Crown Royal on his lips, but I resist. I've become the master of denying myself with Cash. Scaling our walls in one night is not what I want. We still have a lot to talk about, but he's here, and that's all that matters.

"I'm glad you're here," I admit. His hand firmly grips my thigh, holding me tight as if I'll disappear.

He chuckles as I run my fingers through his messy hair.

"I've exclusively been yours since the moment I moved back, Rem. You know that, right?"

"I do now," I say. "Thank you. I don't share."

"Fuck, me neither. Tonight, I wanted to beat the fuck out of Archie."

"You're the only man I want, Cash. That's the truth. I just have to figure out how to make it work."

"I know," I say. "And you will."

I love the way he smells, and I wish he knew how much I've craved having his muscular arms wrapped around me just like this. Before the rest of the restraint I have left falters, I create space and stand because I know where this leads, especially when he looks at me with fire in his eyes.

I'm wobbly on my feet but keep them firmly planted.

His hazel eyes sweep me from my head down to my toes. "Damn, *Valentine*. Being that gorgeous should be illegal."

"It's illegal for *you*," I say with a smirk.

"That's the fucking truth," he murmurs.

Unspoken words stream between us, and we hold a silent conversation—one that might take me under as the liquid courage swims through my veins.

I'm happy about the lowered inhibitions. It's made having this conversation more manageable. I've dreaded it since we spoke earlier.

"I'm going to change clothes, I think."

I need to create more space before I do something I shouldn't.

"Sure," he says, watching me leave as I break the tether of temptation between us.

My heart hammers as I walk down the hallway to my room. Once inside, I slide out of the dress and put on some pajama shorts and a tank. After a few minutes, I braid my hair and return to the living room. Cash stands at the table. Before announcing I'm back, I watch him for a few extra seconds.

Cash is the man of my dreams and my wildest fantasies, the only one who can bring me to the edge and please me in the ways I need. He's my dangerous temptation, which only makes me want him more.

"You still puzzle?" he asks when I'm closer.

"Yes, I usually finish one every other month. It's one of my guilty pleasures."

He picks up a piece and snaps it into place. "What are your others?"

"Reading."

He nods.

"And *you*," I admit.

Cash glances over at me with his brow popped. "When you say things like that—"

"I can't pretend like it's not the truth."

He finds another puzzle piece and clicks it into place. Cash leans against one of the mismatched chairs from under the table, the same one where I've sat countless lonely nights thinking about *him*.

"There are so many things I don't know about you," I say, moving closer, meeting his eyes. "Like, what happened after you left Valentine?"

"Ah, yeah," Cash admits, scanning the scattered pieces I've sorted by color. "What do you want to know? I'll tell you the truth, even if it's not what you wanna hear. You have my word."

Cash's word is as good as gold, almost better than Harrison's favors. I could practically sell them on the black market.

"Beckett mentioned Samantha and you being into her. Was he right?"

A smile plays on his lips. "We never officially dated."

"Oh." *Friends with benefits?*

"I don't start relationships with doctors, Rem, especially those obsessed with career climbing. I worked long days for nearly seven years. Thankfully, Hayden was in Houston, too, and would force me to have dinner with him once a month to keep me in check. He made sure I didn't forget who I was until he moved back. That's when I spiraled and was very hard to be around. You wouldn't have liked who I was, trust me. I was a bastard."

I swallow hard. The world has hardened Cash in ways I didn't imagine. "You believe that?"

"Absolutely. I was obsessed to my detriment. When Beckett told me about buying the Horseshoe Creek Ranch, it woke me up. I looked at my life and asked myself what the fuck I was doing. I had the job of my dreams, made ridiculous money, and was unhappy. After I was offered another five-year contract for triple the money, I refused it. I became an equine vet to be outside, but I barely saw the sun. I had everything but felt empty."

"I thought you were happy. You seemed happy online."

"No. I was miserable," he says. "That's why I came home. Being *here* is happiness. I needed fresh air, Rem. I needed *you*. When you stopped answering my calls and texts, I knew what we had was over. I also knew the longer I stayed away, the greater risk I had of losing you forever. In the chaos, you were the calm in my mind, the light at the end of my tunnel. I came back as soon as I fucking could."

My emotions bubble, and my heart hurts for him. I had no clue.

"Cash," I whisper, understanding the mental anguish he put himself through. I did the same thing. Maybe we're more alike than different.

"Knowing I was coming home to you was the only thing that kept me going. Hayden kept me updated and would always tell me how you were. It felt like you were waiting for me, too."

"I was." I study him. Since he returned, this is the first time we've had the chance to have a serious conversation. Our time has always been rushed, and I cherish this so damn much.

"What we had... *have*... people find once in a lifetime. I'm not walking away from that."

His truths make me smile. "I was lost without you. I searched high and low, trying to find someone who could fill the hole you left in my heart."

His jaw clenched. "And?"

"You're not replaceable."

As I swim in his hazel eyes, I understand he's a dangerous rip current taking me under. Somehow, I'd buried myself so far under his skin he couldn't erase me. However, it goes both ways and now we're swimming in dangerous territory. I want to kiss him so fucking badly, but I know I need to stop this before it starts.

As if he can read my mind, he speaks up. "I should probably get going."

"Will you stay with me tonight?" I ask, not wanting him to leave, not yet.

Since January, we've rushed our time together. For once, I want to slow down with him.

"Do you have extra blankets and pillows?"

"You're not sleeping on the couch," I say, crossing my arms over my chest and smirking.

He tilts his head at me, and I see the desire in his eyes, but Cash doesn't say a word.

"I won't force you to stay if you want to leave," I say. I've grown tired of pretending I don't want him when I know it's just us.

He steps forward and grabs my hands. Sparks fly and flutter when he touches me. "I don't want to leave you."

I let out a relieved sigh.

"Let's go to bed," he says, wrapping his arm around my shoulder as we take the hallway. "Beckett told me Summer was changing your shifts to days."

"I wanted to surprise you," I admit. "Guess not anymore."

He chuckles. "Whoops."

I shake my head. "Gonna have to tell Beckett to stop running his big mouth."

Once we're in my room, I shut the door and look up at him. "Please don't leave me once I'm asleep."

"That won't *ever* happen again."

CHAPTER NINE

CASH

Remi clicks on the lamp, and a warm glow fills the room. I stand with my hands in my pockets, admiring her. Taking a mental snapshot, not wanting to forget how beautiful she is right now, just being herself. The heaviness I felt earlier with her has vanished. Properly communicating and sharing what's in our hearts did that.

"What?" she asks, tilting her head at me, noticing I'm staring. "You have this look on your face."

"Feels like a dream. Trying to make sure it's not," I admit.

She takes a few steps forward and wraps her arms around my waist. "Feels real to me."

I kiss her forehead. "My biggest fear is fucking this up and losing everything and you."

"We can still stop this right now before it goes too far," she says, meeting my eyes.

"We're a runaway train, Remi. You know we'll never be able to stay away from one another, especially now that I'm back. You'd be thinking about me even if you were with another man. Our connection is deep and tightly wound. There's no undoing what we've done or how I'll always feel about you."

"You're right," she whispers. "I'll always want you, Cash."

"If you had gotten married while I was away, would you still have met up with me?" I ask.

She closes her eyes tight. "Yes. And you?" she asks.

"You'll always be my kryptonite," I admit, happy that's not our situation. "It's why we're dangerous apart. We don't care about anyone else. I left a lot of pain in my wake."

"I did, too," she says. "And I wished they were you the whole time."

"I know," I tell her, knowing exactly how much she fucking means to me. I'd do anything for her, even end lifelong friendships, if that's what it took. "Let's spend June getting to know one another again."

"How? Our schedules won't allow it," she says.

"Every day, I'll write a letter for you to read when you return from work. By the end of the month, there will be no secrets."

"Okay," she whispers.

Leaning forward, I gently press my lips against hers, and our tongues slowly brush together. Remi tastes like sugar and alcohol, and I can't get enough. Kissing her comes naturally, and it feels so damn right. My body buzzes as we grow more greedy. This woman has me under her spell. As I slowly pull away, she desperately savors the moment as I crave more of her touch.

"It's only *ever* felt like that with you," she whispers. It's an admission that has my heart lurching.

When I open my eyes, she stares up at me. I run my thumb across her cheek, and she leans into me. "That's why I'm not worried about us, babe. I know what we've got. I feel it, too."

She briefly pauses. "We just need to be sure."

"I want *you* to be sure."

I've waited seven years to be back with her, and I'll wait however long she needs. We're two pieces of a puzzle, made for one another.

She moves to her dresser, slides open the bottom drawer, pulls out a pair of jogging pants, and hands them to me.

"Who do these belong to?" I ask, my brows furrowing.

"Jealous?"

"*Fuck yes.*"

"Good. They belong to *you*," Remi says, opening the drawer wider. "So are these."

Next to one another are a few of my University of Texas T-shirts and shorts. It's a time capsule with items of clothes I haven't seen in a long time. I thought they'd gotten lost in the move.

"You kept these?"

"Thought you might need them one day."

I chuckle. "Seems as if that day has arrived."

"Finally." She studies me, and her gaze lingers from my mouth down to my abs as I remove my belt. I unbutton and unzip my dress pants which drop to the floor. I grab the hem of my collared shirt and pull it off my body.

When I'm standing in my boxers, Remi steps back, drinking me in like a tall glass of water on a hot summer day.

"And just like that, I'm twenty-one again," she says. "Had the best time of my life."

I chuckle, feeling the week catching up with me. "No funny stuff, Rem. I'm putting those rules back in place. When we're together again, it won't be because you drank too much and your inhibitions are fucked."

Disappointment splashes across her face like I've denied her.

"Please don't think I don't want to fuck your brains out right now. I absolutely do."

She grabs my hand, leading me into bed with her.

She leans over and clicks off the lamp, then we lie on our backs, staring at the ceiling. Then Remi slides out of her shorts and panties and throws them on the blankets. I turn my head toward her.

"Rem," I whisper as her hand slides down between her legs, and she gasps as she touches herself.

"I wish you were touching me," she whimpers. "So fucking wet for you."

As she grabs my hand and guides it down to her pussy, my cock grows hard.

"*Please.* I won't regret this," she says as my finger dips between her drenched folds. Remi reaches over and slides her hand inside my joggers, stroking me long and hard. I groan out, my eyes rolling into the back of my head. Any other time we've fooled around, someone has interrupted us, leaving us hanging on the edge.

She lifts her shirt, and I lean over, capturing her perky pink nipple in my mouth as I rub circles on her needy clit. Her hips buck upward as she continues stroking me. I dip the tip of my finger into her tight, warm cunt, and she groans with anticipation as I give her more. Remi rocks against my finger as I continue clit play with my thumb. She winds up quickly, and I can tell by how she moans that she's close.

"Are you going to come for me?" I ask as she strokes me so fucking good. My balls tighten, and I don't know how much longer I'll be able to last. We're too desperate and never satisfied, but this is the first time we've brought each other this close in nearly seven years.

Her muscles tense as her orgasm builds. I slow my pace, not giving it to her immediately, wanting her to know that I still have her—body, wants, and needs—memorized. I know what she craves and her deepest sexual desires.

"Fuck yes," she says, muttering. "Keep going. Yes. Yes. Yes."

Her back arches, and as if a string held her, it snaps, and she pulses around me as I slowly finger fuck her into oblivion.

"Cash, fuck," she says as she continues to come, but I don't stop, just slow my pace, working her up again, giving her two digits.

She opens her legs so fucking wide as I gently rub her clit. Her body tenses again, and she quickly begs.

"I'm..." The sentence ends as she screams out my name. I'm sure the whole town hears her coming, and I kiss her neck. Her pulse races as she crumbles under my touch again. "I've waited so long for that. So fucking long."

I place my fingers in my mouth, tasting how damn sweet she is. "Me too."

Her mouth traces the shell of my ear, and then she moves to my neck before taking my nipple in her mouth. I'm so hard my cock feels like it might break off as she strokes me slowly. My fingers are in her hair; if she keeps this up, I will lose myself.

"Tell me when you're close," she whispers, her hot breath in my ear. "But next time we're together like this, you are fucking me. I want you deep inside my cunt, ripping me in two," she demands.

"Next time, I plan on breaking you in half," I warn as she slows, playing with the sticky precum on the end of my dick. Her touch makes me sensitive. "Goddamn," I hiss, my hips bucking upward as my quads tighten. The orgasm builds fast. I growl out.

Remi pushes my joggers down, and takes me in her hot mouth as she continues to stroke and suck me. Her other hand massages my balls, and when she tries to take me to the back of her throat, I release. She milks and drinks me down, licking me clean.

"I love the way you taste," she says with a smile as she crawls into my arms. "I've missed you so much."

"If you only knew how much I missed you," I say.

"I'm going to write you letters, too," she says.

"Oh, we're going to be pen pals?"

"Absolutely. Ask me whatever you want." She traces hearts and circles on my stomach.

I dig my fingers into her scalp, smelling her hair and skin as she holds onto me like she never wants to let me go. Fuck, I hope she doesn't.

"I will."

Remi yawns, and I smile with pure satisfaction.

"Good night, Valentine."

"Night," she says with a content sigh.

I close my eyes, and relief floods through me. Even if Beckett will never forgive me, I think he'd understand. Love like this only comes once in a lifetime, and I can't pass up the opportunity.

I fucking won't.

THE NEXT MORNING, I wake with my hard cock pressed against Remi's ass. My arm wraps around her stomach, and as I try to pull away from her, she interlocks her fingers with mine, not letting me go.

I hum against the softness of her neck. "Good morning, gorgeous."

"You feel good," she says in her sleepy tone.

"Don't tease me," I warn.

"Hmm?" She rolls onto her back, and her mouth is so damn close to mine. When my hand rests on her hip, she smirks.

"Naughty as fuck. You know exactly what you're doi—"

A knock taps against the front door, and Remi's eyes widen. "Shit. What time is it?"

My phone is inside of my pocket on the floor. It buzzes, and a nagging feeling appears.

"Who do you think it is?" I ask her as she rushes out of bed.

Remi grabs one blanket from her bed and a spare pillow and throws it on the couch. "Go to the bathroom," she says, picking up my clothes and shoving them into my arms. "Now."

I get up and do what she says as she closes her door, then rushes down the hallway as the knocking turns into pounding. Remi speaks to someone, and they respond in a deep voice. But I can't distinguish who it is. Jealousy creeps up. What if she has been seeing someone? Didn't she say we were exclusive?

I'm too far away, and I need to confirm who the fuck it is. After a few minutes, I flush the toilet and wash my hands. There's no use hiding out; my truck is outside, and everyone knows what I drive. If it's not one of her brothers, I might lose my fucking cool.

I put on yesterday's clothes and put my joggers in the hamper. I meet her in the living room with my fist tight and am relieved to see Colt. Had it been some other man, I'd have knocked him the fuck out.

"Good morning," I say, giving him a firm handshake, and he smiles.

"What were y'all up to last night?" His brows lift.

I stand firm, my expression not changing because he's giving Remi a hard time, as he always has.

"Absolutely nothing," Remi states, narrowing her eyes at him. One of her biggest pet peeves is being teased about us. It's usually the truth, though.

He laughs, leans back, and pats the pillow Remi threw at the end. "Cash, how's your back from sleeping on this board last night?"

"Perfect," I tell him, meeting his narrowed eyes. "Gonna grab some coffee from Grinding Beans. Would either of you like one?" I ask, changing the subject.

"No, thanks," Colt says.

"Me," she responds. "Black like—"

"Your soul. I know," I say.

"Already finishing each other's sentences?" Colt asks, wearing a cheeky grin. "Interesting, sis."

I don't waste any time and give them their space.

CHAPTER TEN

REMI

When the door closes, I turn my body toward my twin brother. "What's wrong with you?"

"This is fucking ridiculous. Why aren't you two open with what's going on? It's obvious."

I roll my eyes. "Pfft. We hardly speak to one another in public."

"You don't have to," he says. "I know you. And after last night when you were chatting with Archie, I had no doubts about the two of you. Cash glared at him like he was going to fuck him up."

I snicker. "Did he? I didn't notice."

"Tell me what you're worried about," he says.

"My relationships are none of your business. Why are you here?"

He shakes his head. "You're stubborn. The quicker you rip off the Band-aid, the sooner Beckett will get the fuck over it. If Kinsley told him to stay away from Summer, do you think he would've?"

"Please, stop," I whisper. My twin brother already knows the truth because I can't hide anything from him. "It's different."

"You told me you were in love with him, *Remington*," Colt says, using my full name. It just reminds me of being in trouble as a kid.

I thought he'd forgotten. I'd hoped he had. "It doesn't matter."

He shrugs. "Have you told Mom and Dad you're seeing Cash? I'm sure they'd be happy to know that. After last night, though, I'm sure they know."

"Goodbye, ol' brother of mine," I say, grabbing him, but he's so tall and muscular he doesn't budge. My brothers are all built the same.

Instead of leaving, he kicks off his running shoes and places his feet on my coffee table. He's wearing his glasses today, the same shape I have, but it was an accidental twinning moment. I don't always wear mine, though, just when reading. Colt's eyesight is worse.

He places his hands behind his head. "I'm thinking about buying another house."

"This is what you wanted to talk about at seven in the morning? You know I work the night shift."

He grins. "You were up with *Dr. Johnson*. But anyway, you know the old Riley house."

My brows furrow. "The *haunted* one?"

"The *abandoned* one," he corrects and chuckles.

"It's falling apart."

"Oh, it's in horrible shape," he says. "But I stopped by and walked through it. There wasn't a front door, and someone had gone inside and spray-painted some dicks on the walls, but it was sturdy. The structure was solid, so I made them an offer."

"Was it for sale?"

"No," he tells me. "I just drove by it to shoot my shot because it would be a great fixer-upper."

I chuckle. "It needs to be flattened."

"That's the difference between me and you. I see the possibility of things while you take it at face value."

"I do not."

"You do, and that's okay. That's why I wanted to talk to you about this. I'm logical, but I also believe I can do anything. Possibilities aren't reality. If you wish in one hand and shit in the other, well, you know how the saying goes."

"Exactly. Give me more details," I say.

He places his hands behind his head. "Built in the 1800s and has been abandoned since around 1995. It needs new everything, but the bones are solid. I can get the property and the house for fifty thousand. When I finish it, I can live there or flip it and make three hundred and fifty in profit."

My mouth falls open.

"It has five bedrooms and three bathrooms. I'd knock some walls down to open up the living room, and the kitchen overlooks the edge of the Horseshoe Creek Ranch."

"Wow," I say. Anything is possible, but it needs to be probable. "How long will it take you to renovate?"

"Since my other two houses are in perfect condition, it would take a solid year to fix it, working from early morning to dark." He grins. "Can you imagine?"

"If anyone can do it, it's you. I bet it's satisfying, too," I tell him, envisioning it.

"Any dream can be a reality if you want it to be," he says, but I don't think he's talking about the house, not by how his jaw relaxes. "But anyway, how do you feel about it?"

I stare at the painting on the wall. "It sounds like an excellent investment if you can reno quickly."

"Guess that house is *fixing to be mine,* then." He holds up his hand for a high five, and I laugh. "I looked up the tax records before I went over there. The tax records say the property is worth seventy-five. The land also needs a lot of work, but like you said, it's an investment. Five bedrooms is a lot for just me, though," he says.

"Guess you'll have to have a fuckton of kids to fill it."

He laughs. "Fuck them kids."

"Yeah, I feel ya. I'm not ready for that yet. I want to see how it goes for Summer. If it sucks, she'll be truthful. Kinsley will probably be pregnant next year because they always promised to have kids together. We're in the clear for a long time, thankfully."

"I've come to terms with not finding anyone. A stork needs to drop a woman on my door because there ain't anyone around here."

"What about Haley?" I ask.

He gives me a look. "No."

I yawn, wishing I had that coffee. "She's fun."

"We're not compatible," he says. "Plus, Haley's into Emmett. Not trying to steal my brother's girl."

I lift a brow. "How'd you know that?"

He shakes his head. "It's like you don't realize how transparent you are."

The door swings open, and Cash carries two coffees. Cash looks at me, and my expression softens. He hands me one cup, and I immediately remove the lid because I've learned my lesson.

"That right there." Colt stands and points between us.

"What are you talking about? He handed me a drink," I say.

Cash seems confused, too.

"You're like a flash in the dark. If someone's not paying attention, they'd miss how you look at one another. To me, it's crystal clear."

I make a face at him.

"Anyway, have fun. I'm about to buy a house," he says, patting Cash on his shoulder as he walks past him.

When we hear his truck pulling away, Cash turns to me. "What the fuck was that about?"

I shake my head. "He knows about us."

"Yeah, about that," he says, sipping his drink. "There are many people on that list."

"Like who?" I ask.

"Kinsley, Hayden, Grace, Harrison, Colt, Christine, and Archer."

"Archie."

He rolls his eyes. "I don't care what his name is. Who else knows?"

"Haley. Lexi. Emmett." I sigh. "I just don't know how. We've avoided each other the way we'd planned. How we look at one another is speculation and gossip. There is zero proof."

"Maybe we were messy," he says. "I think Harrison knows something more, considering his snide comments. It's only a matter of time until the walls close on us, babe. When will Beckett find out?"

I contemplate his question.

"Are you prepared for that?" he asks.

"I thought we'd have more time."

He shakes his head. "We don't. It seems like the avalanche started, and there's no stopping it now. Colt just confirmed that for me. Actually, Hayden did yesterday."

I pat the couch cushion next to me and then turn my body toward him. Cash clicks the button on his phone and glances down.

"What did Hayden say?"

"In a roundabout way, he told me to fight for you," he explains, but a smile plays on his lips. They've been friends for nearly as long as he and Beckett. They also lived in Houston at the same time until Hayden returned to Valentine last year to try his second chance with Kinsley.

It makes me laugh. "Okay, we should tally how many people are against this."

"Two," he says. "Harrison and Beckett."

"So, how do we get them on our side?" I ask, and it grows quiet as the gears turn.

When an idea hits me, I gasp. "I think I might have a plan."

He shakes his head. "I already don't like the sound of this or the look on your face."

"It's perfect," I say, standing up and smiling. "Beckett said he didn't want to see me sad anymore, right? Well, guess who will be doom and gloom around him."

"You're not a great actress."

"I can try. I have a lot of pent-up emotions," I admit.

Now that Cash's back, many of my struggles have vanished.

"I need to tell him I broke up with Eric because he was right. Then, a week later, tell him I realized I'm in love with *you*. Then I'll explain how you've denied me because of *him*, and he's the reason my life sucks."

"Or we could tell him the truth and let him deal with it in his own way?" His lips part. "Honesty is the best policy."

"Nah. This is sibling revenge. He keeps trying to control my relationships and will do the same thing to Fenix, London, and Vera. It's up to me to stop this for my younger sisters. I'll let him think he's the puppet master. Give him a taste of his own medicine."

"Rem, sometimes you're too smart for your own good. This could backfire," he says, trying to be the voice of reason.

My mind is made. "We'll try my way, and if it doesn't work, we'll tell him the truth. But in the end, we're together."

"Okay," he says, shaking his head, but he gives me a cute little grin. He's always allowed me to call the shots when navigating my family. Right now, we should tell the truth, but I'm determined to teach Beckett a lesson. I'm matching his energy.

"You're going to destroy him. I can see it in your eyes."

I move toward him, wrapping my arm around his waist and looking into his eyes. "As long as he doesn't destroy us, I don't care. If I let him keep doing this, my unhappiness *will* be in his hands, just like before. He needs to understand that enough is enough."

His brows lift. "And what about Harrison?"

"I think I can fool him, too, but he'll be harder because we're closer. Also, he has no proof. His side comments were probably because he caught us standing too close. He saw nothing other than me pouncing on you. Oh, and not to mention, *the girl code* is enacted. If he messes with any of my relationships, Grace has promised to cut him off to keep him in line."

He bursts into laughter like I'm kidding. I'm not. "Wait, you're serious."

"Dead serious. I have Summer on board, too. If they interfere with my love life, I'll *end* theirs."

I think about this more closely. "Sometimes you're scary."

"Only when it comes to you. Are you prepared for what people say when I tell them how much I want you?"

"You'll actually go that far?" He doesn't sound convinced.

"They need to get used to hearing my truth," I say. My body buzzes as I think about it.

His eyes darken, and I'm tempted to steal a kiss when he tilts my chin upward.

"And what happens at the end of our ninety days in this place?" he asks.

"Maybe you should propose," I say with a wink.

"Mm. And if I did, what would your answer be?" He studies me.

"I guess you'll have to wait and see."

He licks his lips and smirks.

I think I might die and go to heaven.

CHAPTER ELEVEN

CASH

It's been twenty-six days since Remi and I moved in together. I've passed her on the way to work as she's headed home. She's blown me kisses each time. I can't believe how our shifts are exactly at the wrong times. All month, I've had emergency calls on the weekends, and somehow, I've missed her in the afternoons, too. It's almost comical how it has worked out because whenever we've thought we'd see one another, she has to stay over, or I'm out of the office.

However, knowing I'm in her space, even when she's not there, brings a smile to my face. After the first week of missing one another, we poured more of our hearts and souls into the notebook we pass back and forth each day. It was awkward at first, but it quickly became our confession. It's how we've asked the hard questions. A spiral notebook is our safe place where we share our deepest secrets.

Sitting at the two-person breakfast nook with a freshly brewed cup of coffee, I open the five-subject spiral college-lined notebook. This has made the days pass quicker and has given me something to look forward to when I'm missing her. Somehow, we're closer than ever.

Each morning when I wake up alone, I know her beautiful mind awaits me since we write them before we leave for the day.

I pick up the pen and scribble away, knowing she'll read this in an hour when she comes home. If I didn't live and die by my schedule, I'd wait for her, but unfortunately, I can't skip my appointments. She wouldn't want me to, anyway.

My Valentine,

I woke up this morning with you on my mind. There's nothing new about that, though.

Last night, I dreamed you left the B+B and crawled into bed with me.

I must've been exhausted because I could've sworn you were home until I rolled over and you weren't there.

The bed was cold, too. I laid awake for an hour before I fell back asleep, contemplating if I should've driven to the B+B to see you.

However, I didn't want to ruin the plan.

Eyes wander out in the middle of nowhere, too, especially when Summer has cameras everywhere outside of the property and in the common areas.

Anyway, I miss you so damn much, and I can't wait until this weekend when I get to see you finally.

Yesterday, I asked what you wanted for your birthday, and you never answered.

So, I have two questions for you today:

1. What do you want for your birthday?

2. What's your favorite memory of us?

Now, to answer yours.

You asked what was on my mind the first time I saw you in that coffee shop seven summers ago.

I FLICK the pen between my fingers, thinking back to the memory with a smile.

Sometimes, there are moments in our lives that are so monumental it's impossible to forget the minute details.

I noticed you as soon as you walked in.

What I remember the most was how your hair was down, and it looked windblown like you'd driven with the windows down.

Familiarity crept in, and at first glance, I thought you were Kinsley. I'd been away for too long to realize who you were. I was preparing to get my balls busted because that's just how Kinsley is.

After you ordered and noticed me sitting at my favorite table in the corner, my life changed.

With one dirty look, I was caught: hook, line, and sinker.

I don't know what I expected when I sat with you, but it wasn't to give you my number or have you text me. You started something I wasn't prepared for.

You may have always had your eye on me and fallen first... but I fell harder.

As I mentioned several times before, falling in love is the easy part. Keeping it is when it gets complicated.

This time, I won't let you go unless you want me to. I guess that would be a discussion for September 1st.

However, know that I'm a workhorse, babe. I was married to my job, devoted, and forever faithful.

If you choose me, you'll be my new career. I want more time with you. It's the one thing we can never buy more of.

Time is fucking precious, and the older I get, the more I realize that. The truth is, I don't want to waste another minute. When you know, you know.

There are days when I still regret going to Houston, but lately, I've tried to flip the script.

Leaving made me realize what we had, and this time, I'm determined to keep it.

Just like you mentioned, I worry about Harrison and Beckett. I respect them and don't want to lose my brothers. But if I'm forced to choose you're my choice.

I've always known that. Do you?

There are only four more working days until your birthday, and then we'll finally be on the same schedule.

I'm marking days off on my calendar at work like I'm being released from prison.

Not seeing or talking to you until your birthday is hell, but I know a light is at the end of the tunnel. Somehow, it's <u>always you</u> who keeps me going.

I'm not sure I'll be able to keep my eyes off you at your party—not that you care, because I think you enjoy knowing you're the end game.

But maybe you can clear that up for me? Do you notice how I look at you?

Would that be considered another question?

Even though you're not here, the ghost of you is, and it always haunts me. I'm not sure I'll ever be able to get enough of you, Rem.

Your heart. Your mind. Your soul. I love everything about you.

SATURDAY CAN'T GET HERE FAST ENOUGH.

I LOOK FORWARD TO READING YOUR REPLY WHEN I
GET HOME TODAY. SWEET DREAMS AND EARLY HAPPY
BIRTHDAY.

$

I TOP my to-go coffee and then drive to work. I check the time, knowing it's another day when we won't cross paths. When she gets off today, I'll be in the Davis Mountain area because I have a barn call this afternoon.

It will be worth the wait.

The morning sun rises above the horizon, and fog floats over the country road as I drive to the clinic. Dew droplets coat the ground, and I can tell it will be a hot day. June in this area is always hot, but I prefer it because it's dry heat instead of sticky heat, like in Houston.

When I arrive at the clinic, I walk inside and turn on the lights. A stack of files waits for me on my desk for the appointments I have scheduled today. Three horses need their teeth floated over at the Granger ranch. Two others need their yearly shots. Mr. Armstrong wants to know if his mare is ready for breeding. It's going to be a long as fuck day, but at least I'll be busy.

As I sip my coffee, the clinic door opens, and I glance at the clock on my wall. It's barely past seven. Moments later, I hear heavy footsteps clunking down the hallway. Then Beckett is standing in my doorway, holding a box of donuts.

"Hungry?" he asks.

"I knew it was you based on your cadence." I laugh. "Actually, I am. I was gonna make some toast or some shit before I left for the day," I tell him.

He sits, plopping the box down onto my desk. Sticky, fat donuts are stuffed in the box, and they smell like sugar and sin. I snag one. "Shit, they're still warm."

"Yeah, Sadie hooked me up," Beckett says, grabbing one.

Sadie owns the bakery in town, and she's married to an ex-bullriding champ.

"So, how's things been going lately?" Beckett asks.

"Fine," I tell him. "Been working my ass off non-stop this month. However, I'm happy to be home," I admit. "Grateful, actually."

He nods. "Yeah, I noticed you're out on calls a lot. Stopped by the other day to see if you wanted to join me for lunch, but you were already gone."

"Shoulda texted me."

"I spoke with Melody, and she said you were in Alpine."

"Oh, yeah. Last Wednesday. This man thought his horse was colicking. It was one of those days I could've lived without, if you know what I mean. However, the horse is fine. Full recovery. It was bad, though."

"Yeah. I can't imagine how difficult that is."

"I thought I'd eventually be desensitized to it, but nah. Not sure that ever goes away," I explain. "But anyway, what's up with you lately?"

"Summer got a call yesterday from this man called Andrew Callo, and he offered her fifty thousand dollars to rent the B&B until Sunday."

My mouth nearly falls to the ground. "Holy shit."

"I know. She canceled all the reservations we had."

I shake my head. "I guess it's true that with enough money, a person can buy anything they want."

Beckett shrugs. "We only had three people staying this week, but she found them somewhere else to go and hooked them up with free training lessons, so it all worked out."

"What if this guy is a weirdo?" I think about Remi working

there at night alone with this man, but the thought doesn't settle well with me.

Beckett shrugs. "Then I'll fuck him up."

I laugh. He's always been a bulldog, and he will bite. Some people run their mouths. He means it. It's how I know we'd fight if he knew the truth about me and Remi. It's why I'm always prepared.

"How's it been living with Remi?" he asks, but he zeroes in on me.

I think about the plan she's enacting next week. I don't know if it's the right decision.

"We've not crossed paths once since I moved in. We need a bigger bathroom, though."

I'd rather live with her in a house we build together, one we can make our own, but I don't dare say that out loud.

He chuckles. "Yeah. I didn't realize how fucking gross Summer was until I lived with her. She does this thing where she puts strands of hair on the shower wall. I'll come home, and there's long hair slapped on the tile. I've cleaned it up for the past month, and she hasn't noticed. Not even once."

"Do you still have a weak stomach?"

I thought he grew out of this. Beckett used to dry heave when it came to literal shit. His parents had this cattle dog when we were kids, and if it had an accident in the house, he'd clean it and complain while gagging. He refused to deal with his baby siblings. He seems like a hard ass.

"Yeah."

I burst into laughter and snag another donut. "This kid is going to kill you. They're *disgusting*."

"I know. I'll be gagging my way through a diaper change. And spit up." He makes a face and shakes his head. "I'm hoping I become desensitized to it. Praying, actually."

"Doubt it," I tell him.

"I was going to ask you how Remi has been acting lately. She told me last week that she and Eric broke up," he says. "She seems down."

"Really?" I ask, knowing this is part of the plan.

"I'm concerned," he tells me. "I know her schedule is changing next week, but will you please keep an eye on her?"

"Yes, of course."

"Thank you," he sighs.

The main door opens and closes. Beckett and I turn our heads to see Melody. She smiles at him. "Good morning," she says.

"Would you like a donut?" Beckett asks.

"No thanks. But do any of you know Lexi Matthews?"

We're both confused.

"Yeah," Beckett says.

"This guy just approached me when I was walking out of the diner and asked me if I could give him information about her. It was creepy."

Beckett's brows furrow. "Someone asked Kinsley and Remi."

"Why? What's going on?"

Melody pulls her phone from her pocket. "I researched her, and she's dating Easton Calloway."

"Who's that?" Beckett asks.

"Are you serious?" she asks. "You don't know who he is?"

Beckett glances at me, and I shrug.

"They call him the Prince of Diamonds. Calloway Diamonds. None of that rings a bell?"

I make a face. "We don't keep up with shit like that."

"Anyway, Alexis is dating him. They're like the real deal. She's from here, right?"

"Yeah, she is," Beckett says. "Just seems weird. How'd they meet?"

"Not sure." She turns her phone around and shows us a picture of them sitting together in the park. They look *happy*. The spark is undeniable.

It makes me wonder if that's what everyone sees with me and Remi, and that's why they're convinced something is going on. It's the only way because we're hardly together, even privately.

I can count on my two hands how many times we've seen one another since I moved back. Seeing her sometimes is better than never, but now I want *always and forever.*

"Is that her?" Melody asks, swiping through other photos of them leaving an event. Seeing Lexi in that setting is odd, but they're a perfect match. He's darkness, and she's sunshine.

"Yeah." Beckett shakes his head. "They're here to get information about her. *Bastards.* We protect our own 'round here, so no one better talk."

She locks her phone. "They offered me $100 for a statement."

"Shoulda negotiated," I tell her.

"Hell no. They were rude. One guy grabbed my arm to stop me, and I nearly drop-kicked him, then sprayed him with mace."

"Shoulda. Then told them to get fucked," Beckett says, and his phone rings, pulling his attention away. He turns it around, and I see Harrison's name on the screen.

As he stands, he offers me more donuts, and I shake my head. "See ya," he says, answering.

Melody walks further into my office and sits where Beckett just was. "How are things going?"

"Great."

I try to check in with her weekly, even if it's five or ten minutes to catch up since she's my right-hand woman.

"How are you liking things?" I ask.

"I'm shocked you grew up here. Like really? No wonder you're the way you are. Southern is a lifestyle in this part of the state."

I laugh. "I know. Horses have always been a major part of my life. My dad's a breeder, so it's ingrained in me. Anyway, how'd you like to stay after your internship?"

A smile fills her face. "Are you kidding?"

"Dead serious. It's busy around here. I can only handle so much, and you've been doing an incredible job running the office while I'm out. Several people have told me how great you were with their dogs and cats. They like you 'round here a lot."

Her grin doesn't falter.

"Obviously, you don't have to decide right now. You have two months of the internship left, but I'd like to know thirty days before your contract ends. I can get Stephanie, my lawyer, to help me draw up another one and make a new offer to keep you on. We can discuss pay and all of that," I tell her. "I don't want to work like a dog for the rest of my life. Having help would give me the work-life balance I haven't had since I graduated."

"Dr. Johnson, I don't need time to think about it. I'd be honored to have this position."

"Great to hear." I hold out my hand, and she gives me a firm shake. "I look forward to working with you."

"Thank you for the opportunity. I appreciate it. My med school friends are going to be jealous. I'm the first to snag a permanent job."

I chuckle. "That must feel good. I was the first in my class, too."

"Yeah, but you're the best in the state. Everyone knows that."

"I lost a lot getting there," I tell her.

"But the experience is what people dream of having. You can work anywhere in the world."

"That's true. However, I'm exactly where I want to be."

She tilts her head. "Was it hard? Working for the clinic? And the horse track?"

"It's very competitive and cutthroat. You can't have a soul. I trusted no one because they all wanted to be where I was.

Sabotage is real. Working in that type of environment after med school wasn't healthy."

"I heard that, actually," she says. "I did my research on you before I took the position. A college friend helped."

My brow pops. "And?"

"I know your credentials. Her brother worked with you at the animal hospital in Houston. She asked him what he thought about you."

I cross my arms, actually enjoying this conversation. "Oh, really?"

"Apparently, you're feared," she says. "You were called an assertive asshole who'd fire someone without question if the protocol wasn't followed properly. He said you were difficult, but if I passed up the opportunity to work beside you, I was fucking stupid. You're respected. The best."

"My reputation often precedes me."

"I was prepared to deal with this gigantic asshole," she says. "You're a puppy."

"There are fewer people and fewer sick animals here, but I'm still an asshole. You do what you should, so I don't have to act that way. If you'd made a mistake the first week, I'd have terminated you and found someone else. Your standards match mine, so I have no issues."

She nods. "I know."

"What do you think Rob will say?" I ask. "Is he getting along okay in Valentine?"

Rob is Melody's fiancé who moved to the middle of nowhere, Texas, to be with her. It must be true love because Valentine doesn't have much to offer other than small-town living. There is an allure to that, though. I missed it after living in Austin and Dallas through my twenties and almost half of my thirties.

Coming home was nostalgic for many reasons.

"Are you kidding me? He loves it here." She laughs. "More

than me. He's been driving to Big Bend once a month to hike. I've joined him several times, but he's really into it. His parents are considering moving here if we end up staying."

I grin. "Guess you can share the good news."

"Yeah. This was a pleasant talk. Thank you again." Her smart watch buzzes, and she twists her wrist to look at it. "Gotta get ready for my first appointment. Annual shots."

"Ah. I have to get going, too. If you need anything today, call me. I don't care what's going on, okay?"

She nods. "Yes, Dr. Johnson. Have a safe day."

"You, too," I tell her, then walk to my truck. I grab my medical bag and double-check the supplies I have on board. After I close the door, the growls of Remi's Mustang grab my attention.

I take a step back and watch her pass by. She picks up speed, kicking up gravel and dust. I shake my head and smirk, imagining the smile on her perfect face.

Her car roars to life as she turns onto the country road. I watch until the red of her taillights fades into the distance, and she's out of sight. I wish she would've stopped. However, we're still playing it safe and agreed we wouldn't see each other until her birthday. The anticipation might kill me.

I'd die a thousand deaths if I could live with her for just one lifetime.

CHAPTER TWELVE

REMI

As I drive past the Valentine Veterinary Clinic, Cash stands outside of his truck with a stethoscope around his neck, carrying his medical bag. He turns toward me, but I know he can't see me because the windows of my Mustang are too dark. A smile touches my lips.

I want to turn my car around, but I continue forward.

We agreed to wait to see one another until my birthday. It's been over three weeks, and I don't know how I'll survive the next four days, but I'm trying. It sounds wild, but the distance allows us to grow closer. I've learned things I've never known about him, and I love how raw he is with his words.

Is it possible to fall for him harder *without* sex? Yes.

I turn onto the country road and head toward our condo, ready to read the letter he left me an hour ago. Each day, he rips himself open and pours words on a page before he starts his day. It's love letters I never knew I wanted.

As I walk in the door, our notebook sits on the counter. I sit at the breakfast nook and open it to the last page he wrote. My eyes slide over it, and my heart flutters with each word.

EVEN THOUGH YOU'RE NOT HERE, THE GHOST OF YOU IS, AND IT ALWAYS HAUNTS ME.

I'M NOT SURE I'LL EVER BE ABLE TO GET ENOUGH OF YOU, REM. YOUR HEART. YOUR MIND. YOUR SOUL. I LOVE EVERYTHING ABOUT YOU.

That's when my emotions take over, and tears fall down my cheeks. I don't deserve him. I glance at the dollar signs he wrote on the bottom and smile before closing the notebook with him on my mind.

He's all I want, all I've ever wanted. I *crave* seeing Cash—smelling, kissing, and touching him—and I can't wait to see him on my birthday.

I WAKE up at four and need to be at work by five. After I've filled a mug full of coffee, I sit in the chair and open the next page in our notebook. I grab a pen and write to him, knowing he'll read it when he gets home.

My Valentine,

I woke up this afternoon wishing you were home so I could talk to you directly.

Before I fell asleep, you were on my mind. I hoped I'd dream while I slept, but I didn't.

Yes, I know you asked me what I wanted for my

birthday, and I didn't answer because I didn't know what to say.

So I'm just going to be honest: I want you. Nothing else.

I want your lips.
I want to have you buried between my legs.
I want every part of you.

IMAGINING HIS TOUCH, the way he makes me feel, me squeezing my thighs together. I continue.

Now, you asked what my favorite memory of us is.

Easy, the night we escaped the crowd on my twenty-first birthday.

We snuck away and laid on a blanket and made wishes upon the stars that fell, leaving glittery trails.

Do you remember what you told me?

I SMILE, thinking about it.

You told me you were falling in love with me, kissed me for the first time, and stole my breath away.

I never wanted the night to end.

I was already stupidly in love with you but was too scared to admit it was more than a fling and a stupid crush then.

What I'd quickly felt for you ran much deeper, and it happened so fast that I think my head is still spinning.

I still remember the sound of your laugh and how you tasted like chocolate cake and tequila.

You held me in your arms, and we watched the Milky Way rise. That night was magical, one I will never forget. It was the first time I imagined my life with you.

Sometimes, that summer replays in my daydreams chronologically.

Another memory that plays in my mind is our last goodbye. It fucking hurt to let you go.

I know I told you to leave and didn't want you to stay, but I secretly hoped you would. It's one of my regrets.

The past seven years without you have made me appreciate the small things.

I'll never wonder if I was with you because you were my first love. Now it's confirmed that you're my one and only.

Time apart allowed me to grow up, learn what was out there, and face my fear of losing you forever.

You're my end-all, be-all.

I hope you know that.
I've always wanted you, Cash, and always will.

THE WORDS SCRIBBLE across the page like a confession, but I keep going.

We'll see how July goes.
Today, I cried to Beckett about breaking up with Eric. The tears were real because I thought about life without you.

It was fucking awful, and I never want to relive that again.

Beckett was ready to ride at dawn. It's another reason I think this plan will work great.

While I'm grateful for brothers who care about me and have my best interests in mind, I want them to stop.

You're an incredible man, smart and strong, and you love hard.

They should be honored that you want me when you could have anyone.

You're a catch, and you're also mine. ;)

Anyway, my question of the day:
1. What does your dream life look like?

I can't wait to see you—only four more days.

Also, I'm happy we're pen pals. I love being honest with you and reading your thoughts each day.

Your story is my favorite.

Can we keep doing this even when we're on the same schedule? Pretty please?

Oh, and before I go, I love how you look at me. The intensity makes the world around me disappear.

It's why I believe we can exist without constraints. I'll wish for that when I blow out my twenty-eight candles.

Will you be my birthday present?
You're all I want.

Please say yes to it all,
—Your Valentine

I FINISH MY COFFEE, pull my hair into a ponytail, and head to the B&B.

As soon as I walk in, Summer approaches me. "I'm so glad you're here," she says, nearly bursting into tears.

"Oh, goodness. What's going on?"

"It's my hormones. I cried over a plant dying at lunch."

My eyes widen. "Summer, you kill plants daily."

More tears fall. "I know! This pregnancy is going to be awful if this is where I already am. I'm a plant murderer!"

I chuckle and place my hands on her shoulders. "Didn't you just buy some new bath bombs that smell like strawberry cobbler? You should go home and take a nice relaxing bath, and

I'll throw a middle finger to every dead plant I see today just for you."

She sniffles.

"Okay?" I ask.

"Yes, that sounds nice."

"It will be, especially in that tub."

She covers her face with her hands. "What if these plants are signs telling me I can't raise a kid?"

"You're given what you can handle. My ma always told me that." My face softens. "Also, you're gonna be a great mom. You're caring. You're smart. And you know what? Sometimes, you kill plants. My mom raised ten kids and started popping them out at nineteen. She had five kids by the time she was your age. Trust me when I say you can handle one."

"You're right," she says.

I make a mental note to text Beckett to let him know Summer is in pregnancy meltdown mode today. "Anything I need to know before you go have that incredible bath?"

"Yes, Andrew Callo will be here in about an hour. I wrote some notes on the pad next to the phone. I've decided I'm still making him pancakes in the morning because it's nice to do, especially after paying fifty thousand dollars for the B&B."

I nod, knowing there is no reasoning with her. "If I need anything, I'll call you without hesitation."

I grab her purse and keys from the counter and hand them to her. Then, I walk her through the common area and everything that happened during my shifts over the past week. Summer has been more emotional than usual, but this is the first time I've seen tears. I've been a friend, but I'm also walking on eggshells because I know I can be blunt and don't want to hurt her. I can control what I say about work, so I do that instead.

After she's gone, I read over the note she left about Andrew Callo.

He will have guests with him and would like his privacy. No housekeeping is needed.

"Perfect," I whisper, then I check each room to ensure plenty of towels and toiletries are stocked. The beds are made, and every surface is clean.

I walk to the kitchen, grab some cookies from the fridge, and preheat the oven. Fresh-baked cookies can make the unhappiest of people smile. I've tested it.

Once the oven is heated, I place the cookies on the tray and set a fifteen-minute timer. While I wait, I scroll through social media, then I text Haley.

> REMI
>
> How's work?

She immediately texts me back with a picture of herself sitting in one of the comfy chairs, reading a book.

I laugh.

> REMI
>
> We have the best jobs.

> HALEY
>
> Heck yeah, we do. Are you excited about your birthday?

The question has me smiling wide.

> REMI
>
> You have no idea. I'm more excited about this one than any of the others.

> HALEY
>
> Ooh, you've missed beer pong that much?

> REMI
>
> Ha! I'm mainly excited because it will be my first day off all month, and then I will switch to the day schedule. Let's hit up some of those painting classes. I'll bring the wine.

HALEY

Yes! I'd love that! I haven't been to Spirit
Painting in a long time.

IT's an adult painting class that's B.Y.O.B. I walk since it's only a
few blocks from my condo and drink an entire bottle of wine.
I've gone alone several times but have not visited since I moved
to the night shift. My schedule is shit, but it's almost over. I'm
happy to do whatever Summer needs because she gave me this
job when I needed it the most.

Working at the B&B is the easiest job I've ever had. My
sister-in-law is an incredible boss, letting me do whatever I
want. In my last job, I was micromanaged to death until I was
nothing but a corporate corpse. It's why I stopped coding, even
if I was damn good at it. Now, I read romance books and bake
cookies all night and day with the occasional towel delivery or
sheet change. Most people who visit deny room services.

REMI

Have you been chatting with Emmett?

As I WAIT for her reply, the timer beeps. I remove the cookies
and place them on top of the oven. The sweet smell wafts
through the room. Even though they're still warm, I put them
on a decorative platter. Just as I'm taking the last one off, the
bell Summer placed on the counter dings. The sound pierces the
air as it travels through the quiet house.

I grow nervous, not knowing what to expect from a man
who offered an excessive amount of money for five nights here.
It's suspicious, but it's not my business.

I grab my plate of cookies and leave the kitchen to greet him.

Moving toward the counter, I see my good friend, Lexi. The woman Harrison almost married, Stephanie, is her cousin, but we've never held that against her.

"Oh, my goodness! What're you doin' here?" I ask, so damn excited to see her and in disbelief that she stopped by to visit. She's supposed to be in New York. We texted last week, and she told me she might have someone for me to meet. I didn't think she was serious, though.

"Surprise!" she says, and she hugs me tight. "Happy early birthday!"

I laugh and step back, and then I notice the tall, dark-haired, handsome man beside her. My eyes trail from his shoes, up his suit pants, to his stark white button-up shirt rolled to his elbows. Detailed tattoos are inked to his wrists and stop precisely where his shirt sleeve would fall. Everything about him screams power and money. I meet his blue eyes, and he's stone-cold.

"Damn, you're *intimidating*," I say, not sure how I should respond. I'm not sure he's real, as he gives off protective German shepherd energy. "*Wow.*"

"I've been told that on more than one occasion. I'm Easton Calloway. And you are?" His tone oozes with confidence.

"Remington Valentine." I hold out my hand, and we exchange a firm handshake. I continue, "But call me Remi. Anyone who uses my full name gets punched in the dick."

I shoot him a grin but playfully hold up my fist. I glance at Lexi; she looks at him like he roped the moon for her.

"Noted. Well, it's very nice to meet you, Remi." He chuckles. "We'd like to check in, please."

I shake my head, and my ponytail swooshes. "I'm sorry, but I don't have a reservation in either of your names, and we're currently booked until Sunday."

He glances at Lexi and then back at me. "It should be under

Andrew Callo. It's an alias I often use when I travel, so I can't be tracked."

Lexi turns to him like this is new information.

"Wow, you're the guy who rented the entire B&B through the weekend?" I ask, shocked. I wonder how long they've been together.

Easton nods. "I like my privacy."

He knows what he wants. I can't say I've met many men who confidently do.

I move behind the counter and login to the laptop. "I've got a note about that right here. No one will bother you, guaranteed. I'll pretend like you don't exist."

He may think I'm joking, but I'm not. My favorite guests are the ones who don't want to be bothered.

"That's appreciated," he states as his cell phone rings. He pulls it from his pants pocket and glances down at it. Lexi's eyes meet his.

"I need to take this," he says.

"Sure," she tells him as he strolls to the common room. His voice is inaudible.

I lean across the desk, grinning. "He's the one you texted me about, isn't he?"

Last week, she texted me asking how I knew if she was in love. Hilariously enough, we're in the same place in our relationship. I saw the way Easton looked at her. The twinkle in her eye is undeniable.

"Yep. That's him, in the flesh."

She glances over her shoulder at her man. He checks his watch and meets her eyes as if she summoned his attention. A smile meets his lips, and he nods but continues his conversation. That man is fire, and together, they're an inferno. He's older, too. If I had to guess, he's mid-thirties. Maybe they have the same age difference as me and Cash, but it doesn't matter. They look great together.

"You didn't say he looked like that. *My God.* I'm moving to New York." It's a joke, but damn, he's made different.

"I know," she whispers, shaking her head. "I'm so screwed."

"I can tell."

Another tall, dark-haired God enters through the front door. "Oh, who is he?" I ask.

"Brody, the bodyguard." She snickers.

I have so many questions for her but now is not the time. So, instead, I turn and grab all the keys from the locked cabinet.

"He rented all the rooms. Do you need all of these?" I ask, setting the ten keys on the counter.

"How did he pull it off?" she asks, looking down at them.

I tilt my head at her. "He made an offer Summer couldn't refuse."

"I bet he did," she says.

"But now that she and Beckett are expecting—"

"What? I didn't know. I bet she's so happy. Oh goodness, that means you're going to be an aunt. Congrats!"

I smile about Beckett and Summer, who are adding a baby Valentine to the family. They are going to be so spoiled. "Thanks. I'm excited about it, but Kinsley has already claimed the favorite aunt title."

They've been best friends since they were kids, so I'll let her have this one. I log in to the laptop and type into the reservation system to log what time they checked in. I glance over to see Easton still on his phone, and then I meet Lexi's gaze. "There are other things that have been going on, though. Recently, I've noticed a lot of outsiders visiting."

"It's my fault," she whispers.

"I know. They offered me a hundred bucks to talk about you. I told them to get fucked, though. So did Kinsley. Pretty much everyone has."

"Beau didn't," she admits.

Beau is her ex-boyfriend who cheated on her and knocked

up another woman. He's a bastard, and if he were on fire, I wouldn't piss to put him out.

My eyes narrow. I don't like it when people mess with my friends. I'm loyal to a T.

"What the fuck?" I ask.

Before she can continue, Easton and Brody walk over.

Lexi turns to Easton. "Here are our keys."

"Which goes to the suite?" Easton asks.

I sort through them and hold up the keys to our largest room. "This one."

"And which room is the farthest away from that one?"

I pick them up, and Easton gives them to Brody. He places them in his pocket, not once cracking a smile. They're all serious, except for Lexi, who's like Southern sunshine.

"Thank you. We don't need any others," Easton confirms.

I chuckle, knowing he paid fifty grand for two rooms. "I already like you."

Lexi grins wide. This man already has my stamp of approval. I can get on board with someone who's no bullshit and likes to be left alone. The two of us may be cut from the same cloth.

"And do we contact you if we need anything else?" Easton asks.

"I'll be here during the night shift today, tomorrow, and Friday. Summer will arrive in the morning around seven, and breakfast will be served at eight. She loves to make pancakes. Just eat them, okay? She's pregnant, and she'll cry at the drop of a hat if you refuse," I explain. After how emotional she was today, the last thing she needs is a man like Easton refusing to eat her food. She might go into full meltdown mode.

"I don't like pancakes," Easton says, and Lexi elbows him. "I'll learn to love them. Thank you, Remi." Then, he turns to Lexi. "Ready to go to our room, darling?"

"Yes," she says. With one glance, they're lost in one another's world.

"Thank you," Lexi whispers to me over her shoulder.

I give her a thumbs-up as they approach the narrow staircase. When I turn my head, I realize Brody is still standing there.

"You're just as intimidating as him."

He laughs. "He's not intimidating."

"Okay, you won the prize," I tell him, my eyes slide up the tattoos on his arm. "You were a Marine?"

"Yeah," he says.

"Do you like cookies?" I ask.

He snags a few with a nod.

"If you need anything else, let me know," I say.

He lifts his duffel over his shoulder and moves to the stairs. Once I hear his door snap closed, I pull my phone from my pocket and move outside to sit on the rocking chair on the back porch to enjoy the early summer evening. The crickets are out, and I love how warmth floats in the fresh breeze. I open my texts with Haley and see she never answered my last text message asking about Emmett. I'll ignore it this time.

REMI

Lexi is in town!

After the breakup that had her questioning everything, Haley, Lexi, and I were three peas in a pod. When she moved to New York, I was sad. I've missed her.

HALEY

Omg! Is she coming to your party? I want to see her!

REMI

She better! She's staying at the B&B this week.

HALEY

Finally, the three musketeers are back together again.

REMI

Wait until you meet her boyfriend. We are not worthy.

I SIT on the back porch for five minutes. I hear a door close and walk through the house to see Easton standing in the common room, flipping a key in his hand.

"You need some help?" I ask.

"Sure," he says with a smile. His demeanor has spun one-hundred-and-eighty degrees since I saw him ten minutes ago. I narrow my eyes at him. "Why are you so happy?"

He chuckles. "Where is my room located?"

I stare at him for several seconds. Something is off about him. "You're *not* Easton."

Brody comes down the stairs and sees him, then shakes his hand.

"Which room?" he asks Brody.

"Upstairs at the end of the hallway to the left," he tells him.

I glance at Brody. "Who was that?"

"Family business," he says.

"I don't care what you say. That man wasn't Easton."

"How do you know?" he asks with a brow lifted. For a moment, I nearly gaslight myself into believing it is Easton.

"That man wasn't the same," I explain. "He had a unique energy. I can sense that."

I hear knocking on the door upstairs. Brody and I listen.

"*Open up!*" he says, in the same voice and tone as earlier.

Was that Easton, and then Lexi just locked him out?

The door squeaks open and is followed by yelling. I move past Brody, and he grabs my wrist, not letting me go.

He shakes his head.

"Let me go. If my friend gets hurt, you'll regret it." If he doesn't, I'll take him down like I've taken down my brothers, with a knee to the junk.

"Lexi is fine," he confirms, his expression unchanged. "I promise. Don't get involved."

Brody releases me, and I narrow my eyes at him. Moments later, Easton walks down the stairs and out the front door. I follow him and see the white vintage Mustang in front of the house. I admire the Shelby Cobra Mustang, and my mouth falls open as I stare at it. From above, the window slides open.

I turn and look at Lexi, who's grinning wide.

"Are you kidding me?" I yell, and my voice echoes in the distance. "This is … oh my God!"

Lexi laughs. "I drove it."

"No way. Let me, *please*," I beg as I look inside at the red interior.

Easton shakes his head and speaks loud enough for me to hear. "Absolutely not."

Lexi snickers. "You'll have to ask his brother. He's the only one who gives the keys away."

"Brother?" I ask as the guy I spoke to minutes prior steps off the porch and walks toward me. "Twins. I *knew* it. You seemed … *different*."

"You might win the record of the person who figured it out within the first few minutes. I'm Weston Calloway. Nice to meet you," he says, holding his hand out to me.

I take it, and he kisses my knuckles, meeting my eyes. "Remi. I also have a twin. I see through that shit."

"Ah," he asks. "That's how you knew. Are you identical?"

"No, I have a brother, but you're not as transparent as you think. It's a different vibe."

He chuckles and lets go of my hand. "It's not the first time I've heard that. Lovely to meet you, Remi. I'll be staying while they're here. Can you give me a set of keys to my room?"

I glance over my shoulder at Easton and Lexi, who are lost in one another.

"Are they always like this?" I ask him.

"*Always.* I'm responsible for them getting together."

I laugh. "Really, you're a matchmaker?"

"You better fucking believe it," Weston says.

CHAPTER THIRTEEN

CASH

THREE DAYS LATER

It's Friday night, and after I finish my last appointment, I drive back to the clinic to repack my medical bag just in case there is an emergency call in the middle of the night. The lights are off, so I flick them on and move to the sink to wash my hands and arms with antibacterial soap. My employees are already gone for the day.

Some days, I do routine check-ups; others, I'm elbow-deep in places. The problem with horses is it's impossible to do ultrasounds from the outside. It's one hundred percent an inside job.

After I restock my supplies, I return them to my truck. It's fading to dark, and soon the sun will fully set. In the distance, the B&B sits on a hill, and the lights glow yellow. Remi's car is on the side of the B&B, and I wonder what she's doing.

I drive home with her on my mind. As soon as I walk into our condo, the notebook awaits me on the counter. When I see it, nothing else matters.

My Valentine,

Happy Friday!

Can you believe my birthday is tomorrow? I can't.

Twenty-eight.

It feels like a weird age, somewhere between still too young and old enough to know better.

Don't worry; I'm not having a meltdown about it.

Age doesn't matter to me. Growing old is better than the alternative.

When I get off work in the morning, I'm crawling into bed with you, so wait for me.

I want to be wrapped in your arms and held until I fall asleep, then wake with you next to me.

Sitting here, I think about how we've lived together for nearly a month and haven't seen one another even once. Isn't that strange?

Somehow, I've felt closer to you in the past twenty-seven days than ever before. Am I alone in that?

They say absence makes the heart grow fonder, and I believe in that statement now.

You asked me how many people I dated after you.

I don't know—a lot. If you want to know how many people I've had sex with, the answer is three, including you.

I'm sure you don't want to read about my past relationships, but I think it's crucial for you to know.

There was a man named Noah.

He was ten years older than me, and we used each other for sex.

We were broken people who needed someone to fill the void. He'd divorced the love of his life, and I'd lost you. It was physical only. We ended it when he found a woman he wanted to date seriously.

Soon after, I met Landon. He was your age.

We'd dated for two years and lived together for a year.

I moved to Alpine, and we rented a house in town while I worked online for the tech company. I believed I'd healed and had finally moved on from you.

Time was supposed to heal those wounds.

It didn't work out, though. Obviously.

If you're wondering what happened, we broke up because of you.

That probably comes as a shock, but that breakup made me realize I had a lot of shit to work through for you.

It was my wake-up call, and confirmed I was still in love with you.

After that relationship ended, I moved back in with

my parents into my old bedroom until Grace asked me to be her roommate.

I'd committed to my single-girl era, telling myself I'd have you or no one. I needed to be in a better place mentally before I started another relationship.

Every stressor in my life was removed, including my toxic job. Kinsley encouraged it, but I was grateful and felt free. Then I moved in with Grace, and I think she understood how fucked up I was.

For months, I was worried I'd never find love again.

But when you came home, I knew I'd never lost it.

I STOP READING and sit back in my chair, sitting in her words for a few minutes. This breaks my fucking heart. Nothing about this makes me happy.

I'm sure you're curious how you had anything to do with my breakup, considering I pretended you didn't exist.

It's funny how a person's subconscious doesn't forget things.

We'd drank a lot at a bar down the street and stumbled home.

When we were having sex, I called him Cash.

He'd known about us, about you. It wasn't the first

time it'd happened either.

The following day, he broke up with me.

We broke our lease and went our separate ways, and though I apologized a thousand times, he said he couldn't be second place in my life.

He was a good man and treated me right, but I knew I wouldn't be happy with him because he'd never be you.

"REM," I whisper, shaking my head and exhaling.

I was upset for months and kept it to myself.

Even now, no one knows why we broke up because neither of us could admit what happened.

I never got over you, and I was so mad at myself.

Landon saw the writing on the wall, and he was right. I hurt him, and I'll always regret that.

Did I mention you're the only man who's ever made me come?

Anytime I was with someone else, I imagined it was you.

I had wished it were you, so I shouldn't have been surprised when I whispered your name.

Honestly, I'd have broken up with me for that, too. I deserved it because it was a slap in the face.

There hasn't been a day since you kissed me on my birthday that I haven't thought about you.

Tomorrow will be seven years since we first kissed.

There were days when I wished I could erase every memory of us because I knew no one would ever compare.

You broke me, and you are the only one who can glue me back together. And come September 1st, if you want to end this, my feelings won't change.

You ruined me, Cash.

You're the only person who can satisfy me emotionally and physically. And now that you know that, what will you do?

I'm risking my heart, but somehow, you're still risking more. It scares me. I want you to be happy and have it all. It's what I wish for.

So, what's your confession? The secret you've been hiding from me?

Less than twenty-four hours to go!

I'm not counting down to my birthday but to seeing you. Can't wait.

—Still Your Valentine
(I always will be)

I CLOSE the notebook and stare at the wall, speechless, until my vision blurs.

CHAPTER FOURTEEN

REMI

As soon as it clicks to midnight, I do what I do every year: text my brother.

REMI

Happy Birthday! I love you! I am happy to share this day with you.

COLT

Happy Birthday, Sis! You're my favorite. I love you! I hope all your dreams come true!

REMI

You too, bubba.

I smile, wondering what my brother is doing. I hear the front door open and expect to see Weston and Brody since they left a few hours ago. When I look up, Cash walks toward me carrying a bouquet of pink flowers.

I stand up to greet him, shocked by his public display of affection. "What—?"

His mouth crashes against mine, and his hand twists through my hair. We're needy and breathless, a force that can't be

126

reckoned with. Moans escape me as his fingertips massage into my scalp. I'm dreaming.

I must've fallen asleep at work, and I'm imagining it all.

"Happy birthday, Valentine," he says with his forehead pressed against mine, and I laugh.

"You're not supposed to be here," I say as he hands me the flowers.

"Fuck the rules," he says as I search his eyes. Tonight, they look blue-green, and I want to swim in them.

His palm presses against my cheek, gently capturing my lips one last time.

"I couldn't wait to see you any longer," he whispers. "I couldn't sleep. Your letter kept repeating in my mind."

"Ahem," I hear from behind me. It's Easton. He walks over to us with his hand in his pocket. He's dressed in a T-shirt and plaid pajama pants. It's much different from his suits or Polo shirts.

"Nice to see you again, doctor," he says. Cash takes his hand, and they exchange a firm shake. They met yesterday and hung out with Lexi's brothers last night.

"Please explain why you aren't together," Easton says.

It's a blunt question, but I stick to routine and dodge it.

"Excuse me?" I ask him, narrowing my eyes.

"I see two adults sneaking around like teenagers."

"Pfft," I say, carrying the pink daisies to the counter. I fill a vase with water—considering Summer loves flowers and plants, there are plenty here—and then I set them on the counter for everyone to enjoy.

"This has been going on for seven years," Cash confirms.

The first time we kissed was on my twenty-first birthday. The first time we hooked up was on the Fourth of July.

Disdain spreads across Easton's face. "Why? Were you seeing other people?"

"No, it's my brothers," I confirm. If I were a teenager when we started hooking up, I'd understand why Beckett and Harrison are so against it. When we first got together, we were consenting adults.

"Sometimes you have to ask yourself what you want and not concern yourself with others," he says.

I scoff and brush him off, but he hit the nail on the head. "I didn't need your unsolicited opinion."

"It's the truth," Easton states. "I took you for someone who could handle it."

"I can," I tell him, even if I run from it often.

"Hmm." Easton isn't convinced.

Weston and Brody stumble through the front door. They're laughing and shouting about something. I narrow my eyes at Weston, but I shoot him a smile. He pops his brows at me, his eyes trailing from head to toe, and he smirks before glancing at Cash. The man isn't intimidated by the tiger standing next to me, ready to rip out his jugular for looking at me like that.

Since the moment Weston arrived, he's been flirty as fuck, but I'm used to his type.

I grab Cash's hand and rub my thumb against his. He immediately relaxes.

"I didn't realize you had a twin." Cash brings his attention back to Easton.

"Yeah, and looks are the *only* thing we have in common," Easton tells him.

Weston and Brody continue to the back porch, and I notice a bottle of whiskey in their hand. They're tipsy.

The screen door slams, but I still hear them going on about something.

"Anyway, don't fuck this up," Easton states, and it's a demand. "Love is always on time, and when you're ready for it, it finds you. I searched 20 years for what you've ignored for nearly a decade. What the fuck?"

Cash's expression softens, and a dozen unspoken

conversations stream between us. Easton's right, and the three of us know it.

"Why don't you two take a key to a room? There are seven extra to choose from. No one will bother you the rest of the night. I'll text Summer and tell her I sent you home for your birthday."

A smile touches my lips. "You're serious?"

"Yes. Choose an adventure and cherish the tiny moments. It was the best decision I ever made." Easton grins before snagging a chocolate chip cookie off the tray and heads back upstairs. "Happy birthday, Remi."

"Thank you," I say as his footsteps echo from above. A few moments later, the door to his room clicks closed. I glance around the B&B, and everything is in place. Easton and Lexi are upstairs. The drunk ones are on the back porch, howling with laughter. No one needs anything.

Cash studies me, and I say, "He's right."

"I know," Cash says.

"We'll stick to the plan. It's going to work flawlessly," I say. "I'm having lunch with my daddy next week, and I will be a tattletale."

Cash bursts into laughter. "You make me cherish being an only child."

I take a step forward, wrapping my arms around his neck. "I'm so happy you're here. It was a pleasant surprise."

"Me too," he whispers.

When I pull away, I grab his hand and snatch the key for the executive suite at the end of the hallway, then lead him up the stairs.

I look at him over my shoulder as we climb the wooden stairs. They creak with each step, and I smile. His gaze locks on me; I'm the bullseye of his target.

I've always wanted to be, and right now I am. The intensity of his eyes on me causes goosebumps to flood my body. I don't know how this is my life or how, after all this time, we've only gotten better together. If this man told me to get down on my knees and beg for him, I fucking would, and I beg no one.

As soon as we're in the room, I lock the door, and he pushes me against it. I grab his shirt in my fist, inhaling his skin. He smells like citrus and fresh mountain air. My hands dive under his shirt, sliding up his carved abs and down to the button and zipper on his jeans. When I glance down, he's so damn hard his cock looks like it will burst the seams of his dark-washed jeans.

He gently grabs my wrists and then places them above my head as he kisses my neck and nibbles my ear. "There's no taking it back if we keep going. This isn't a game to me, Remi," he mutters, then snags my skin between his teeth.

"I want this—*you*. I won't let you go again." Moans escape me as he lifts my jaw. I give him more access to me as he holds my wrists with one hand, and the other slides down my body. "Please."

He lets go of my wrists, and his hands rest on my hips.

Cash flicks off the overhead lights. We're in the bed-and-breakfast executive suite. It's called the executive suite because a wooden desk overlooks the prairies.

We move to the bed, and his hands are in my hair, and our lips crash together.

"This is what you want? I'm what you want?" I ask, wanting to make sure we're on the same page.

"Fuck yes," he tells me. "Never been more sure about anything in my whole damn life."

It's music to my ears. We've reached this point over the past few months but never went all the way. It's been a perpetual state of teasing and blue balls. Something has always stopped us. Fear or other people nearly catching us.

His movements are slow.

"You asked for my confession," he says; the moonlight beams through the window, and the room glows a pale white.

My breaths come out ragged. "Yes."

With his hands on my shoulders, he grins, and I notice his dimple showing. "When I told you I was falling in love with you all those years ago, the truth was I'd already fallen."

He searches my face, kissing me and smiling.

"I didn't hook up with anyone after us."

My lips part. "At all?"

"Since you, it's only been you, and it will only ever be you," he whispers.

Butterflies flutter in my stomach, and his admission leaves me speechless.

"I'm sorry for breaking you, Rem."

"I'm not," I admit, tugging his lip into mine. "You just made sure I'd always be yours."

His finger traces my jaw. "I tried to move on, but I couldn't."

I search his face. "What if I'd have gotten married?"

The question fills the silence, but I know the answer, and the thought breaks my heart.

"I'd have married my career and stayed single for the rest of my life."

"Cash." I grab his cheeks with my hands. I'd decided the same: either I had him or I wasn't dating anymore. That's why I've relentlessly stayed in my single-girl era. My heart belongs to him; if I dated anyone else, I'd hurt them. The realization weighs on me. "We're in too deep."

"I'll go to the bottom for you."

Tears threaten to spill over. He leans forward and kisses my forehead. "No crying on your birthday, Valentine."

"I tried to erase you, Cash."

He holds me tight against him. "Tried," he mutters. "And fucking failed."

I capture his lips as he pushes me back on the bed, and I kick off my sandals. He kisses up my stomach and pushes up my shirt, removing it along with my bra. His scruff tickles my skin as he carefully unbuttons and unzips my jeans, and I wiggle out of them.

Cash takes a step back and admires my naked body in the moonlight. He removes his shirt, kicks off his shoes, and then drops to his knees. He slides his firm hands under my ass and scoots me to the edge of the bed. The anticipation of having his mouth on me again is almost too much for me to handle. I open my thighs, giving him full access to me.

He drops kisses inside my inner thigh, teasing my bare pussy with the scruff of his face as he moves to the opposite leg. When he does it again, I rock my hips upward, and I feel him smile against me as he gives my needy clit one suck.

"Fuck," I hiss, growing greedy. "I need this."

Cash's hand glides up my body, and he tweaks my nipple, then he splits me open, and his mouth is on me, then he impales me with his tongue. I think I see stars when he moves to my clit, gently sucking and massaging my hard nub. My body instantly responds to him, and the orgasm builds.

"Mm. Should I make you wait?" he growls against my pussy, grabbing my ass.

"No," I whisper, wanting more of this. "Please, I've waited so long."

He laps me up at an agonizingly slow pace, and I melt under him as every one of my muscles tense as he dips and curls his giant finger inside me. A cry releases from my throat as my body releases. "Make love to me," I say.

He stands. "I didn't bring a condom."

"I want to feel you, just you."

"Are you on birth control?" he asks.

"Yes," I whisper. "I need you so bad."

"You've got me," he says. Cash removes his boxers as we move up the bed. His thick cock waits at my entrance, and the anticipation of feeling him again almost becomes too much.

"I'll go slow," he whispers at the nape of my neck. He has always been caring, and he puts my needs first.

I open my thighs wide, and I adjust to how large he is and how he fills me full. I enjoy how my body molds around him. When our ends meet, I sigh in relief and enjoy his pressure. Cash's mouth is on mine, and I'm so fucking greedy for him. "You feel so fucking good," he moans, sliding out.

My pleasure is on his tongue, and I taste myself. "I don't want you to be gentle," I admit.

With slow movements, he thrusts in and out, my body rocking to the rhythm of him. He pumps into me, and his soft pants are in my ear. "Rem."

"I want you to break me, for real. I want to feel you all day tomorrow."

His thick cock slides deep inside my slick walls, and then he slams into me. I lift my arms above my head, arching my back, needing more of him, knowing I can barely handle him as is.

Cash is the only man who has ever had his mouth on me, and he's also the only man who's ever been able to bring me to the edge. My body belongs to him and has since the moment I secretly gave him my virginity.

"Cash," I whisper. It comes out as a strained moan between pants.

He nibbles on my ear and slams into me. "I fucking love it when you say my name."

"You own me." I gasp, nearly ragged, as he slams into me, slow and arduous, filling me so goddamn full I might split in half.

He places his hand on my neck and barely squeezes. My pussy clenches around him, and I growl out his name.

"You're a bad fucking girl," he says in a low rasp.

"Yes, yes," I whisper. I want this, need this, and he delivers, tightening his grip, slamming harder but keeping the same pace.

Even after all these years, he remembered what I love and

desperately crave. I want to be choked and bitten, my hair tugged, and my ass slapped.

Guttural groans release from my throat, and I'm unable to form words. I scratch my nails down Cash's back. He hits my G-spot over and over. My pussy pulses with anticipation, and the orgasm builds deep inside. Every muscle tightens as he slides in and out, giving the extra push.

"I'm so..." I come so hard I leave my body. His name falls from my mouth like a whispered prayer as I come.

I needed this. I needed *him*.

As Cash wages war on my pussy, gripping my ass, giving me all of him, I'm catapulted into outer space.

"Rem," he whispers as he releases, and warmth pools inside me. We stay connected, gasping for air, trying to return to reality.

I don't know what planet I'm on, but I might have transcended to another dimension as I wrap my arms around his neck and capture his mouth. Cash meets my eyes, pushing my hair away from my face.

"You're the best present I've ever had," I whisper, smiling, wanting to remember this moment and him just like this.

He chuckles as he runs his fingers through my hair. "Babe, I'm the gift that keeps on giving."

After he kisses me and pulls away, Cash meets my eyes. "I'm in love with you, Valentine."

"I'm in love with you, too."

CHAPTER FIFTEEN

CASH

Hearing her admit that she's in love with me changes things. It's what dreams are made from. Maybe now we'll finally be able to move forward. I've waited years for this moment, to hear her say it, to have her choose me. I've never forced our relationship and have been patient, waiting for my girl to see what she has—a man who'd worship her from sunrise to sunset.

After we clean up, we settle naked in bed. I hold her against me, promising myself that I will never let her go again. The thought is unbearable.

But as Beckett has always told me: When two people are meant to be together, love finds a way. I know he was referring to him and Summer, but there is truth in that statement.

"Mm, you're so comfortable to snuggle with," she says.

It's always *been* her, no matter the challenges, and it will always *be* her.

"Let's go home," I say, smelling her hair and the sweet scent of her shampoo. Having her pressed against me is heaven on earth, but I peel away.

"Home, I like the way that sounds," she admits.

"I want to hold you as we fall asleep and wake up with you in my arms in the morning," I say, not wanting this to end right now. When we walk out of the room, I don't want it to be over. Hell no, this is just the beginning.

"I'd love that," she says, removing the space I created, not letting me go.

"I parked behind the clinic so no one would see my truck." I don't want to sneak around, but I also don't need anyone speculating shit.

"Do you want me to drive you?" she asks with her head on my chest. My fingers trail on the outside of her arm, and goose bumps line her skin.

"No, I'll walk. The milky way is out." And I need to clear my mind.

I slide out of bed and put on the clothes she just peeled off of me. Remi props herself up on her elbow, her naked body on full display for me. When she looks at me like that, it's hard for me to fucking leave, to walk away.

"Rem," I say, buttoning my shirt, not able to break away. "You're a cocktease."

She snickers, but she knows what she does to me. It's crystal fucking clear.

"We'll pick up where we left off," she says.

A smile touches her lips.

She stalks toward me and her legs tremble with each step forward.

"I feel you already," she says with a sexy grin.

I wrap my arm around her waist. "Happy fucking birthday, Valentine."

"It's been my favorite one."

I grin. "Wow. That's an accomplishment. Guess I hold first and second place."

"You hold all the places," she says with hooded eyes, and I

know if I don't go now, we'll never leave this room. Wouldn't be the worst thing that ever happened though.

"I should go," I say, unlocking my phone and checking the time. It's just past midnight, and no one should be on the ranch.

"Should you?"

It makes me realize that I'm the one who walks away when things get serious. Maybe I'm avoiding shit as much as her. I pull her in for a kiss and grip her bare ass. She arches herself against me and whimpers. Dirty thoughts fill my mind, and if she doesn't stop, I'll have her for round two right here on the goddamn floor.

"It's hard to watch you go," she whispers.

"You've *never* asked me to stay," I say, and it's the raw truth, one that cuts deeper than I thought.

"I didn't ask you to return, either, but here you are," she tells me, not taking my shit. It's what I love the most about her.

I smirk. "You're right. Here I am, still fucking obsessed and under your spell."

"You're not innocent," she says.

"You're damn right about that." My hand fists into her scalp, and she groans against me, always insatiable for my touch. "My only regret is not coming back sooner to claim what's mine."

"I've always been yours," she says.

"Then tell everyone," I say, forcing her to meet my eyes.

"I will," she says.

"I'm waiting for you, Valentine," I say, letting go of her. "I want to be with you."

"Everything is on the line."

"I'll fucking risk it all, I don't care," I whisper. She doesn't know the brunt of it. She doesn't understand that without her, I will lose myself in my work. If she calls this off, I will leave Valentine behind and never return again. There's more at risk than my clinic and a chance at love; my entire existence is on the line.

During a dark time, I imagined returning to Valentine, to be with her just like this. It's the only thing that got me through because my heart knows this woman will lead me to true happiness.

"Then I'll tell the world. If you're willing to risk everything, knowing how fucked up I am, then fine. There are better choices for you. Don't you see that?" Remi says.

"Fuck that," I say, moving her onto the bed, capturing her mouth as she moans against me. "You're the only woman on this entire fucking planet I want, Rem. *You.*"

She leans forward and undoes my belt and jeans, and then I'm buried deep inside of her. We're desperate and eager.

"You have me," she whispers.

"Prove it," I say, kissing her neck as I slam into her. We race to the finish line, fucking out our frustrations.

"I will," she groans out. "I promise."

And then I empty deep inside of her. "Okay," I say breathlessly. "Okay."

We stay holding one another until our heart rates settle. Then I kiss her one more time.

"Worshipable," I say.

"Speak for yourself," she says, and I leave.

Before I close the door behind me, I turn and meet her sparkling eyes, taking a mental snapshot of how pretty she is, naked and smiling at me, with the moonlight splashed across the floor.

With a grin, I walk down the hallway to the bottom floor of the B&B. I pass no one as I exit the front door and take the side trail that leads down the property line to my clinic.

A smile touches my lips as I look up at the stars and inhale fresh mountain air. It's comfortable outside as a symphony of crickets fills the space. It's *finally* happening.

Fifteen minutes later, I walk up to my truck and Harrison walks out of the shadows.

"Where were you?" he glares at me.

Only problem is I'm not intimidated by him. "At the B&B." I always told myself that if any of them confronted me, I'd be truthful. Today is Harrison's day, and it only took seven years.

"I thought you were better than this."

"Say it," I say between gritted teeth with my feet firmly planted, ready for the attack.

"You're *fucking* my little sister," he seethes.

"How do you know that?" I meet his eyes, growing agitated, then I smirk. "Did you *watch?*"

"Fuck *you*," he growls with flared nostrils. "I saw you two at Beckett's wedding. Grace and I were in the treehouse and watched the entire fucking thing go down. I'm going to tell you this one fucking time, leave Remi alone."

"Ahh, so you did," I say. "I've wondered why you started acting weird as fuck."

"Leave. Her. Alone."

"No," I state. "I can't do that."

Harrison goes into a blind rage and throws punches that I dodge.

"You're going to hurt her like you did before," Harrison says. "And I can't let that happen again."

His words catch me off-guard, and his fist slams into my mouth. My head falls back, and the world blinks black for a second before I come to. I deserved that, and I'll give him one.

"You took her virginity, you fucking bastard. Didn't think anyone would figure it out? I saw you two together all those summers ago. I should've stopped this bullshit then." Harrison uses his strength to tackle me onto the ground.

He falls to his knees with hopes to pummel me, but I twist away. Somehow, I'm faster. Seconds later, my knee is in his chest, and my tight grip is on his throat. He gasps for air, reaching for me.

"I'm sorry it has to be like this. But this ain't any of your goddamn business," I say between clenched teeth as I rear back and slam my fist into his face. It only takes one hit, and he's out.

I stand over him, shaking out my hand with my foot resting on his neck. We're not kids anymore. I'm too fucking old for this, but I won't take an ass beating from anyone, especially not Harrison Valentine.

When he finally rouses, he glares at me standing over him. I smile like the Cheshire cat. "Don't you *ever* fucking disrespect me like that again, do you understand me? I think you've forgotten who the fuck you're messing with." I spit in his face.

He stares up at me like I'm crazed, and as I push him away, my own dizziness takes over. The bastard must've given me a concussion. My bottom lip bleeds from where his wedding ring caught me, and I wipe the blood on the sleeve of my shirt.

"Let it be known that if you hurt her like you did before, I will fucking come for you, Cash. And I'll tell Beckett what I saw with my own two eyes. *Past and present.* You ruin her again, and I'll ruin you. That's a promise."

"Do you think I'm scared of your empty as fuck threats? I *dare* you to tell him," I say, meaning every fucking word.

"You're going to get what you deserve." He tries to sit up.

I place my foot on top of his chest, pinning him back down with my weight. "You're right. I'm going to marry your sister, Harrison. And you're going to fucking accept it because we're good together, and I love her."

"And she loves you back?" he asks.

"Yes."

"She actually said that?" he asks, rolling away from me and standing. For a moment, he might be preparing for round two, but then he backs away, staring at me. "Did she tell you she loved you?"

It's not a question I can answer, but my silence does it for me. She told me she was in love with me, but I know it's not the same. Those three words hold weight.

"She *hasn't* said I love you," Harrison says with a sarcastic laugh, and it wounds me deeper than a fist to my fucking face. "That tells me *everything* I need to know about this relationship."

"Get the fuck out of my barn," I demand. "And think twice before you start shit again. Next time, I'm going to drop your ass without question."

He walks away, flipping me off, and I shake my head as I climb into my truck. I shake off the creeping headache and rest my head against the seat. "Fucking *asshole*," I hiss, hating he knew exactly what to say to get under my skin, just like an annoying little brother.

I rub my hand over my swollen knuckles, then pull out of the barn and carefully make my way to town. Hayden warned me about fighting. I didn't expect it to be so soon.

Driving with a concussion is the last thing I should be doing, but I want to be home now.

Remi has never said *I love you.*

She does, though. I can see it in her eyes.

Or am I imagining it?

With a tight grip on the steering wheel, I drive slowly and easily.

When I arrive home, I let out a sigh of relief, but need to sit down.

Remi is at the table, puzzling in a tiny T-shirt and shorts. She turns to me with shiny eyes, but the bright smile on her face disappears immediately.

"What happened? Who did this?" she asks, approaching me and noticing the blood on my shirt and then glancing up at my lip. She touches it when I place my hand on her hip. Right now, I want her close.

"Harrison."

Her eyes narrow, and her jaw clenches tight.

CHAPTER SIXTEEN

REMI

Blood and dirt are on his shirt, his hair is disheveled, and his lip is busted. "Did you say *Harrison?*"

"Rem, please don't," he says, gently grabbing my wrist. "I took care of it."

"Do you need to go to the hospital?" I grab his cheeks, studying him. Slight bruising blooms along his jaw.

"I'm fine. I might have a concussion, but I'll survive. No medical attention is needed." He shakes his head and lightly touches my elbows.

"You sure you're okay?" I ask.

"Yes." He moves to the couch and kicks off his shoes. "I just need to shake it off. Bastard distracted me."

"What did he say?" I ask.

He pauses for a moment, and I see a flash of something on his face. Sadness? Hurt? I can't place it, but I don't like it.

"He knows about us. Confirmed."

I swallow hard, meeting his eyes. "And he told you to stay away from me, didn't he?"

"*Valentine,*" he whispers, looking at me, begging me to stop with his gaze. "It *doesn't* matter."

"It matters to me." I grab my keys off the bar top and approach the front door. I know how my brother is, and I'd bet money that Harrison threatened him. "His bullshit stops tonight."

Cash stands and moves to me, hooking his hand around my hip. "What can I do to convince you to stay? Tell me. Anything, *it's yours.*"

His voice is as *smooth as whiskey.*

"You *almost* had me." I place my palm on his cheek, angry Harrison had the damn audacity to do this. "I'll be back in an hour. Get some rest."

He pulls his keys from his pocket and drops them in my palm. "Take my truck."

"Why?" I look down at the key fob.

"Because I worry about you traveling on the roads late at night. I'd prefer you drive a tank."

I find it endearing that he's concerned. "You know I have to do this."

"I know," he says, "but there are better ways. You're going to roll up on him in the middle of the night and do what?"

"Give him what he deserves," I admit.

"When you said you'd tell people about us, I didn't expect you to go vigilante over me."

I snicker. "Should've."

This is a family matter, and being stubborn is a Valentine family trait; something all of my brothers and sisters deal with. Cash has been around long enough to understand.

"Hurry back to me," he says, grabbing my shirt with his fist and kissing me. It quickly deepens, and his tongue darts into my mouth as he presses against me. A moan escapes me as he palms my ass with a firm hand.

We pull away, and I smile against his mouth. "Good try. So close."

He huffs. "*Please* go easy on him. I fucked him up pretty good."

"I'll match *his* energy."

Cash watches me with his arms crossed over his chest as I turn toward the door. I glance back at him before I leave and he shakes his head, but he's smiling. "Defiant."

"To my core."

When I'm outside, I unlock his jacked-up Chevy and step onto the running board. While I love my Mustang, big trucks with diesel engines feel like home. I drove one until I purchased my dream car.

With my foot on the gas, I back out of the condo, and the engine sounds angry. The loud noise bounces off the walls of the downtown buildings as I head to my parents' ranch.

His truck has that new car smell that's mixed with leather and hay. A lead rope and a pair of boots are on the passenger floorboard. A saddle is in the back, and I wonder if he's been taking the horses out at his parents' place. Cash has been riding longer than I've been alive. It's how he and Beckett became friends. Southern isn't a lifestyle, it's a way of life. They live the cowboy way.

The last time I was in the saddle was during Harrison's first wedding, the one where he almost married the wrong woman.

Watching Cash ride horses with my brothers did things to teenage me. There's nothing sexier than a man in a saddle.

I take the curves with fervor, hugging them as I drive to my parents. The game warden sits on the side of the road and I glance down at the speedometer, making sure I'm not speeding. That's when I notice a picture tucked inside. It's dark, but the glow of the dashboard gives enough light to see he's holding a woman in his arms.

Her back is facing the view, and her long brown hair is down. My jealousy flares. Who the fuck is that?

I grip the steering wheel tightly, traveling faster to

Harrison's house. When I arrive, I park beside his truck and press the horn. It's loud and angry, and the blaring noise echoes across the property. I'm sure my parents will ask questions, but my brother can answer for that. He's the one who started this.

Moments later, the front door swings open, and Harrison stands shirtless with his hands on his hips. His eyes narrow, and I turn on the brights. He covers his face, blocking the light as anger floods him. With a tight fist, he steps off the porch, approaching the vehicle.

"Didn't get enough?" he yells.

I clutch my courage and then step out of the truck, moving toward him, kneeing him as hard as I can in his dick.

Harrison groans and hunches over, looking up at me. "What the hell, Remi?"

"Leave me alone. Leave Cash alone. Stay out of my life," I yell.

"You're too young for him, and you were too fucking young for him back then, too. You're keeping your relationship a secret. Why?" He screams back at me as he grabs himself with furrowed brows.

"That's none of your damn business, Harrison. Stay out of it!"

Moments later, Grace steps onto the porch with her housecoat on. Her brows furrow when she hears me screaming at Harrison, but it's directed at him.

"What have you done?" Grace asks him as she approaches.

She's *livid*.

"Gracie." Harrison keeps his voice calm as he straightens his stance.

"What have you done?" she asks through gritted teeth.

When he doesn't answer, I speak up for him.

"He fought and threatened Cash," I explain. "He started shit, and now I'm finishing it."

My brother found the trouble he was searching for tonight.

"If you mess up *my* chance at love, so help you God..."

He swallows my truth like poison. I'm so frustrated with Harrison that I don't have to lie.

Grace's hands find her hips. "Cash is a *good* man. Any woman is lucky to be with him, especially your *sister*. What's wrong with you? Don't you want the best for her?"

"It's not like that," Harrison says.

"Yes, it *is*," Grace says, and I'm so thankful she has my back. She's the only person he'll listen to when he gets like this. She's the only one who can get reality through his thick skull.

Harrison glares at me. "Do you love him?"

I move toward my brother.

"Yes, I *do*," I say, the truth spilling from my lips without hesitation.

His mouth parts, and he's shocked. He didn't expect me to say it, and I didn't either, but it's the damn truth.

I take another step and jab my finger into Harrison's shoulder. *"And you're going to accept it."*

"Remi." His voice softens, and he tries to stop me, but I pull away.

Gracie shakes her head and walks toward their house.

When the front door slams closed, I glare at him. "Stop trying to ruin my life."

The headlights illuminate my brother in the dark as I walk away from him.

"Sis, I'm trying to help you," Harrison says.

"You're doing a shitty job of it." As I stand on the running board of Cash's truck, I speak to Harrison in a scarily calm voice. "I deserve to be with my person as much as you deserve to be with Grace. I would've never forced you to admit your feelings when you weren't ready. I helped you and you're hurting me."

"What are you afraid of, Remi?" he barks out.

"Hurting him." It's the truth.

"Sis."

I slam the door, then back out of the driveway, kicking up gravel, not looking back as I drive away.

A few tears spill down my cheeks, and before I turn onto the country road, I put the truck in park and lean against the steering wheel.

I want to be happy like Harrison and Grace or Beckett and Summer. I'd even take a second chance at love like Kinsley and Hayden. Am I capable of having love like that?

If Cash will risk it all, what do I have to lose? *Him.*

As I look down at the dashboard, I see that picture again. I turn on the overhead lamp and pull it out to look closer.

It's him and *who?*

I flip it over, and on the back, it says: *us.*

Knowing he's looking at this picture with him and some other woman each day he drives around doesn't settle well with me. He said there was no one else, and I *believed* him. Was all of this for nothing?

I take my time driving home as my thoughts eat away at me. I kill the engine and snag the photo from Cash's dash before I walk in. Part of me wonders if he subconsciously told me to drive his truck so I'd find it.

When I enter the condo, the lights are off. I lock the door and then drop his keys on the bar top before walking to the end of the hallway. I slowly push open the door to his room and enter. The side lamp by his bed makes the room glow yellow.

"Finally," he says, rolling over with a grin. "Come here."

I crawl on the bed and fall into his arms, holding him tight. He's freshly showered and smells like mountain rain.

"Did everything go okay? What's wrong?" he asks, noticing my shift. "Are you okay?"

"Yes. It went fine. Who's that woman in the picture?"

The room grows quiet. "What are you talking about?"

I pull it from my back pocket and hand it to him.

He looks at it with his brows furrowed. "Oh."

"What the hell?"

He sits up in bed, pulling me close. He wraps his arm around me and holds the picture out for me to see.

"The woman who has my heart," he says. "I met her a long time ago."

This confession has me dying inside, and I think I might be sick. "Before me and you?" I whisper.

"Same time." His eyes soften as he looks at the photo. "My absolute everything. It's funny, though. I've just been waiting around for her to wake the fuck up."

"So you can go to her?" Maybe she was his other summer fling.

"If I said yes, would you be jealous?" he asks.

"You know I would," I say, chewing on the inside of my cheek, not able to imagine him with someone else.

He tucks loose strands of hair behind my ear. "It's me and you, when we snuck away to Florida together. We took a lot of photos that week."

I didn't recognize myself or remember the pictures. I look closer and laugh, but also cry. Tonight has been too much.

"Aww," he says. "I'm sorry. It was a bad joke. When I told you there was no one else, I meant it, Valentine. It's just you."

I laugh, wiping away my tears. "I don't want to imagine you with someone else. It's too much."

"Babe, I couldn't be with anyone else. Just you," he whispers. "I've carried that photo with me since the day I left to go to Houston. It's always been with me wherever I go."

Knowing he drives around with a photo of *us* on his dashboard has my body buzzing.

I breathe out his name. "*Cash.*"

"When I told you I thought about you every fucking day I was gone, I meant it."

I shake my head. "I didn't realize..."

"That you're *it* for me? *You are.*"

Our lips crash together, and the need to have him consumes me.

"Rem," he says, pushing hair from my face. "On September first, I'm not letting you go."

"I hope you're not making a mistake."

"I'm not," he confidently says with his full chest. "One day you'll see that."

I WAKE with Cash's body molded against mine and his muscular arm holding my bare back to his chest. My eyes flutter open, and the early morning sunlight leaks through the curtains. At first, I'm not sure where I am, but then memories of last night flood in, and I realize I'm naked.

It's the first night I slept in Cash's room *with* him. Over the past month, I crawled between his sheets just to feel close.

He nuzzles into my neck. "Morning, my *beautiful* girl."

I roll over and meet his lazy grin before kissing him. "I love waking up to you like this," I admit, used to him leaving me.

He runs his fingers through my hair. "Good, because you're sleeping with me from here on out. How'd you sleep?"

"Incredible," I say, admiring how gorgeous he is with diamond eyes and long lashes.

"Want to have breakfast with me?" His voice is full of promise.

"In public?" I ask.

"Yeah. Are you allowed to eat with me? Or shall we ask your brothers for permission first?"

"Don't be an asshole."

"I'm over it, Rem. After chatting with Easton yesterday and

beating Harrison's ass, I don't care anymore. You can continue with your plan, but I'm going to be honest."

"But—"

He stops me from talking by kissing me.

"Are you embarrassed of us?" His tone is feral, unfuckable with.

"What? *No.*" I laugh. "You're a wet fucking dream."

He doesn't look convinced. "I don't understand."

"Sometimes I don't feel good enough for you. Now that I'm older, it's not quite as bad. But I'm the Wednesday Addams of my brothers and sisters, and you're Dr. Cash Johnson, animal saver."

Laughter falls from his lips. "I don't think you realize what you have to offer. Is this a middle child thing?"

"Fuck, probably. Is getting what you want an only child thing?" I ask with my hand on his cheek. I trace his bottom lip with my thumb.

"You better fucking believe it," he tells me, his hand glides down my body. "And you spoil me."

"Can I have *you* for breakfast?" I run my fingers through his hair.

"I'll never deny you," he desperately whispers with his fingertips pressed into my skin.

I push him onto his back and kiss down his body until his eyes flutter closed. With my fingers in the band of his boxers, I tug them down, freeing him. Pre-cum pools on the tip, and I lick and suck him. He groans out as I work him so damn good.

"I want to feel you," I whisper, and he nods as I straddle him.

His firm hands grab my ass as I ease down onto his cock, steadying myself with my hands on his stomach.

"Rem," he sighs as I adjust the positioning of my thighs to take him in slowly. I gasp when I sink to his base and buck my hips forward. Pleasure floods through me, holding me tight as I rock against him. One of his hands reaches up to my peaked nipple, and he tweaks it between his fingers. "So goddamn gorgeous."

I sigh, closing the space between our mouths and devouring his lips and tongue. Can I really have this man as mine? When we're together like this, I believe it's possible and that it will all work out.

His teeth graze along my jaw until he's licking and sucking my collarbone. The sensation of his mouth kissing me in private places where only he's been has me begging for more.

"Cash," I whisper, my pussy already quivering at how full he fills me. "You were made for me."

"Actually," he says. "You were made for *me*."

With a shaky breath, I steady myself, and tiny cries release from my lips. But he feels so good. The warmth quickly spreads through me as he watches me take what I need. I love being the center of his attention, just like this, with the morning sunlight peeking through the blinds.

I smile, and so does he. His strong hands glide over my bare skin. He leaves a trail of heat where he touches, and he can mold me into whatever he wants. As the orgasm threatens to take over, I take his mouth, fucking him so good a groan chokes in his throat. With my fingers knotted in his hair, I nuzzle into his neck.

"I'm about to come," I whisper, tracing the shell of his ear with my mouth.

His hands are on my ass and he's pumping into me, giving me every thick inch of him until I crumble around him. Seconds later, he's losing himself. Warmth spreads inside me.

I collapse onto his chest. With his arms wrapped around me, he holds me against him, kissing my hair and forehead. Our want and need still buzzes in the air, but I don't want to move, not when I'm encapsulated by him. He kisses my shoulder and traces up to my jaw with his scruff.

"Ready for second breakfast?" he asks.

"Can't wait," I say.

We shower together and then leave the condo once we're dressed. My lips are as swollen as his, and guilt is written on our faces. He's my best kept secret, but we can't stay this way forever.

As we walk down the street, his fingers brush against mine. I quickly hook my finger with his and hold it briefly before letting him go. I'm not ready to show public affection yet, but as soon as I have Beckett on board, I will be. Hopefully, Harrison keeps his big mouth shut.

When we arrive at the diner, people are waiting outside on the sidewalk. Not surprising since it's just past nine on a Saturday morning. The whole town is here, or at least that's how it feels.

The sounds of chatter and plates and silverware clanking fill the waiting area. Ten minutes later, a girl who I believe graduated with my younger sister, Vera, leads us to a table in the middle of the room.

"Relax, roomie," Cash whispers as he pulls out my chair, noticing I'm tense. We never go out in public together, and I feel eyes on us.

After our coffee is delivered and we order, he focuses his attention on me with warm eyes. "What are you thinking about?" Cash asks before taking a sip of coffee.

"Us," I say.

"That reminds me of something." Cash pulls his phone from his pocket and clicks around. Seconds later, he hands it over to me, and inside is a photo album he created of us. It's full of selfies and pictures we took. There are tons and I scroll through them.

"We were so young."

It's impossible to ignore how we looked at one another. I'm positive the intensity hasn't changed.

"I think we need an updated one," I say. As I slide into the chair beside him, my heart rate ticks upward. I ignore my nerves and hold up his phone to take a picture.

We look at each other on the screen and I stick out my tongue and snap a few before handing it to him. "A few more to add to the collection."

When I'm back in front of him, his gaze softens.

This man is exclusively mine, and when he glances at me like that, the world around me fades away. Being lost in one another like this has haunted me over the years. When he licks his perfect lips, it nearly takes me under, burying me alive.

The only thing that breaks us away is the server reaching for our coffee mugs to refill them.

Once we're alone, he leans forward. "You're gonna have to stop looking at me like that."

I press my lips together and smirk. "I've always been told I can do whatever I want on my birthday."

"Suppose you're right," he says, shooting me a wink, and I think back to the first time we kissed. It's similar words I told him that night.

SEVEN YEARS PRIOR

It was too loud inside the house where the party was popping, so I stepped out on the back porch. I sat on the steps and looked up at the stars; the alcohol buzzed through my veins. Laughter took over as I rested my chin on my knees.

"Rem," Cash said and sat next to me. "You ditched your party?"

"I want to escape," I said, leaning into the warmth of his body. He'd been home for a month, and we'd chatted and seen each other every day in secret. Yesterday, he'd met me in the treehouse in my parent's backyard. We talked about life until the sun rose. Mom knew because she threw up Ziplock bags with sandwiches inside around midnight.

He stood. "I'll be right back, okay?"

I nodded and smiled. Two minutes passed, and he returned with a backpack thrown over his shoulder. One thing about Cash was his preparedness in most situations. He held out his hand, and I took it but quickly let him go. As we walked down the trail to the pond and firepit, I reached over and interlocked my fingers with his. His thumb brushed against mine, causing my body to react. I was still a virgin, but I wanted to give myself to this man.

We teetered the line of friends and flirting, but that night, I knew I wanted more with him.

When we reached the trail's end, Cash opened his bag and pulled out a blanket. He laid it on the ground, and I sat next to him. He grabbed my hand and pulled me back with him. It was platonic as we laughed and pointed out constellations, making up folklore about them.

Stars fell, and we made wishes upon them, but he told me I got two because it was my birthday. It's just how the wish distribution system worked, he explained.

Cash propped himself up on his elbow and glanced at me. When I met his gaze, my breath hitched. The stars sparkled around him, and he was magic.

"Kiss me," I whispered, not wanting to pretend any longer.

"I shouldn't," he said.

I smirk. "I've always been told I can do whatever I want on my birthday. Are you denying me?"

"Absolutely fucking not."

With his hand on my cheek, he leaned in and gently pressed his mouth against mine. Time slowed when our tongues danced together. Fireworks are the only way it could be explained, as my willpower escaped me. Cash's thumb brushed my cheek, and I never wanted the moment to end. It'd never felt that way with anyone else or had the intense need to squeeze my thighs together when he barely touched me.

When we pulled away, I kept my eyes closed and lips parted. "I'm so fucked."

"God, me too." He laughed against my mouth and returned for seconds, which I happily accepted. I wanted to taste more of his tongue *as we floated to a different world where we could be together with no worries. I straddled him, and he was hard. It was the first time I'd had a man hard and below me. I rocked against him, feeling heat pooling between my legs, a sensation I'd never experienced.*

Cash grabbed my hips, stopping me from slowly grinding against him. We'd crossed an unimaginable line, one we'd teetered for weeks.

"I think I'm falling for you, Rem," he admitted.

"I know," I said because I'd felt it too.

Knowing how forbidden it was, knowing Beckett would never accept me being with Cash, made me want him even more. But even without that, the attraction and chemistry were undeniable.

When I got home that night, my panties were soaking wet. I didn't know how it felt to be touched by a man and had never touched myself before. I wanted more of him, just like a drug, and that summer I was determined to overdose. I did.

THE CLATTER of plates beside me snaps me back to reality and I smile up at him. "Thanks for breakfast. I needed this."

"Welcome." His eyes slide from my eyes to my lips. One brow slightly pops up, and I'm tempted to go home before breakfast is served and have him for brunch.

"Check yourself," I say, knowing that look.

"Hell no," he tells me, unashamed, as he blatantly eye fucks me, chewing on the corner of his lip with those perfect teeth.

Having him openly flirt without apology makes me feel pretty and wanted. Maybe I am the woman this gorgeous man is obsessed with.

Our plates slide across the table before us, and silverware is handed over. As I cut open my sunny-side eggs and watch the yolk ooze into my hash browns, I wonder how we got here. It could've been the countless stars we made wishes on the summer we spent together.

"I think I want to go riding soon," I admit.

He tilts his head at me. "Really?"

"Before Harrison's wedding, the last person I'd ridden with was you. You know it hasn't been the same since Majesty." That was my childhood horse, and after he was gone, I stopped riding. That animal was one of my only friends growing up, besides my twin. Majesty was my escape, and he took care of me on our adventures in the woods together.

Cash knew how safe I'd felt with that horse and how lost I was after he was gone. I'd shared it with him, knowing he'd understood on a deeper level.

"No more punishing yourself," he says. "You say when, and I'm yours. I'll saddle a horse, and we'll ride double like old times."

"You mean it?"

"Absofuckinglutely."

CHAPTER SEVENTEEN

CASH

After breakfast, we stop by the coffee shop and grab mochas.

When we're outside, I turn to Remi. "Want to visit Hayden?"

"Sure," she says. We make our way to Main Street Books, and as we're crossing the street, my phone buzzes and I answer.

"Dr. Johnson," a man says. I notice the strain in his voice. "This is Walter Travis."

"Yes, sir. How can I help you?"

"I'm sorry to call on the weekend, but I was wonderin' if you can come out to my ranch?"

"What's goin' on?" I ask, glancing over at Remi.

She grins, but I was hoping I wouldn't have any calls today so we could spend time together. I've been waiting all month to see her, so this seems cruel.

"One of my mares got into something, and she's cut up pretty bad on her chest. Skin is flappin'."

"Text me your address," I say without hesitation, picking up my pace as we cross the road. "And some pictures."

He hangs up on me.

157

"Is everything okay?" Remi asks, taking double the steps to keep in stride with me.

"I have an emergency. Want to ride along?"

"Promised my parents I'd see them for a few hours," she says. "Mom baked me a chocolate cake with extra icing. I was hoping to bring you with me."

"Aww, Rem. I'm so sorry." This would've been the perfect opportunity to be with her alone with her folks. I'm annoyed that I won't be able to join her.

"Hey, don't worry about it. I hadn't originally planned to see you until tonight, anyway. Since last night, it's all been extra time with you. I've enjoyed it," she says.

My phone buzzes, and I open the text clicking on the man's address. It's fifteen minutes away, but I can be there in twelve. I look at the pictures, seeing the deep gash across her breast. Even though there's blood on her leg, she looks happy without a care in the world with her ears pointed upright at full attention. That's good news. Wounds like this usually seem worse than what they are, and it's unnerving to find an animal in that condition.

I immediately call him back and he answers on the first ring.

"Get her in a stall, and if you see a lot of blood dripping, get some gauze—anything you have—and add a lot of pressure until I get there. Is she acting weird, fatigued, or anything?"

"Not yet. Let me take care of her," he says, hanging up on me again.

Remi's hand brushes across mine, and the electrical current is almost too much.

I pull my keys from my pocket and remotely start my truck when it comes into view in front of the condo to get the air conditioner going.

My medical supply bag sits by my bedroom door, and I walk in and plop it on my bed, ensuring I don't need to stop by the clinic first. Packing after every shift is a habit that guarantees I always have what I need. I once learned a very hard lesson and will never be caught unprepared again.

Remi watches me from the doorway. "Seeing you in doctor mode is so *hot*."

Laughter escapes me as I glance over my shoulder at her. She's eye fucking me with her hands tucked into her pockets. "Keep it up, and I'll call Melody to go out there."

I pick up the bag and move toward her. When I'm close enough to pull her into my arms, I do.

"Hurry back to me," she whispers, sliding her lips across mine.

Sweet mocha is on her tongue. As I pepper kisses along her neck, I grab a handful of her perfect ass. "I will, birthday girl. I left a gift for you on your bed."

"What? You didn't have to get me anything. You're enough."

I smirk. "I'll see you tonight."

Remi allows me to pass her, follows me through the house, and watches me climb inside my truck. With a wave, I back out of the driveway with thoughts of her at the forefront.

Once I'm traveling out of town, I glance down at the photo of us and smirk. I knew she'd eventually find it. That photo has been tucked into the dash of every vehicle I've driven since the day I left her with a silent promise that I'd return.

When I arrive at the Travis Ranch, a big Ram truck is parked by the big red barn. I park, grab my supplies, and rush inside.

"Dr. Johnson," he says, relieved to see me. "This way."

When I enter the stall, there's blood, but not as much as I expected. The cut is deep and stretches across ten inches, but it's in a manageable place.

I immediately take the mare's vitals. Her heart rate is regular, and she has a strong pulse. I walk around her, checking the temperature of her legs and making sure there are no other wounds.

I pet her neck, then administer some meds as the owner removes the bandages he temporarily placed to cover the cut.

He steps out of the stall, giving me more space to work. She jerks her head back as I numb the area. "I know, I know, I'm sorry."

I focus on rinsing and disinfecting the area because it's one of the most critical steps.

"What did you get into, girl? I'm not going to hurt you." I keep my voice level as she lowers her head, and I run my hand down the softness of her nose.

In Houston, they'd call me the horse whisperer because even the bastards calmed when I got close.

"Is my Molly gonna be alright?" Walter is distraught.

Owners typically blame themselves for accidents, but horses are curious creatures by nature. They find trouble.

With a smile, I speak in the same calm voice I used on his mare. "Yeah. She will be. The upper chest area has a good blood supply, so wounds like this usually heal fine without many issues. All that muscle helps. It could've been *a lot* worse," I say. After the shit I've seen at the animal hospital and the racetrack, this is nothing. "We need to find what she got into, though. Make sure a hazard isn't lurking for others."

"I got my boys coming out to search the pasture before dark to see if we can figure it out."

"Good idea. Don't want it to happen again. Might not be so lucky."

Some of the things I've experienced are what my nightmares are made of, but I keep that to myself. While my job is typically rewarding, sometimes there are pitfalls. A part of me dies whenever there's an animal I can't save, no matter how hard I try.

Nearly two hours later, Molly is stitched and more than ready to leave the stall. I recheck vitals, administer an updated tetanus shot; then I call it a day. Everything is manageable, which is the outcome I always hope for on emergency calls.

I remove my gloves and grab my supply kit.

"You have a sink?" I ask.

"Yeah, over here," Mr. Travis says, leading me into a nice tack room. I love the smell of leather saddles in a storage room. There ain't nothing like it.

After I wash and dry my hands, he walks me to my truck.

"Thank you for comin' out here. You were quick as lightning," he says, shaking my hand. "I was worried."

"It all worked out," I say. "If you need anything else, call, okay? I'll order some antibiotics."

"Thanks, Dr. Johnson. I'll contact the office on Monday," he says with a firm handshake.

When I leave the property, I stop by the clinic to replenish my supplies. In the distance, music plays from the barn and Beckett is there. He designed the building so he could use it as an event space at the drop of a hat. The entire family loves a party.

While Remi visits her parents, I waste some time and drive to the training barn with my windows down. I hop out of the truck and round the corner, seeing Beckett's already moved all the saddle horses and training equipment to the tack room.

"Why do you have that look on your face?" Beckett asks when he looks up at me.

I realize I'm smiling. I'm fucking happy.

"Did you just get finished seeing someone?" he asks with a popped brow.

"Please," I tell him. "I just sewed up a horse at the Travis ranch."

"Oh," he says, carrying a table across the room as Alan Jackson blares over the speakers in the corners. "What happened to your lip?"

By habit I lick it. Thankfully, the swelling went down. "Accident."

"Weird, you and Harrison both got into *accidents*."

"A coincidence," I tell him, remembering last night, then change the subject. "So, beer pong?"

"Hell yeah. Harrison and I are going to rule the table. We've been practicing every lunch break for the past two months," he admits.

I chuckle. "Remind me not to play tonight. You're both gonna be annoying about how good you are."

"Probably," Beckett says, tilting his head at me. "Something's going on with you."

"You can be direct and ask," I offer, ready to answer his questions, the ones he never asks.

He shakes his head. "Nah. I already know the answer."

"You're gonna have to be specific," I say just as Harrison rounds the corner.

He meets my eyes, and we hold an intense but silent conversation but say nothing before he walks away.

"He's been like that all day," Beckett says. "I think Grace cut him off or pissed in his cereal this morning."

I snicker. "Deserves both. So, what time does the party start?"

"At dark. Kegs are getting delivered in a few hours, though. We can start the party early if you wanna join me."

"Just like old times." I chuckle. "Start before the sun sets. Wake before the sun rises."

"The cowboy way," Beckett tells me. I glance down at my phone and check the time, knowing I need to take a shower. "I'll see you soon, okay?"

"Hell yeah, man. Tonight."

It's mid-afternoon when I arrive home. After I set my supply bag on the floor, I notice our confession book in its usual place on the bar top. I sit and flip it to the last page with her handwriting. Today's date is scribbled in the corner.

> *My Valentine,*
>
> *I was serious about staying pen pals, but there's a reason for that.*
>
> *I know I need to be honest with myself and my family, but most importantly, <u>I need to be honest</u>.*
>
> *Since the pages have become our confessions, the truths of our hearts, I have more to share.*
>
> *After my last breakup, I went to therapy weekly for over a year, and my incredible therapist suggested I write letters to you with the intention of you <u>never</u> reading them.*
>
> *She believed I had communication issues, and I agree. Sometimes, it's hard for me to share how I feel, but writing makes it easier.*
>
> *So, when you suggested we do this, it was almost as if you knew what I'd been doing all along. It felt like a sign.*
>
> *Anyway, I left the notebooks I filled with the letters to you on your bed.*
>
> *I'd secretly hoped one day I could share my thoughts with you. They're about you, anyway.*
>
> *Also, I want you to know that Harrison asked me what I was afraid of.*

His words have haunted me since last night.

I'm so scared of hurting you, of who I'll become without you.

I'm worried you'll fall out of love with me and realize I was a mistake, a fling that was only supposed to last a summer.

We're incredible right now, but will it last? When the chase is over, will you still want me? I hope you do.

You said you didn't care about the risk, and if you don't, I won't either. Or at least I'll try.

I don't want to play games anymore, but I need time to tell Beckett and my parents. I will, though—this month. Seven years is long enough.

I'll probably be visiting with my parents for the rest of the afternoon.

I hope everything went okay with your visit today and it had a happy ending. You're so good at what you do. It takes a kind heart to help sick and hurt animals. I admire you so damn much.

It's only been a few hours, and I already miss you.

Thank you for the beautiful earrings.

Each time I wear them, I'll think about you.

Meet you at the party. Can't wait to see and kiss you again.

—Your Valentine every day of the year

. . .

I SIT BACK in the chair with happiness as a wide smile fills my face.

I walk to my room and see the stack of notebooks on my bed. I flip through them, glancing across her handwriting. I open the first page and my eyes scan over it.

LETTER # 1 - TWO YEARS TO THE DATE.

Cash,

I'm supposed to try an exercise where I write you letters daily, full of truth.

My therapist said to pen them as if you'll never read them.

Is it wrong that I secretly hope you do? My defiance got me into this mess. I knew you were off-limits, but I went after you anyway.

At first, I approached you to rebel, to be with an older man knowing my brother would lose his shit.

Sneaking around became a fantasy, but I never expected something to form between us.

I was drawn to you.

After crushing on you, I wanted you as my summer fling. Then we kissed, I wanted you forever.

Now, we're strangers.

It's sad how that happens.

Sometimes, I must remind myself we were together and that you weren't a fleeting fantasy.

Years later, it still feels like an anchor is tied around my feet, ruining my thoughts, ruining my life.

I haven't spoken to you since you left, but somehow, I'm drowning in thoughts of you and every day asking myself why.

It's torture knowing you're living your best life like I don't exist.

I ghosted you, hoping to erase you, but it hasn't worked.

I dream about your happy life with a happy wife and a house full of kids and a pasture full of horses knowing I could be that woman but was too chickenshit to go after what I wanted.

I was too young to understand what we had.

I don't know if I deserve love, especially not yours. I know I hurt you by ignoring you, but I'm sorry. It's too painful to speak to you or even hear your name.

Still secretly feeling this way about you is a blessing and a curse.

It's not your fault, though. I'm not mad at you but at our circumstances.

We spent an incredible summer together, and I look back on it with a cruel heart, knowing our forever is now never.

People ask if it's better to have loved and lost than to have never loved at all.

I think the correct answer is the latter. That way I wouldn't have to think about you every damn day and know exactly what I'm missing.

Years ago, I thought it was a stupid crush, something I'd get over.

It wasn't.

I know that now. And I'll spend the rest of my life searching for how you always made me feel.

—Somehow, still your Valentine

I can't stop reading. I want to binge these letters, the confessions she wrote for me when I dreamed about being with her.

LETTER #2 - NEXT DAY, TWO YEARS PRIOR.

Cash,

I reread my last letter, and I sound pathetic, like a sad, hopeless woman writing to her first lover.

That's reality, I guess, but hopefully, it's only temporary.

My therapist told me I shouldn't read them again, but I'm a rule breaker.

You know that, so you'll understand.

And if you're not smiling when you read that sentence, I haven't done a good job of showing you who I really am.

She suggested that I keep writing about what comes to my mind until I'm satisfied discussing it.

Honestly, I don't know what satisfaction feels like anymore, not since you left.

It's cruel of you to capture my heart, but what's crueler is you have no idea.

When Beckett mentioned you coming home, I considered texting you.

I didn't want to reach out to you first. I wasn't strong enough to be friend-zoned and knew we'd fall back into talking every night.

I just want to know HOW to get over you.

How did you get over me?

I lose the ability to form words when I think about that.

You make it seem easy, still smiling in photos with your friends. You should write a book and teach people how to get over heartbreak.

When I've had too much wine, I think about calling you.

Your number is still the same, and I never deleted

you from my contacts. I want to hear your voice again. It's smooth as whiskey.

Other than that, everything around here is good.

I haven't gone horseback riding since you left.

You made me love it again, but now it reminds me of you, of us.

It hurts too much, almost as bad as when I lost Majesty.

Anyway, Kinsley has been burning spell candles.

Each week, she asks me to send her my wish energetically.

Okay, don't laugh, but I'm manifesting you coming home, coming back to me.

So, if you're sitting on our bed in the house we live in together and reading these letters, know it was Kinsley's candles.

It's false hope, but she has me convinced it will happen. I guess we'll see.

Hmm. Where are you right now as you read this?

Tell me if it came true.

Are you mine? Fuck, I hope so.

My mouth falls open, and I pull my phone from my pocket and call her. It's something I hardly do, but I don't care that she's at her parents' house even though she'll act weird. "Hi," she says, and I can imagine how awkward she's being as her mom stares at her.

"I got your letter."

"Yes," she says.

"Maybe I should say *letters*," I correct. "Anyway, I thought you'd enjoy this line." I read it for her. "It came true two years later. Tell Kinsley thanks."

She gasps. "Seriously?"

"Yeah." I laugh.

She doesn't say anything for a few seconds.

"Oh God," she mutters. "You have no idea what I told her to manifest."

"Do I *want* to know?" I ask.

"Uh. It's all really great things."

"Promise you'll tell me when it happens."

"I will," she says, then lowers her voice. "I'll see you tonight. Miss you."

"Miss you too, Valentine," I say, and we end the call. I read the rest of the page, then flip it over to the back.

> When I think back to that summer we spent together, I remember how magical it was.
>
> Sometimes, I wonder if I dreamed it all. If we ever really knew one another, especially now that the memories have faded into a haze.
>
> Is it better in my mind than it actually was, or did we have the real deal?
>
> It feels real, but I'm gaslighting myself into believing it wasn't. As more time passes, I don't know what our truth is anymore.
>
> It's scary to know that pieces and memories of you are being deleted from my mind.

Eventually, will I forget we ever existed?

Years ago, when I stood outside in the sunshine and closed my eyes, I imagined you and could almost hear my name on your lips.

I don't know what your voice sounds like anymore, but sometimes, I dream about it.

<u>This is pathetic, isn't it?</u>

I'm shaking my head at myself, and I'm frustrated.

But I'll keep writing you these letters for science. The truth is, you were my match, and I'm waiting for you to come back home and light me up again.

I might wait forever.

I love you, Cash, and it's your fault for being so goddamn good to me.

I never told you because I was scared, and now I never can.

I always worried that you wouldn't say it back and that maybe I was in too deep, so I kept it to myself.

Writing that made me realize that I keep a lot of things to myself.

I need to do better.

When you come home, I promise I'll try harder.

Yes, I still miss you.

—Your shackled Valentine

.

.

P.S. I really do hope you're happy. You're living the dream life you worked so hard for, and I'm proud of you. You're making a difference and changing lives. You totally changed mine.

She loves me, and nothing else in the whole goddamn world matters. I have zero doubts about how my girl feels about me. And while she hasn't said it yet, she will when she's ready. But after reading this, I could die a happy man. Remi loves me.

I flip through the notebooks, noticing how she faithfully wrote to me.

Fuck, I can't wait to see her tonight.

CHAPTER EIGHTEEN

REMI

HOURS EARLIER

After eating too much cake and hanging out with my folks, I arrive at the condo. Cash isn't home yet, so I take my time writing him a letter. I sign the bottom then go to my closet and pull out the notebooks of old letters I'd written him. I flip through them seeing my emotions spilled across the pages. I set them on his bed.

The day has finally come, I think. He deserves to know what was on my mind before he returned.

After a quick shower, I get dressed and leave for my party. I text Colt to make sure he's on his way so we can meet up. Twenty minutes later, I'm sitting in my car in front of the B&B waiting for my twin. My nerves take hold, but I don't know why.

Before I get out of my car, I pull the visor down, check my makeup, and adjust the crown on my head. My mom got it for me, and I promised to wear it. I glance at the heart-shaped earrings Cash gifted me. He's the only man to give me jewelry other than my father.

When Colt parks next to me, I leave my car and greet him. He's wearing a crown that's fit for a king. We shake our heads and walk to the barn.

"The only reason I'm wearing this ridiculous crown is for the pictures later," Colt tells me.

"Same," I tell him, as we take the path. The sky grows dark, and nightfall is upon us. "How are things with Cash?" he asks, not giving any fucks.

"Great." We walk a few more steps. "He's a good man."

Colt nods. "He's good for you, sis. Even if you don't want to admit it."

"That's changing." I look up at the sky as we stand behind the barn. "One day, I'm gonna marry him."

"I know you are." Colt smiles and pulls me into a tight hug. "Don't let anyone make decisions for you, okay? Do what makes you happy."

"I will." I squeeze him, not wanting to let him go. Growing up, we had each other's backs and still do. He knows how Beckett and Harrison have been with my relationships.

When Colt lets me go, he creates space between us and looks past me.

"Hey, man. It's good to see you."

I turn to see the man of my dreams standing close.

"Yeah, absolutely," Cash tells him. Hearing his voice sends shivers up my spine, and I lick my lips.

My brother pats my shoulder, and they exchange a firm handshake before walking away.

A minute later, it's just the two of us standing in the summer breeze. "Hi."

"Howdy." His gaze trails down to my cleavage, my shorts that leave nothing to the imagination.

"Damn, Valentine, you look *good* tonight," he says.

His black button-up is rolled to his elbows, and I love it when he wears that old, worn baseball hat. Cash, standing before me dressed like this, is what my fantasies are always made from. "This is how you dress in my fantasies," I whisper.

"I know," he mutters, removing the space between us until our mouths crash together. His hand fists through my hair, and we're dangerous and desperate, out in the open, where anyone can stumble across us. It feels like another seven years have passed since I saw him, but it's only been hours. I'm addicted to every part of him and have been since the moment he kissed me under the stars.

"Cash," I whisper when my back touches the barn, and his hard cock presses into me. I grab his hand, sliding it down my shorts and into my panties. His finger dips inside of me, and I gasp out, knowing it's too reckless. I'm breathless, wanting and needing him just like this as he gives me two digits.

"You're so wet," he whispers, sliding his fingers to the knuckle, and I rock against him. "But we *can't* do this here," he says, removing his hand and placing his fingers into his mouth, sucking and licking as he watches me.

"All of a sudden, I want to skip my party," I say, and the thought nearly takes over.

He smirks. "Make your move, Valentine."

The need is so intense.

"I can't do that to Beckett. He's planned this for months," I whisper. "But I want to."

"And I'd let you." He pulls away with a strand of my hair between his fingers. "You're my kryptonite, Rem."

"Let's leave early," I say, blinking up at him, needing relief. It's going to be a long as fuck night.

He takes a step forward, gently brushing his lips across mine. "I'm leaving when you are."

"Okay," I whisper, guiding my hand over his hardness.

"I won't be able to take my eyes off you all night."

"Please don't," I say, wrapping my arms around him. "I'll meet you inside."

"Okay," he says, stealing one last kiss, then we break apart.

I swallow hard, glancing back at him as we separate. The warm light from the barn splashes across his face, lighting him up.

"They're waiting for you, birthday girl," he whispers with a grin.

In another lifetime, I'd walk in holding his hand for everyone to see that Dr. Cash Johnson belongs to me and that I'm his. One day, I promise myself. Hopefully, sooner rather than later.

I glide down the hallway to the big room in the barn with my heart fluttering. The lights are dimmed, but as soon as I enter, Beckett yells and points in my direction.

"There's Remi," he says, whistling. Heads turn toward me, and my eyes scan around the room. Moments later, Cash pops up behind Beckett, smirking. I'm lost in his gaze as I give him a small smile.

Colt moves toward me, grabbing my attention. While we stand beside one another, the seventy people in the room sing Happy Birthday.

"I almost feel like a celebrity." Colt covers his mouth so no one can read his lips as he speaks to me.

"Isn't this song weird?" I whisper back. "It's so awkward."

We've had this same conversation during this song since we were old enough to talk. Since we're twins, the family makes a bigger deal out of this day than they should.

"I'm glad I get to share this day with you," I tell him, and we hug.

"And many more," Kinsley and Sterling yell from the back of the barn. Harrison makes a fart noise, and everyone chuckles, then the music is cranked loud enough for dancing but still low enough for conversations.

"So glad we could get that out of the way already," Colt says. "But I bet you five bucks it won't be the last time we hear it."

He holds out his hand, wanting me to shake.

"Not taking that one," I say, slapping him away. The more everyone drinks, the more times it's sung. We used to count. I think the record is thirty-seven times.

Before anyone can approach us, Colt and I escape to the keg and pour ourselves a cold one.

"Cheers," I say. Haley comes over and hugs me. She's carrying a bright pink bag, and when she hands it over, by the weight alone, I know it's a book.

"It better be dirty," I whisper in her ear.

"The *filthiest*. It's about a hot veterinarian with *skills* and a massive you know what," she says, wagging her brows.

Laughter escapes me. Colt shakes his head as he walks away.

Cash stands by the entrance chatting with Hayden. They're laughing about something, and I love it when he smiles like that, showing his perfect teeth. As if I summoned him to turn his head, he glances in my direction, then focuses on me.

We're entranced, lost in a cosmic tumble.

"Am I imagining things, or is Cash eye fucking you from across the room?" Haley asks with a brow popped. "You don't even have to answer. I fucking *knew* it."

I glance at her and take a sip of my beer.

"Oh my God," she whispers. "*You've had sex.*"

"Haley, I haven't said a word, and you've already made up the whole scenario in your head."

"I read a lot, okay? Don't blame me," she says. "Please tell me it's incredible."

"Better than incredible," I whisper, trying to hold back a smile.

Telling the truth sets my soul on fire.

She squeals, but then she freezes in place, and her mouth falls open. "Oh goodness. Someone just spilled three beers on Emmett."

I turn my head to catch Emmett tossing his soaked T-shirt to the side, grinning wide. With his abs out and his pants hanging low on his hips, he leaves no room for the imagination.

"He's a thirst-trap," I say, shaking my head. The keyword in that sentence is trap."

"Great, because if he's showing, I'm one hundred percent looking," she says with zero shame. "Wow. I didn't realize he had so many tattoos. He's giving me bad boy vibes, which does *all sorts* of things for me," she continues.

Haley narrows in on him as he throws a ball toward the red plastic cup. It sinks inside and he high-fives one of the ranch hands. I don't remember his name because he just started working for my parents.

"I need to grow some balls and just ask him on a date," Haley says.

I smile and witness Emmett glancing at her. The chemistry is there, and damn, it's intense. "He'd probably say yes. But you should be careful with him. He might be quiet, but they're usually the ones a girl can't trust."

"I don't want to marry him. I want him to wreck me." Haley chuckles.

"He will," I tell her. "Just watching out for you and your heart."

"I no longer have a heart," Haley says. "I'll be fine."

About an hour after the party starts, I'm three beers in, and my inhibitions are slowly fading away. That's a bad thing because it gets to a point where I don't give a fuck about anything.

Haley and I laugh with Kinsley as she fills us in on the local tea she just learned. Then she turns to me. "Heard you fucked Harrison up."

"Yeah, and did he tell you why?" I ask her, knowing they're close.

"No," she admits. "He wouldn't say, but I have an idea why."

"I want to date who I want to date. Period."

"Ah, knew it has something to do with that. I could just tell. And Beckett?"

"He doesn't know yet," I confirm. "I don't want to hide anymore."

My sister grins wide. "Then don't."

I meet her eyes. "Do you remember a long time ago when you used to text me about sending wishes to the universe?"

She snickers. "Oh God, yes."

"Kins, some of them are coming true." I look at her, studying her face. She grabs my hand and leads me away from everyone, and we lean against the wall in the corner of the room. Hayden is still chatting with Cash.

Her expression grows serious. "He's in love with you, Remi."

"I'm in love with him, too," I admit. "So madly, deeply, stupid in love with him, and I'm going to fuck up everything. I know it."

She places her hand on my shoulder. "Are you manifesting fucking it up?"

"Probably."

"I want you to start telling yourself that everything is going to work out, and it's going to be fucking wonderful and easy! Speak that shit into existence like you did before. I've got your back, sis. So does Hayden." Kinsley pulls me into a tight hug. "Claim your man."

We grab another drink, then join Haley. As I glance toward the entrance, Easton and Lexi enter the barn, and I swear everyone freezes in place.

Lexi and I chat and hug and her being here was a surprise I didn't know I needed. Seeing her in love and happy gives me hope, too. After a few minutes, they get in line to play beer pong.

When they're across the room, Haley chuckles. "You were right. He is intimidating."

"Right?"

The overhead lights dim and a colored disco light twirls above. Emmett excuses himself and then Haley speaks up. "I'll be right back."

I search the room for Cash, but I don't see him. I stand on my tiptoes, wondering where he went. I always find him.

"Searching for someone?" that familiar voice says from behind. I turn and he's close, almost too close.

"People will talk," I say, smirking, knowing more than my family fills this room.

"Do you care?" he asks, placing his hand on my hip. Electricity buzzes through me as he leans in and whispers in my ear. "Because I have *no more* fucks to give."

"I don't care. Not on my birthday," I say.

"Then dance with me." He holds out his hand, and I take his fingers in mine. This gorgeous man leads me to the middle of the room and places his hands on my waist as we sway to the music. The only time we've ever danced was under the stars, alone, and in secret. It was only ever me, him, and the crickets.

When he pulls me close, I meet his warm hazel eyes. Today they look blue.

"Now what happens?"

"I guess we wait to see if someone wants to fight me at your party," he says, twirling me around.

I laugh, holding onto him and grabbing my crown so it doesn't fall to the ground. As soon as he lifts me upward, I snort.

When I catch sight of Lexi and Easton dancing, I focus back on Cash.

"Do you think we look at each other that way?" I ask, wishing and wanting to capture his lips.

"Without a fucking doubt," he mutters, moving in close.

As my eyes flutter closed and we're a millimeter away from kissing, I hear a man yelling Lexi's name.

I look around, trying to see who it is. They're on the other side of the room.

"No," Lexi says with anger in her voice. "I have *nothing* to say to you."

I stand up on my tiptoes and see her ex-boyfriend Beau reaching for her hand.

Easton steps forward, and I think he might snap Beau's wrist off his body. *"Don't. Touch. Her.* And if I were you, I'd take a step back."

"Oh shit," I whisper. "Fuck, we need Beckett and Harrison to pay attention."

Lexi's brothers Brett and Chris step beside Easton, and they have that look in their eyes like they want blood. The last thing we need is the deputy called out here.

Beau yells something. Then Lexi's voice is crystal clear. All that theater she's done has helped her project over an audience. "You cheated on me!"

The music stops, and I hear gasps and chatter. With each passing second, it grows out of hand, so I rush to my brothers.

I shove my fingers into my mouth and whistle like my mama used to do. Their heads pop up and they turn toward me. "Fight!" I yell, pointing to the center of the room.

Beckett and Harrison go from happy to pissed in two seconds. I push through the crowd with Cash's hand in mine.

"You have the audacity to call *me* a liar after everything you put me through? You're a cheating bastard!" Lexi yells.

I move in front of Beau with my hands on my waist and I grow angrier by the second. Cash stands behind me, ready to break his neck if he lays a finger on me. Beckett and Harrison push through the crowd and join us.

"You won't be ruining my birthday, Beau. Please leave," I say, keeping my tone cool. I'm not here to instigate, I just want them to stop.

No words come out of his mouth.

"Out you go," Beckett pushes forward, grabbing Beau's

shoulder. Harrison grips his other one, and they lead him outside.

Easton takes Lexi's hand, and they escape, but I understand. There are too many eyes on them, and they're already being watched.

I turn to Cash, and his finger hooks my belt loop. He tugs me closer to him. "Are you good?"

"Yes," I say, happy that he's this close, tempted to nibble his lip. "I am now."

"Rem," he growls as my fingers brush against his cock. He's had a semi since his fingers were buried inside of me.

"I need you," I whisper. Just as he opens his mouth to speak, the microphone comes on. Feedback echoes and Harrison speaks with his mouth too close, so it sounds like a jumbled mess.

"Sorry about that, ladies and gentlemen; I thought we said pricks weren't invited! Let the good times roll," he says, and he seems like he's in a good mood.

Everyone laughs, and then the music continues like nothing happened.

"I'll be right back," I tell Cash, and he nods. Before Harrison can return to Grace, I loop my arm in his. "Can we talk?"

"I guess." Harrison leads me down the hallway to his office. He walks in and looks around, making a face. "Someone had sex in here."

"Ew," I tell him. "It wasn't me, I swear."

We move to the supply room. He shuts the door and crosses his arms over his broad chest.

"I owe you an apology," he says. "I'm sorry for ever questioning you. I love you, and I want the best for you. I wanted to make sure you weren't being used. I know you two were together the last time he was here, okay? And I know more than I should. But at the end of the day, this is your relationship, not mine. You said you loved him, and that's enough for me," Harrison explains.

My bottom lip quivers. "Thank you. I'm sorry, too."

"I still think he's too fucking old for you, but it is what it is," he says.

I adjust the crown on my head. "The heart wants what it wants."

"You're *really* into him."

"It's love like you have," I say.

My brother nods, and his grin catches me off guard. "Does Cash know?"

I meet his blue eyes.

He shakes his head. "Have you told him how you feel?"

"I—"

"I asked him directly, Remi," Harrison flatly says. "I asked if you'd said 'I love you'. It's not words we throw around lightly. When he couldn't answer, I thought your relationship was bullshit."

"It's not though." My heart rate increases, and I remember all the times we've been together and how we've never exchanged those three words. It's not that I haven't wanted to tell him, it's just, well, I don't know what I'm afraid of.

"I know that now. If you love someone and you're madly fucking in love with them, you have to say something, sister. Don't make the same stupid mistake I did, okay? It was awful. I wouldn't wish that upon you. Promise me."

"I promise," I whisper as my brother hugs me. "Did you tell Beckett?" I ask as I squeeze him.

He creates space, holding his hands tight on my arms. "No. That's your problem to deal with."

"Thanks," I say, pulling away. "I'll tell him soon."

"Good, and until then, I'll keep your secrets," Harrison says. "But also, if Cash hurts you, he'll wish he were dead."

"That's not funny."

"I'm not laughing." He doesn't crack a smile.

We walk down the hallway together. "Happy birthday, sister. I hope your dreams come true."

"They already have," I say when I meet Cash's gaze. I smile at Harrison and walk away.

Electricity pulls me toward him, and when I'm close, I lead him outside.

"Everything okay?" he asks.

"Perfect," I tell him, knowing I need to tell him how I feel.

When we're alone, I push him against the barn. His fingers are in my hair, and I desperately kiss him. It's hot and passionate, and I need more of him, all of him.

"I have a confession," I moan against his mouth.

"Remi? Cash?" Lexi says. She's on Easton's lap, and I realize we ruined *their* moment.

"You didn't see us," I say, walking back inside, giving them privacy.

Cash joins me. "You were saying?"

"Can we leave now?" I ask, turning to him.

"Whatever you want, birthday girl. It's your night," he says.

I grab his hand and lead us away from it all.

Right now, I need to be alone with him. Our future depends on it.

CHAPTER NINETEEN

CASH

I interlock my fingers with her as we walk in the dark down the path that leads straight to the B&B. The stars above sparkle and shine, and she smiles when one skips across the sky.

"Two wishes," I mutter, grinning at her. It was a rule that if I saw a shooting star on my birthday, I got two. I remember telling her that before.

She can have ten wishes, and I'll try to make every single one of them come true. Hell, for my girl, there is no limit.

Remi's eyes flutter closed, and our walking pace slows. A smile plays on her plump lips, and her eyes open. She's staring at me like I'm her world. I'll fucking take it.

"Good ones?" I ask as we continue forward.

"The *best*," she confirms. "And the wish you made?"

I laugh, kissing her knuckles. "It never changes."

"Will you tell me when it comes true?"

"Yes," I say, knowing one day it will.

"Don't forget," she says.

"Oh, Rem, I won't trust me."

Before we reach the B&B, I pull her into my arms, and we

dance under the stars to the fading music in the distance. I spin her around, and she laughs, pressing her palms against my chest. She stills as I meet her eyes.

"I love you," she whispers into the summer night as the sounds of crickets and frogs surround us.

A warm smile spreads across my face as her mouth slams against mine. "Fuck, I love you, too. So damn much, Valentine."

She grabs my shirt. "I've loved you for years, and I'm so deeply, madly, obsessively in love with you. I'm sorry for not telling you."

"Don't apologize. Better late than never," I whisper across her mouth with a smile, picking her up and carrying her the rest of the way to the B&B.

"I knew you loved me, Rem. I read a few of your letters."

"My truths," she exhales.

"Yes," I say, setting her on her feet before we climb the back porch stairs.

"Where are you two going?" Weston asks from a rocking chair in the corner. I wonder how long he's been watching us.

Remi takes a step back, startled. "None of your business."

"Did you hear the news?" he asks.

"What news?" she impatiently waits with swollen lips.

"Easton proposed to Lexi," he happily announces.

I burst into a giddy laughter. "Amazing. And on my birthday."

"Anyway, have fun," Weston tells her, glancing at me.

We enter the B&B and greedily stumble up the stairs. She fumbles with the doorknob, and we burst inside, unable to keep our hands off the other. The bed is a mess from last night, with sheets and blankets crumpled in a pile just how we left it.

With my foot, I kick the door closed as Remi leads me to the bed. The need is like nothing I've ever experienced as her hand slides down and grabs all of me. We're a boiling pot of water; if we keep this up, we'll spill over.

"Remi." Her name falls from my mouth like a prayer, and I want to worship her from now until the end of fucking time.

"Make love to me," she whispers, removing her shirt and dropping it to the floor in a pile.

I grasp her waist. "That's how babies are made."

She smiles. "I'd have yours."

I lick my lips. "Keep that up, and we'll make one. Fuck, putting a baby inside of you has me so fucking hard."

"One day," she whispers, setting her birthday crown on the side table before peeling my shirt off my body. Reaching behind me, I pull it over my head and drop it on top of hers. As she unzips and unbuttons my jeans, her eyes are zeroed in on my cock. Remi pushes them down, then she falls to her knees before me with her hot mouth open.

She licks the sticky pre-cum from the tip of my cock before hollowing her cheeks and taking me in slowly. My eyes flutter closed as she cups my balls, working me so goddamn good. When I hit the back of her throat, her muscles tighten around me.

"Fuck," I hiss out, knotting my hand in her silky strands. Remi unsnaps her bra, showing me her full breasts and perky pink nipples that are standing at full attention. I reach down and tweak one, and she moans with me between her lips.

Remi's hand slides down between her legs, and I lift a brow.

"Touching yourself for me?" I whisper, her blue eyes blinking up at me as she slides her fingers between her legs.

She nods with my cock in her throat. "Such a good girl not speaking with your mouth full."

I watch as she rubs circles on her cute little clit, and it makes me want to spill deep inside of her. "You said no one could make you come but me. Did that include yourself?" I ask.

She pulls me out of her mouth. "No one. Just *you*. The first time I came since being with you was with you. I tried, but I couldn't get off. I needed *you*."

"Tonight." I pull her to her feet, then lean in and trace my mouth around the shell of her ear. "I'm going to watch you pleasure yourself, and then we're making love until you come twenty-eight times, birthday girl. One for each year."

"And one to grow on?" she whispers with desire written on her face as she removes the rest of her clothes and moves the blankets to the side.

"Fuck, yes," I say as Remi climbs on the mattress and leans back.

I chuckle, noticing a bottle of whiskey on the table. Beside it is a note. "Compliments of Easton Calloway," I tell her, pouring myself a glass.

"Walk me through it," she says with soft eyes. I slide down her mouth, her breasts, down her navel to her pussy that's sparkling with wetness.

"You know what my body likes."

"I absolutely fucking do," I mutter. "Lie back on the bed and show yourself to me."

She chews on her lip, lying back on the bed. Her hands take the same trail down her body that my eyes just took.

"I want you to touch yourself, too. As you watch me," she says.

Our eyes meet, and I nod, grabbing my shaft. I grunt, already needing to come, considering I've had a hard-on since I tasted her earlier.

"Slide your fingers down your slit and barely touch your clit," I say, moving to sit in the chair in the corner of the room. I sip the whiskey, exhaling as Remi lets out a hot pant.

"Mm," she says. "I love having you watch me. It turns me on."

"Do it for me again," I say, smirking. "And give yourself a finger. All the way out and then back in again."

She closes her eyes and follows my instructions, sliding her finger deep inside. Her breathing slightly increases.

"Again," I say, noticing how her breasts rise and fall and the slight thrust of her hips. I can see and hear how wet she is.

Her fingers play at her entrance as she goes in again.

"Mm. Taste yourself."

Remi places her finger into her mouth and moans.

"I fucking love the flavor of you," I whisper. "Now return."

She slides her finger back out and in again as she holds herself upright on her elbow. Her nipples are at full attention.

"Back to your clit like a good girl," I tell her, wanting to touch her, needing to fuck her as she rubs circles between her legs. "Just like that, I'll tell you when to slow down. Two fingers, baby girl. Put two fingers deep inside your greedy cunt for me."

"I wish it were you." Her mouth falls open, and Remi opens her legs wider. Watching her has my cock throbbing for her sweet pussy.

"Cash," she whimpers. "*Cash.*"

"Mm. It feels so good, doesn't it? Imagine me buried between your legs, devouring you, sucking on you, thrusting my fingers inside your tight holes. I love how you sink on them, letting me tickle that g-spot."

She moans out. "Fuck. Your dirty talk has me so worked up. God, I need you."

"Three fingers, Valentine," I say, and they disappear inside her. She rocks her hips, pumping herself, panting. "Use your other hand and ravage that needy clit as you pump deep inside your dripping wet pussy. Just like that."

She gasps.

"You have permission, Rem," I say. "Your body is fucking begging for it. Come for me."

Her head rolls back on her shoulders, and her body seizes. She's teetering on the edge, her hands slowing to a dangerous pace. Knowing she's never pleasured herself and is so damn close for me has me stroking so slowly. I can't come yet, but God watching her is working me up.

"My greedy girl is so fucking close, isn't she?"

"Mmhm." She whimpers, her body shuttering. "I'm thinking about you. Imagining it's you, like I always have," she admits, slowing her pace on her clit. Her toes are pointed as she scales the wall leading to her intense release. "I'm yours, Cash."

"I'm yours, too, Valentine. Now, *come. For. Me.*"

Her eyes meet mine, and the orgasm rips through her. I move to the bed, dropping to my knees before her, sliding my hands on her ass, bringing her pussy to my mouth. I lick up every drop of her sticky cum, loving how she tastes as her pussy pulses around my tongue.

"Coming for me on command," I say, burying my face between her legs as she rocks against my face. "My favorite fucking flavor."

When her hips rock, I realize she's building up to the next one.

"Your scruff," she chokes out as I lick and suck her swollen nub. "Fuck. *You feel so good.*"

I'm merciless with how I devour her. She squirms against me, trying to create more friction, nearly begging me to allow her to come again. "*Please.*"

"I'll think about it." I impale her wet cunt with my tongue, wishing it was my cock. I reach down and grab myself, rubbing the pre-cum across my tip. Her muscles are so tight as she teeters on the brink of pure ecstasy. She wraps her legs around my neck, and I'm hungry for more of her and enjoy her pleasure, enjoy the fact that I'm the one leading her to the edge —the only one who ever has or will.

I'm her first and her last.

Her groans ring out. My girl has always been greedy and never satisfied. I hope she never is.

She will come at any second and knows as much as she covers her mouth with her hand. We're not alone in the B&B. We both know that. But I don't give a fuck who hears her call my name. I want the whole damn town to know who owns this pussy, and very soon, they will, as I continue to give her more orgasms.

"Enjoy it, Valentine. We've got all fucking night." Giving her a finger, curling it at the end as I return to her clit in long, torturous sucks with a random flick. In a blink, she's screaming out, begging for *more more more* as she bucks against me.

She gasps for air. "I want forever."

I smile against her sensitive skin, allowing her to fall from her high before returning my mouth to her perfect little pussy.

"I want to give you forever."

Each time I think she's done, she releases another one and falls apart again. "Is that five already?" I hum against her inner thigh, pepper kisses, seeing how she's already soaked the bed with her pleasure.

"I want more," my horny girl mutters. "Until I'm *nothing*."

"*Rem*."

"Tonight, I want you to ruin me."

I meet her blue eyes. "That's truly what you want?"

"Yes. Make my fantasies come true."

"I plan on it, birthday girl."

CHAPTER TWENTY

REMI

I want to be torn down and rebuilt by him, and as he hovers above me, his thickness waits at my entrance.

"I love you, Rem, but I'm gonna fuck you like I hate you," he says, his voice a rasp as he barely gives me the tip.

"Do it," I say, digging my heels into his ass, forcing him inside of me.

I want it all.

I want him to plunge so deep inside of me he breaks me into two halves and then glues me back together again. He's already destroyed me once, imprinted himself on my body and soul, and I'm okay with him doing it again as long as we can have this very moment.

"God, yes," I whisper as he glides inside my slick walls. The pressure and heat of him spread through me. His strong hand is on my hip, creating more friction as he slams into me. It's deep and dangerous as his cock plummets inside of me, shattering me from the inside out.

I see stars as I whimper with each magnified thrust, each deep pump a promise that he'll never fucking let me go. I hope he doesn't.

My back arches, and I drown in the sensation of him, but he's always pulled me under. Cash is a dangerous rip current, and I'll sink to the bottom with him.

"That's all you've got?" I growl out, wanting to be sore, wanting to feel how he wrecked me tomorrow.

A grunt releases from him as he pounds deeper. The pleasure grows so intense that heat and emotions swarm through. My core tightens. The impending orgasm has me in a choke hold, and I don't know how much longer I can hold on. As I teeter on edge, I feel as if I've transcended with his mouth and teeth and breath on my neck and my shoulder and my breasts. His mouth memorizes me, and I never want him to forget.

"You feel so fucking good," he says, knowing I'm close. "So. Fucking. Good."

I capture his mouth, his movements slow, as he brushes strands of hair from my face.

"Rem. I love you," he whispers into the moonlight, sounding more like a plea than an admission. It's desperate and fierce, causing my heart to flutter away when he repeats it across my lips.

With my fingers threaded through his hair, I say it back. "I love you. I love you so much," I say just as I spill over, my body nearly collapsing as the orgasm takes me under. I clench around his thick cock in thick hard pulses that have my body almost flying off the mattress.

It's euphoric and mind-numbing as the sensation of finding love and being loved overtakes me. His movements grow more ragged, and he escapes with me, emptying every drop deep into my core. The sensation is overwhelming and intense, and tears drip from my eyes. It's raw happiness knowing the man I've secretly loved is mine.

"Rem," Cash says, kissing away my tears, looking at me with sad eyes. We're still connected. The warmth of him pools inside of me. "Valentine?"

I smile, cupping his cheeks as I lift my mouth upward. "I have you, and I finally know that."

"You've *always* had me," he confirms. "And *always* fucking will."

THE FOLLOWING DAY, I roll over to Cash, who is lying next to me. I wrap my arms around his body, kissing his muscular back. He turns toward me, smiling, with sleepy eyes, giving me that dimple I love.

"Good morning, gorgeous," he mutters against my lips.

"Morning," I say.

"Did you survive your twenty-eighth birthday?" he asks with a chuckle.

I squeeze my legs together. "Barely. I think you've carved yourself inside of me."

"That happened a long time ago."

A deep voice responds to a high-pitched one, and I glance outside, trying to figure out what time it is by where the sun is in the sky. It must be check-out time.

"I want to tell Lexi congrats before she leaves," I say, laughing, rolling out of bed. As soon as my feet are on the floor, I stop mid-stride. "Shit."

I glance over my shoulder at Cash, and he looks at me with his bedroom eyes. "Mission accomplished?"

"I feel you in places I didn't know were possible," I say, leaning over the bed to steal a kiss. His large hand is on my ass, and I moan into his mouth.

"Hurry back to me," he says, nibbling and sucking on my bottom lip.

"I will," I say, glancing down at the blanket. His cock makes it look like a circus tent. "Keep that *up* for me."

Cash slides his hand under the blanket and strokes himself slowly. "Oh, I will."

"Shit, I want to stay so bad."

"Go," he tells me, patting my ass. I hurry and wiggle into the clothes I wore to my party and quickly empty my bladder.

The stairs squeak, and I rush to the top of the banister, hoping I don't miss them.

Lexi looks up at me with wide eyes. "Hi, what are you ..."

I smile and move down the stairs toward her. "I heard the news. And on my birthday. I'll never forget the day. I'm so happy for you."

My friend holds out her hand, and the pink diamond engagement ring sparkles bright in the sunlight. Pink is her favorite color, too. I guess Easton thought of everything.

"It's perfectly you, Lexi," I say. It's the truth. That's all I have to offer these days.

"Thank you." She can't stop grinning. Hell, I wouldn't either.

I haven't. I immediately think about Cash. We have the same age difference, and no one has batted an eye at them.

Easton tucks his hands into his pockets, and I glance at him. I'll forever be grateful for him giving us a room in the B&B to escape into. It was the little nudge we needed to cross the line.

"You two are fire," I say.

"I played matchmaker," Weston interrupts us like I was speaking to him. "Kinda made this whole thing happen."

He's too cocky.

Brody rolls his eyes. "No, you didn't."

"Why are you working the day after your birthday?" Lexi asks with a smile.

I lift a brow. "I'm not."

She glances over my shoulder. "Are you *alone*?"

Last night, she saw Cash and me with her own eyes. By the

expression on her face, she knows who's upstairs waiting for me. I imagine him naked between the sheets, and I grow hot thinking about it. I hope my face isn't red.

Weston laughs, and before he can comment, considering he saw me arrive with Cash last night, I turn to him. "Shut up."

"Feisty little Texas girls," Weston says, but he keeps my secrets as he lifts the leather duffel over his shoulder.

Brody does the same, and they make their way toward the door.

"Don't be a stranger, either of you," I tell Easton and Lexi, and then I glance at Weston. "But that one can stay in New York."

He laughs as he grabs the knob to the front door. "Oh, come on. I didn't give you *that* hard of a time."

"Worse than my brothers," I say.

"Damn," Lexi quips, glancing at her man. "That's pretty bad."

Easton looks at Lexi like she's his whole world. It's what movie magic moments are made from, something Grace is obsessed with. But I get it now. I recognize the spark, but with them, it's an inferno.

My friend and I hold a silent conversation—the secrets we could share. One day, I hope to tell her everything.

Easton speaks up. "We should leave if we're going to make dinner tonight."

I follow them to the front of the house, and Easton holds out his hand to give me a handshake. I pull him into a hug. I like him a lot, and I can tell he has a kind heart.

"I'm sure it's known, but if you hurt my friend, I will chop off your balls."

"Great," he says, his crystal blue eyes meeting mine. "Her other friend has my cock. So, you two can have a party."

"It was Carlee," Lexi confirms.

"I knew I liked her." I nod, knowing it's one of Lexi's old

college friends. Carlee is good company and also grew up in Merryville, a Christmas town a few hours from Valentine.

"I'll see you soon," Lexi offers, and I pull her into a hug.

"He's mad about you," I whisper, wanting her to know I see it. Her past relationship messed her up, but it was clear Beau wasn't into her. With Easton, it's different. It's the real deal.

Their driver loads their suitcases, and they climb inside the SUV. And just like that, the Calloway entourage disappears into the distance.

I move inside the B&B, and the house is silent as I glance at the stairs. With a smile, I climb them and walk into the executive suite. The shower runs, and I push open the door to study Cash standing under the steamy stream.

"Join me," he says, and I shut the bathroom door and lock it. It's an immediate yes.

I strip out of my clothes and step in behind him. He turns around, his strong hands on my shoulders, massaging my sore muscles. Being with him like that last night was a full-body workout, but I fucked him in ways unimaginable, in positions I never thought were possible, on the bed, the floor, the desk, against the wall, and even the chair.

He gave me twenty-eight orgasms, with one to grow on. I'm already looking forward to my next birthday.

The hot stream washes over me, and his mouth magnetizes to mine. His soapy hands memorize the shape of my body. With light fingertips, he trails between my breasts, down my stomach, and then over my sensitive bud.

I let out a gasp, and Cash smirks, knowing I'm putty in his goddamn hands. This man can mold me however he likes.

"Remi?" I hear a deep voice ask on the other side of the door.

"Shit," I whisper, then clear my throat. "Yeah?"

Footsteps slide across the floor, and I immediately know who it is. So does Cash.

"Are you okay?"

My pussy clamps around Cash's finger when he dives inside of me.

"Yes," I state, shuttering.

"Did you stay here last night?" Beckett asks. I imagine him looking around the room, seeing the half-empty whiskey bottle on the desk, my birthday crown on the nightstand, and a bed with crumpled blankets.

Cash's brows raise as he tweaks one of my nipples.

"Yeah, Easton gave me a room, so I didn't have to go far after the party. Just showering. I'll be done soon," I say as Cash's finger slides between my wet folds.

"Hmm. Have you seen Cash?"

He smirks at me, waiting for me to speak—my *forbidden love.*

"Nope," I mutter, meeting his hazel eyes.

Cash mouths *fucking liar.*

"Hmm. His truck is at the clinic, but he's nowhere to be found," Beckett says. "I checked the property."

"I don't know. Maybe he went home with someone." Cash gives me two digits, moving his fingers slowly in, giving it to me deep. I grab onto his shoulders, steadying myself.

Beckett laughs. "Pfft."

"I went home with his little sister," he mutters in my ear.

His hot mouth is on me and he rolls circles on my clit. My eyes slam shut, and Cash covers my mouth with his hand just as I'm about to moan out.

"Shh. Shh," he says softly, humming against my neck. "Don't want him to know my fingers are buried inside of you."

With my back pressed against the shower wall, I give him full access to me. My body buzzes with anticipation. I race to the end, riding against his fingers, needing to come so damn bad nothing in the world matters. Just us, just him, just this moment.

"Have you noticed him acting *strange* lately?" Beckett asks.

I almost forgot he was fucking there. Go away, I want to scream.

I want to cry out with pleasure as Cash works my pussy so fucking good my knees nearly buckle.

"Remi?"

"He's always like that," I hurry and say. It takes every ounce of strength I have to keep my voice steady.

"Only when it comes to you," Cash whispers, capturing my nipple between his teeth and twirling it with his tongue as I thread my fingers through his damp hair. Knowing we could get caught has me so horny I'm about to explode.

"Hope you had a wonderful birthday," Beckett says.

"The best," I mutter as Cash touches my neck with soft fingertips, kissing my jaw. My mouth falls open, and he wraps his arm around me, holding me up as every muscle in my body tenses. He knows I'm teetering on edge and pumps his big fingers inside of me as he works my clit until my body crumbles and convulses. I sink my teeth into his shoulder, biting down, riding my release out on his fingers.

I can barely think. I can barely stand. No sound releasing from my throat is a miracle.

"You know you can tell me anything, right?" My brother's voice lowers. Is this my chance to be honest?

"Yeah," I say, with my head resting against Cash's shoulder. He holds me tight under the stream with his hand on my back, embracing me. "I'm in love," I whisper, but not loud enough for my brother to hear. Guilt and intense pleasure flood over me.

Beckett's cell phone rings. "Shit. I gotta go. It's Summer. Anyway, if you see Cash, tell him to text me."

"Okay," I say as footsteps move across the wooden floor.

A minute passes, and I pull away from Cash, meeting his sparkling eyes.

"My brother wants you to text him."

"*You're a bad fucking girl,*" he mumbles, tugging on my lip with his teeth. He tilts my chin upright. "You're addicted to the thrill of getting caught."

"Yes, but I'm more addicted to *you*." I'm still trying to return to planet Earth. My breasts rise and fall with every ragged inhale. I grab his cock, gliding up and down him, admiring his thick vein.

"You can't keep lying, Rem," he says, his tone serious.

"I know," I whisper, dropping to my knees. The stream splashes against my back as I cup his balls, tapping him against my tongue.

Cash clutches my hair. "If he knew I'm about to shove my cock to the back of your throat, he'd bust the door down."

"Am I worth it?" I grab his thigh, taking him in my greedy mouth.

"*Fuck yes.*"

CASH and I leave the B&B separately, playing it safe.

I give Cash a head start just in case Beckett is still wandering around the property. I think he's gone, though, because the barn looks desolate, and I don't hear music playing.

With my arms crossed, I watch Cash turn down the trail that leads along the property line to the clinic. I go upstairs and check the room one last time. My birthday crown is on the nightstand, and I grab it. I'll *never* look at this space the same way, not as I glance around, and replay all the places we were.

I strip the bed now, not wanting to leave any evidence behind, but I do the same for the rooms that Weston, Brody, and Easton stayed in. I'll have a head start for my shift tomorrow. Maybe Summer and I can leave early.

I carry everything downstairs to the laundry room, stuff the commercial-size washer full of sheets and blankets, and then start a load.

I sit on the metal table we use for folding and replay the entire weekend. The minute the clock struck midnight on my birthday, and Cash walked through the doors of the B&B, my world turned upside down in the very best way possible.

A smile sweeps across my lips as I lose myself in my thoughts, and then I text Cash, something I don't do often. It was too dangerous before, but that's changing.

REMI

Hi. Do you have plans for the Fourth of July?

CASH

Not yet.

REMI

Want to be my date for the celebration?

HE DOESN'T IMMEDIATELY text back.

Five minutes pass, and I second-guess myself.

REMI

If you don't want to, please don't feel pressured.

CASH

I'll be beside you wearing fucking bells, Rem. My answer is always yes when it involves being your date. Never doubt that. Sorry, I was chatting with Beckett.

I CHEW on my bottom lip and cross my legs, feeling exactly where he's been.

REMI

It's a date then :)

CASH

It is. I miss you already. Hurry up.

REMI

Thirty minutes max.

CASH

Too damn long.

ONCE THE SHEETS and blankets are finished, I throw them in the dryer. The pink bag with the naughty book is in the back seat of my car. Instead of going straight home to Cash, I drive to my parents' house. My little sister's car is gone, so only my folks are inside.

Vera works at the local nursery, which is the only reason the B&B has live flowers. Summer has a brown thumb and kills plants for a living.

I park behind my dad's truck and step onto the porch, saying a little prayer. I usually call or text to give a heads-up because I walked in on them once and never want to see that again.

When the door swings open, I'm relieved to see my mom on the couch crocheting with a lamp on while Dad watches some space-action movie on TV in his recliner. His feet are kicked up in the recliner, and his white socks poke out from his jeans.

"Pleasant surprise. How was your party?" Mom says.

"Great," I say, sitting in the chair across from them.

"I have to tell you both something," I say, knowing this is where I have to start.

"Are you pregnant?" My mother asks.

"What? *No*," I say, needing to tell them, wanting to claim him. "I'm dating Cash."

Dad doesn't take his eyes off the TV. "We know."

"What?"

"Are you hungover?" Mom laughs. "He visits us more than you do."

"*What?*" My voice raises an entire octave.

"We've been having coffee once a week since he came back in January," Dad says, crisscrossing his ankles in his recliner.

My eyes widen as I glance between them, and then I laugh. "You're joking."

Dad grabs the remote and pauses the TV, then flicks on the light. He gives me a dirty look. The screen is stopped on a battle scene in space. "No."

I try to find my words. "Okay, so Cash visits y'all weekly. What do you talk about?"

Mom drops her crocheting needles into her lap. "It's private. I won't lose my adopted son's trust because you're curious. If you want to know, you can ask him."

Dad points at Mom. "What she said."

"So, you're cool with this?" I ask, and it seems too easy.

Mom smiles. "Honey, *we're cool with it*. Cash is a wonderful young man. He's smart. Kind. Empathetic. But we want *you* to be happy."

I swallow hard and tuck my lips into my mouth. For years, I'd imagined this conversation going a hundred different ways, but the scenario never played out.

Maybe I'm the problem.

This is my goddamn wake-up call.

With my parents on board, Beckett cannot do or say shit.

My father's voice pulls me from my thoughts. "How do you feel about him?"

"I love him with all my heart," I say.

His expression softens, and he smiles. "I knew it. Don't break his heart, *Remington*. That's an order."

When he uses my full name, he's as serious as a rattlesnake. "Why would *I* be the one doing the heartbreaking?"

Mom narrows her eyes at me. "Because you're the only one who's hiding things."

"Beck—"

Dad holds up his hand. "Don't worry about him. This is about you."

"But—"

"Remington," Dad warns. "I won't listen to it. You're twenty-eight years old now, so it's time to act like an adult."

Mom clears her throat and grabs my attention. "Sweetie, are you joining us in the town square for the Fourth of July celebration?"

"I planned on it. Heard Emmett was smoking some brisket."

"He is. You should invite Cash to join us," she says with a smile.

"I already did," I say.

"Perfect." Mom has the look in her eye that Kinsley gets when she's scheming something. It's a Valentine thing that I will not mess with.

"We'll be there," I confirm. "Please don't make it weird."

"Sweetie, the only one who's being weird about this is *you*," she says when I hug her goodbye.

"You tried to hook me up with some other dude," I say, remembering what happened at Beckett's baby announcement party.

Mom grins. "I was testing you."

I shake my head. "That's so evil."

"Sometimes baby birds have to be pushed from nests to see if they will fly, honey. It was just a nudge, and well, it worked, didn't it?" She smirks.

I glance at Dad, and he shrugs. "Love you, Remi. But I really want to get back to my movie."

"Fine," I say.

"Good talk," Dad says. "Tell Cash I said hey."

"This is weird," I mutter as I walk toward the door, as the TV is unmuted. "Love y'all."

"Love you! Don't be late on the Fourth."

"I won't," I say, giving her a wave and closing the door behind me.

I stand on the porch with my hands on my head, staring at the fluffy clouds floating across the blue sky.

Cash has always been traditional to his core, so I shouldn't be shocked. This man has known what he's wanted since he returned, and I've been the only one hesitating. I laugh, bringing my hands to my hips.

Maybe this *will* work out after all.

CHAPTER TWENTY-ONE

CASH

As I sit on the couch and scroll through my phone, the door swings open, and Remi storms inside. She climbs on my lap, and I wrap my arms around her, laughing.

"Hello," I say as she grinds against me.

"Why didn't you tell me you hang out with my parents?"

I lift a brow at her. "Do you care?"

"No," she whispers against my mouth. "You've been drinking coffee with my dad since you came home?"

"Yeah. We have a good time."

"I'm jealous you spent more time with him than me." She laughs. "You're smooth as whiskey."

"If you only knew," I say.

She settles on my lap, creating just enough friction to have me growing hard beneath her.

"So, you gonna tell me what y'all discussed?"

"No," I confirm, digging my thumbs into her hips. "Cowboy's honor. A man doesn't mess with that."

She laughs against my mouth. "I can't believe this."

"Rem. They've known since the beginning," I admit.

She creates space between us so she can look directly into my eyes. "What?"

I tilt my head. "Oh, *come on, Rem.* We spent countless nights talking in the treehouse until the sun rose. Your mom would bring us plates of food when we hadn't stepped inside for hours. Your dad knew when I picked you up to go horseback riding with me, or all the times we met at the firepit. You're the only one who thought they weren't aware of us. The first time your parents asked me about us, I told them the truth. They *never* cared. Okay, well, your dad threatened my life once, but that's not here nor there."

She swallows hard. "I've...I've lied for *years.*"

"The truth *is* the best policy. When I was in Houston, I'd talk to your dad on FaceTime several times a month. We're closer than you think," I say, tucking hair behind her hair. "I'm not considered the eleventh Valentine for nothing. I love your parents like they're my own and couldn't lie when confronted. My word is my life, Rem. I'd rather someone hate the truth than love a lie."

"I understand," she whispers, petting my face. "Today, I told my dad I loved you."

I smile. "And were they shocked?"

"Not at all," she admits, resting her forehead against mine. "Wait, have you been playing matchmaker with my parents the entire time?"

"I'm going to tell them you said that," I say, laughing as her fingers tickle my sides. I wiggle away from her. "Your dad asked me not to give up on you."

Her eyes soften.

"Rem, he knows you're the love of my life. Do *you?*"

"Yes," she whispers, looking up at me with big eyes.

I admire how fucking pretty she is and kiss her slow and sweet. "I told your dad I was gonna marry you," I admit.

She inhales sharply. "Cash."

"When *you're* ready."

"And when will that be?" she asks, painting her mouth across mine. "How will you know?"

I twirl her hair in my fingers as she grinds against me. I'm thick and hard, needing her more than I want her. "There will be signs. There always are."

Remi removes her shorts and panties, and then she removes my jeans, taking all of me out. When my cock is free, she grins, swallowing hard. She straddles me, rubbing me between her slick folds as I wait at her entrance. Remi has control, and she eases down on me until our ends meet.

"Always so fucking needy," I mutter with my hands on her hips, pumping my hips upward as she slams down. It's intense as she takes me from the tip to the base, gasping with each thrust.

"Always so ready to please me," she whispers, racing to the end so desperately as she bounces up and down. "To fuck me. To love me. To own me."

I slide my hand up her throat, rubbing my thumb across her lip. She sucks on my thumb. "Are you already gonna come for me?"

"Come *with* me," she begs, our bodies slamming together, our moans of a symphony of pleasure. "*Please.*"

"Keep going," I whisper until our bodies tense. My eyes slam shut as we float into the abyss, collapsing together. We are nothing and everything at the same time.

FOUR DAYS LATER

Of course, I had an emergency call on a national holiday; it's how the cards *always* fall.

I'm used to it, though, and it's why I'm always prepared. After dealing with a lethargic horse at the Matthews' homestead, I go home and shower. Remi is used to me leaving for emergency calls and is always understanding. I just hate leaving her.

While it's inconvenient for me, accidents never happen at a good time for anyone. It's something I learned a long time ago.

After I'm dressed in shorts and a fishing shirt, I sit at the breakfast nook and flip open our book of confessions to the letter she wrote today.

My Valentine,

Do you remember what happened on the Fourth of July seven years ago?

I smile any time I think about us.

That night we watched each other from across the park instead of the fireworks, and it was fucking explosive.

I'd never looked at anyone who could take my breath away until I met you.

I'm honestly surprised we didn't get caught when I snuck off and met you in your truck.

I'll never forget how you tasted like cotton candy when you kissed me.

209

We drove away with the music blaring and the windows down.

My hair was blowing around, and you grabbed my hand.

You were safe. (Still are.)

I always felt protected. (Still do.)

You were a dream come true, and I couldn't believe you were looking at me like that.

Some days I still don't.

So, to answer your question, that's when I realized I was in love with you.

It happened fast, and I fell hard. It's still one of the most magical summers of my life.

This one wins, though.

After I realized how in love with you I was, I tried to downplay it.

Could the only man I'd ever given my entire self to be my one true love?

It seemed too good to be true, so I waited for the bottom to fall out, for us to argue, for you to replace me, and it never happened.

We were genuinely happy, and I wanted to spend forever with you.

It's funny knowing my parents knew the entire time.

No wonder my mom never believed Eric ever existed.

I'm sure I'll have a lot of explaining to do at some point.

I hope you're there to hear it all. If you were, they might go easier on me!

One reason I love you so deeply is because you're not selfish, and you understand me even when I don't understand myself.

A lot of my insecurities came from Beckett and Harrison, but also because it felt like we were in two different places in our lives.

It finally feels like we're on the same page. I hope it does for you, too.

It makes me wonder if Easton was right about love always being on time.

There is truth in that, and I'm ready.

Mama always said that we're given situations in life that we can handle.

I like to think we were brought back together because neither of us could survive without the other.

No matter what happens tonight, I'm choosing you.

Any time I see fireworks, it reminds me of us and how fucking explosive we were and are together.

I love you with every part of my body, heart, and soul.

You're mine, Valentine, and I will always be yours.

P.S. Please wear that baseball hat for me. I love it.

AFTER I CLOSE THE NOTEBOOK, I lean back in the chair, grinning with my arms folded across my chest. I've been writing back to her each night, so she reads mine before she starts her day. During my free time, I've been reading her old notes and how raw she opened herself for me.

Not sure what I did in a past life to deserve this one.

I slide on my flip-flops and walk into my bedroom, grabbing my hat on my dresser and pulling it down over my eyes. I've had it for decades. It's faded, ripped on the bill, but it's my old faithful. I slide a flask into my pocket and then head to the town square.

Five acres of land are used for special events, like the Fourth of July, the Fall Festival, and the holiday market. In the spring and afternoons, people will take their dogs to the park to play or sit on the lawn and read.

Music echoes off the building walls, and the sun fades in the distance. Pinks and oranges burst across the sky. Golden hour is upon us, and soon, the day will fade into darkness. Laughter and chatter grow louder as I pass the food trucks and carnival rides. Across the way, by the stage where the band will play tonight, is where the Valentine family always sets up.

My palms grow sweaty, not knowing what to expect. This is Remi's insecurity, and she has to work through it. I'll be beside her, supporting her and us every step of the way.

I'm just happy she's finally being honest with herself and everyone else.

It took a lot to get here, but I never gave up on her. I never fucking will.

CHAPTER TWENTY-TWO

REMI

I chat with Kinsley and Fenix as London's band sets up their equipment on the stage. Our little sister Vera is selling pinwheels and sparklers at the local plant nursery booth that's close to the entrance. I gave her a hug and said hello before I met up with the family. She's growing up.

I've barely seen her since she graduated high school last month, but I've also been working nights, so it doesn't surprise me much.

When London spots us staring, she waves and smiles as she adjusts the microphone on the stand and checks her guitar strap. She's wearing rhinestone boots, cut-off jeans, and a tank top. Her long brown hair is down in beach curls, but it's braided out of her face. Tonight, The Heartbreakers are the main entertainment for the celebration and will begin their set list in an hour.

My sister will be famous one day, winning awards and singing in packed stadiums. Her talent is like no other, but her drive is where she shines. At age five, she was playing piano and guitar, and our mom put her in singing lessons soon after. She's a natural.

I could *never*.

Hayden walks over wearing a Main Street Books t-shirt, and Kinsley immediately excuses herself, greeting him with kisses.

"Hey, y'all," Hayden offers, pulling Kinsley into him. They hold a silent conversation, and then he brings his attention back to us. "We're gonna grab a snow cone. Want anything?"

"Nah," I say, and Fenix shakes her head.

"You're missing out," Kinsley says, looping her fingers in his, and they walk away.

Fenix pulls a bottle of wine and two plastic cups from her purse. I chuckle. "You came prepared."

"It's gonna be a long night of seeing everyone with the love of their life," Fenix says. We used to be grumpy about love together. "How have things been with you?"

I meet her eyes and smile. "Amazing. And you?"

"Great," she says, removing the cork of the sweet red.

I know when she's lying.

Fenix has been different since she returned from college, giving up her barrel racing scholarship a year before graduation. She was a state champ, winning trophies, leveling up, and now she never rides. Beckett has begged her to train at his barn, but she's ignored every request.

However, she shouldn't. She's a better rider than Beckett and Harrison combined.

"You're not great," I say, calling it out because no one else is. The only people who kept me honest were my older siblings, so I'll do the same for her.

She pours a cup full and hands me one before doing the same to the other. "You're right, but what can we do about it? No pouting," she says, forcing a smile. "Cheers."

Something happened when she was in school, but she's given some bullshit reason that she was burnt out and tired of competing. I searched her name online because she was well known, and I found nothing. She doesn't need to ride for the college team to be successful. My sister can win championships on her own. It's why she was recruited and given hella scholarships.

"Will you ride again?" I ask, glancing at her.

"Will you?" she throws back.

"You know it hasn't been the same since Majesty." It's different. Her baby is still alive and well. But I know the only exercise her racing horse gets is when Harrison works him weekly. Otherwise, he'd be out of shape. My brother refuses to let that happen.

"Well, things haven't been the same for me, either," she admits. "I'm not ready."

"Will you ever be?" I ask.

"I don't know."

I pat her hand. But I also understand everything has an expiration date, especially the secrets we think we'll keep.

"Just tell me, was there someone?"

She ignores my question, pretending like I didn't ask. When I mention it, she never answers, and I hope one day she will. I've seen that look on my face because I wore that hollow mask for years.

I change the subject. "Anyway, thanks for the wine."

"Anytime," she says.

We sit on a blanket and pick petals from wildflowers like we did as kids. When I pluck the last one, I whisper, "He loves me."

Fenix laughs. "I think you're right about that."

I glance at her, but she's looking past me. Cash walks across the grass with his eyes locked on me. Warmth floods through me when I see he's wearing that hat just for me. Damn.

"Mm," I say out loud, not realizing.

"Oh wow, so that's where you are in this relationship," she says, bumping her body against mine. It's real happiness.

I blush. "I'm no longer hiding us."

"Finally," she whispers, giddy.

I lift a brow at her. "I'm fucking scared."

"Don't be," she hisses. "This is going to be *good*. About damn time."

"Cash," Mom says as soon as he's close. She sets down her metal cup full of lemonade, and I'm positive it's spiked. She and Kathy, Lexi's mom, have been at it all day, talking about everything under the damn sun.

Dad has had his nose stuck in a book since I arrived, ignoring the world. He loves reading those old Westerns, the ones with the real cowboys in them.

My eyes don't leave Cash's as he walks past me and goes straight to my mom and dad. I watch how they interact with one another and how they pull him into tight hugs. They've always acted like this, like he's already a part of the family, maybe because they knew he was my perfect match.

Everyone has been waiting for *me*.

"Did you know they've had coffee once a week since January?" I ask Fenix.

"Seriously?" she asks. "That's *sneaky*."

"I think our parents like him better than me," I admit with a smile.

"Me too," she adds.

Cash glances over at me, and my heart flutters.

Warmth floats in the air, along with unspoken words. Everything around us plays out in slow motions as his eyes slide up and down my body. I lick my lips, hoping he knows what he does to me.

"If you had denied him, I think I would've tried to shoot my shot," Fenix says, drinking her wine.

"Oh, I'm not letting that man go," I say, smiling.

"Don't," she tells me with another shoulder bump, then we chuckle.

This is love. This is happiness.

Beckett carries lawn chairs and an iced chest, and Summer is beside him chatting. Behind them, Harrison is twirling Grace around, singing something. Grace's head is thrown back as she laughs, and he steals kisses from her, then pretends to bite her neck like a vampire. They're adorable together, and my brother loves her so damn much. I think we always knew they'd be together, even if they pretended like they were just friends for way too long.

When I turn my head, Colt walks toward us, eating an ice cream cone. He's gotten a lot of sun since the last time I saw him. Once he's close, he sits on the blanket with me and Fenix.

"How's the house going?" I ask.

"Great," he says, licking the cone.

I look at my twin. "Keep it up, and I will post you doing that online."

Laughter erupts out of him. "Yeah, gonna make me a thirst trap like Emmett?"

"Gross," Fenix says, and I love we can be winos together, or at least until Haley arrives.

"What about me?" Emmett says from behind us. I smile up at him, not realizing he'd arrived.

"Little brother. You're a thirst *trap*," I say.

He laughs, knowing it, and then his expression shifts. If I didn't know better, I'd say he'd just fallen in love. I stand up to see who he's looking at and see Haley typing on her phone.

Seconds later, I get a text message.

HALEY

Is your brother literally eye fucking me right now?

I BURST out laughing and focus on him.

I'd say yes.

"ARE YOU EYE FUCKING MY FRIEND?" I ask him directly.

"Excuse me?" Emmett turns to me, his tattoos on full display. I see mountains, stars, and coyotes.

"I asked if you were eye fucking my friend."

"You have a problem with that?" he asks.

"I have a problem with your reputation. Don't be a fuck boy with her," I say. "Anyone else but Haley."

He narrows his eyes. "I'll keep that in mind."

"Emmett."

I don't like the smile that spreads over his lips.

"I'm serious," I warn.

"Emmett!" Mom says with Kathy next to her, and he nearly jumps out of his skin. "Come here."

When he walks away, I turn to Colt. "Was he always a dick like that?"

"Yes," Fenix answers. "He's always been like that."

"It's always the quiet ones," Haley says when she's close. "That's the ones you have to worry about."

My brother is zeroed in on her, and I shake my head at him.

"He's going to hurt you," I tell her.

"Good," she whispers and laughs. "I'll hurt him back."

My mouth falls open. "You're *serious*."

"I give more than I take, always. I'll *destroy* him." She takes her ChapStick from her tote bag and presses it against her plump lips as she glances his way. "He better watch his ass."

She turns back to me, and I no longer see the woman who was crying about being broken up with during our single-girl era. No, I see a woman who's searching for revenge against men.

"Well. My money is on her," Colt says, sitting back on his

elbow, glancing at me and Fenix. "Anyone want to take that bet?"

"Nope," I say, and Fenix shakes her head.

"Okay, so we're all betting on Haley. Got it." Colt finishes his ice cream and then turns his attention to me. "You should stop by and check out the house in about two weeks. I think it will be in a great place then. At this rate, I think I'll finish it by the end of the year."

"That's incredible," I say. "I thought you said twelve months."

"I'm highly motivated by progress," he admits. "It feels good to fix up the old place."

"Who are we missing?" Mom hollers, and I can smell the brisket.

"Sterling," Fenix answers, pulling her wine from her bag. "Want some wine?"

Colt makes a face at her. "It won't mix with my peach ice cream."

Haley sits down beside her and takes a cup. The three of them start a conversation about something, but I'm lost in watching Cash laughing and showing his perfect smile.

Randomly, his eyes flick in my direction, and I see a smirk on his lips. I get lost in memories of us, wishing he was next to me right now.

"I'll take some more," I say, and Fenix fills me up.

I grow giddy, which can only mean one thing: I'm heading down a dangerous road where my tongue is loose, and I have no fucks to give. "Uh-oh," I say.

"I feel it too," Fenix admits. "This stuff is solid, like moonshine. Thankfully, I have two more bottles."

"Fenix," I say.

"Liquid courage for tonight." She raises her glass, and Colt shakes his head.

The drummer of the first band warms up. After the microphone check and introductions, they start with a few patriotic songs. Soon, they move on to a few country, two-stepping favorites, classics everyone knows.

Moments later, I feel someone hovering over me. My eyes trail from his feet and shorts, up his teal-colored shirt, to Cash's eyes that look blue today.

"Dance with me," he says with a boyish grin.

"Me?" I ask, meeting his gaze with brows raised. I down the rest of my wine and hand Fenix the empty cup.

He holds out his hand, and I take it. Cash pulls me with more force than I expected, and I crash into his muscular chest. Butterflies flutter when he steadies me against him.

"Mm. You sure look good tonight, Valentine." His voice is in a low rasp, a growl almost, and he says it loud enough for me to hear.

"You do, too," I whisper, knowing my entire family is around us, but I tune them out.

"Nervous?" he asks, grinning, spinning me around.

"A little," I admit, but I'm loving this so damn much. I'm sure it's strange for anyone watching us, and it might seem like our relationship went from zero to one hundred. The truth is it took us years to get here.

"Don't be," he whispers in my ear. "All my give-a-fucks are on a road trip. I'm living in my delulu era with you. Join me. It's fun here." He urges me forward. The string lights hanging above light the dance floor, and he looks like a dream.

"Kiss me," I whisper, my eyes fluttering closed.

"Is that what you want?"

Our mouths hover an inch apart, and I wonder if he won't. Just as I feel him move forward to capture my lips, we're interrupted.

My eyes bolt open, and I glare at Beckett, who's standing too close for comfort.

"Sorry to cut in," my brother says, and I can hear his attitude.

I hate it when he gets like this. We can't have this confrontation right here. I don't want the attention.

With narrowed eyes, I glare at Beckett, and Cash creates space, realizing people are watching. The two of them hold a feral but silent conversation.

My heart races, and Cash speaks up as I open my mouth to say something. "I'll be back."

I watch him walk away.

Beckett takes my hand and we two-step around the dance floor.

"Why did you do that?"

"You have something to say to me?" He's being firm and direct, and I don't like it when he becomes that older asshole brother without apology. His tongue is sharp as a sword, and his words will cut through me.

"I–I–" I find it hard to look into his eyes. "I'm sorry."

"For *what?*"

I peel away from my brother. "Actually, I'm *not* sorry. I won't apologize."

"Excuse me?" As he glares at me, my blood pumps faster. "You should be."

"For what, exactly? What did I do wrong?"

He takes a step forward. "What *didn't* you do, Remi?"

"I know I should've told you sooner, Beckett. I'm in love with Cash. We're together."

"Oh, I knew that," Beckett says. "Took you seven years and five days to finally admit that to me and yourself."

"Wait, what do you mean you *knew?* You were counting?"

"Cash told me *years* ago. What took *you* so fucking long?"

"*What?*"

"He waited for you, and you nearly destroyed him."

CHAPTER TWENTY-THREE

CASH

As soon as I round the corner, Remi steps away from Beckett. He's shaking his head, and I imagine the conversation. Beckett has always had my back and was there for me when I wanted to give up.

She says something to him, then glances at me with sad eyes. This is enough.

I know what he's doing, and I don't need or want her to feel guilty.

I walk over and place my hand on Beckett's shoulder. "That's enough."

"You told him?" she asks.

"Beckett's my *best friend*, Remi. Since before you even existed."

"You expected him not to tell me?" Beckett accuses. "That's *fucked* up, sis. Really fucked up."

"I thought...you wouldn't *accept* us."

Beckett crosses his arm over his broad chest and shakes his head. "Cash is my best friend for a reason. Are you kidding me? I bet on you, Remi. Because you're stubborn and so damn wishy-washy, I owe him five *thousand* dollars!"

She bursts into laughter. "Wait, so you knew I gave Cash my virginity?"

"Uh," I mutter. "Beckett, I—"

"What the fuck did you say?" His voice is a roar, and his jaw clenches.

"Shit," Remi squeals as his fist rears back and slams into my face.

I stumble back, planting my feet and lifting my hands, ready to fight if he approaches. "I didn't know until *you* told me at breakfast."

"Eric wasn't *real?*" Beckett yells at Remi. "What is *wrong* with you?"

"Okay, so you didn't tell him everything. Noted," she says with a what-the-fuck expression on her face.

Beckett glares at me.

"I couldn't share *everything*," I explain. I respected Remi's need for privacy.

He's livid, and I can see it as he takes a step forward. Instead of cowering, I stand firm.

"I deserved the first hit," I say. "*Try* to punch me again, and I'll fucking lay you down flat without apology."

Harrison runs over and stands in front of Beckett. "Hey. What's up? No need to fight."

"Did you know Eric wasn't real? And that she slept with..." He glances at Remi but doesn't finish his sentence.

"Yes," Harrison says, patting his brother's shoulder. "I figured that out a long time ago. What did you expect? He's your goddamn friend."

Remi moves between her brothers and pulls Beckett to the side of the stage. "Can we talk?"

He breathes in deeply and goes with her.

A few minutes later, London Valentine steps to the microphone and introduces herself to the crowd, who isn't paying attention to us any longer. She waves at Harrison and me before her eyes slide over to Beckett and Remi. That showmanship smile doesn't falter.

"Hi, I'm London, and we're The Heartbreakers, giving you old and original music. Let's go!" she says and starts it off with Reba.

Harrison glances at me as I rub my hand across my jaw. "Beckett's still got that right hook," he says.

"Fucker. One more Valentine swings at me, and I'm dropping them to the ground first." I chuckle.

He laughs. "What do you think my sister's saying?"

"The truth." Remi glances at me. "Whether or not Beckett can handle it."

"I'm glad it's you," Harrison admits, holding out his hand. We exchange a firm handshake. It's acceptance, and I'll fucking take it with a smirk on my face.

Remi and Beckett hug one another, and then she turns toward me.

"Good luck," Harrison says, patting me on the back.

"I'll fucking need it."

Remi reaches out her hand, pulling me away from everyone. When we're alone, she places her hand where Beckett decked me. "That's the second punch you took for me."

"You're a hazard," I joke, resting my arm on her shoulder.

She lets out a sigh. "I kept you as a secret. You were my biggest lie."

"And I wanted the world to know about us. You were my truth, Rem," I admit.

She shakes her head. "I thought..."

"I wanted *you* to be sure about us. You had to be the one to choose me. My mind was already made." I brush my nose against hers.

"Thank you." Instead of pulling away, she wraps her arms around my neck and slides her tongue into my mouth. She jumps up and wraps her legs around me.

I brace her thigh and ass with my hands, holding her against me. "Thank you for choosing me."

"Is this one of the signs you've been searching for?" she whispers, pressing her forehead against mine.

"Yes," I tell her, and she laughs against my lips. "You're mine, Valentine. I'm gonna make it forever."

"I can't wait," she whispers, and I set her on her feet. A blush hits her cheek as I steal a kiss. "I love you."

"Love you." I lead her away. We're laughing, high on life and love and one another.

"I regret waiting so long," she says. "No more hiding you, *us*. Never again."

I nod, my body buzzing, drunk on her, as we walk hand in hand through the carnival area. It's dark, and the lights of the rides glitter and twinkle.

Remi stops walking. "You said you were worried about losing Beckett. I don't understand why'd you say that if he knew."

"I told him a long time ago that if I moved home to be with you and it didn't work out, I'd move away from Valentine forever," I admit. "I'd disappear and try to pretend like you never existed."

"*No*," Remi whispers, cupping my face in her hands.

"Beckett leased me the property to convince me to come home. It was a deal I couldn't refuse, and he knew that. He wants us both to be happy, Rem."

"He knew you loved me," she says.

"Yes," I nod. "The whole time."

"Cash." My name gets caught in the back of her throat. "I'm so damn sorry."

"Don't be, Valentine. I'd have waited a lifetime for you if I knew there was a damn chance."

Goose bumps trail over her skin. "It feels like you did."

"Y'all want on?" the attendant at the carousel horses asks.

"We don't have any tickets," Remi says with a laugh.

"So? Come on. It's on me," the guy tells us, waving us over.

Remi takes my hand and leads me through the metal gates. As I live the moment, it feels like a hazy dream when we step onto the ride with its glowing bulbs and country music.

Remi walks past a few kids, and we go around to the other side, where it's mostly empty. Once she chooses her pony, she climbs on the seat but keeps her legs hanging to one side.

When the ride starts, the horse goes up and down, and she leans over and steals my lips.

I rest my hand on her back, my thumb brushing the bare skin under her shirt, and the kiss deepens. Around and around we go, lips and tongue and teeth, with her hands massaging the base of my skull. She whimpers so lightly, loud enough for me to hear, and I do.

"Fuck, Rem," I whisper, tugging at her scalp.

She smiles, pulling away and glancing down at my shorts. I reach down and adjust myself. "I'd fuck you right here if it weren't for this audience."

"I know," she says, and I pull away, creating space, needing my cock to calm the hell down. As I lean against one of the decorated horses, I watch her watch me.

"Did you think it would turn out like this?" she asks.

"I knew it would," I say without hesitation. "*Eventually.*"

"Better than never, I guess," she says, grinning, but I see the fire burning behind her eyes.

It's the same one that's *always* been there.

CHAPTER TWENTY-FOUR

REMI

Our eyes lock, and when the carousel stops, he grabs my waist and helps me to my feet. When I meet his gaze everything around us fades away. I'm deeply in love with this man, and when he looks at me like this, there is no doubt about how he feels.

"I'm really fucked this time," I whisper, knowing he's my end game, too.

"Me too. No one else I'd rather be fucked with though," he says, taking my hand as a group of rowdy kids runs past us, laughing. One has a water gun.

I chuckle, nodding at the attendant as we move through the exit. Cash shakes his hand, and the guy stuffs a twenty dollar bill in his pocket.

When we walk away, Cash wraps his arm around my upper back, pulling me to him. He inhales my hair and kisses my head. I hold him around his waist as we stroll toward the center of the town square.

We're *being public* in public, and no one gives a fuck. This is how it should've always been and how it will go forward.

Relief and happiness flood through me, and I squeeze him

tighter, knowing we're flying free. He smiles, and his dimple sets my soul on fire as we cross the plush green grass. Most are waiting for the fireworks show on blankets and lawn chairs. Scents of sweet fried bread float through the air, and my thoughts sprint toward nostalgic memories. This man always intended to come back for me.

"What we had scared the shit out of me. I *wasn't* ready for you."

"Are you now?" he asks, his voice silky smooth.

"*Yes.*" A laugh catches in my throat because it's the truth. "So ready."

"Music to my fucking ears," he whispers as the first boom of fireworks spread above him in the sky. I watch his face light up in shiny blues and reds.

The crowd oohs and ahhs, and I take in the moment, glancing at him with stars in my eyes.

He smirks. "When you look at me like *that...*"

"Like I want you?" I ask, moving in front of him.

"Like you *have* me, Valentine," he says, his hand sliding across my cheek.

"Do I?"

"Absofuckinglutely. You always have." He cups my face, kissing me so intensely that I nearly forget to breathe. We're lost, and neither of us has a map as we navigate forward, soaring full speed ahead. The destination doesn't matter, just as long as we're together.

Glittery fireworks shimmer above, and we're teeth and tongue and pleasure. It quickly grows desperate, just like it does any time we're caught up in the moment. Right now, there is no difference other than not caring who sees us. I want everyone to know this man is mine and has been.

No more hiding.

When we pull away, I'm nearly gasping for air, trying to regain control but wanting to lose it all with him. I laugh against his lips with my fingertips lightly pressed against his cheek.

"Are you happy?" I ask, smiling.

"This is all I've *ever* wanted," he says, lightly painting his lips across mine, causing my heart to flutter.

We stop to watch the sky fill with shimmering colors as the fireworks crackle. Sparkles fall from the sky as my sister London sings her heart out in the distance. When the finale ends, I brush my nose against his, threatening to steal another kiss. I want to leave and end our night right here and right now.

"Cash? *Remi?*" I hear from beside me.

Vera smiles brightly, wearing neon green Ray-Bans on top of her head. Festive red, white, and blue stars are painted on her cheek. I remember what it was like to be eighteen and not have a care in the world.

"Did I miss something? The two of you are making out in public now?"

I glance at Cash, and we laugh. She does not know what's happening—I don't anymore, either.

"Are you *drunk?*" She questions with shock written on her face.

"No," I shake my head.

She holds out her arms. "Hello?"

"We're together. Remi's my girlfriend," Cash says, pulling me close and meeting my eyes. His claim makes me blush.

"*Girlfriend,*" I say, nodding, getting used to the word. It's foreign but oh, so right.

"Please tell me I'm the first one to know!" She's overly excited even if the gossip tea is ice cold.

Cash chuckles. "Not quite."

"I always find out everything *last*—the joys of being the youngest. Well, I've always liked you," she tells Cash, then glances at me. "He always brings donuts when he has coffee with Dad."

My eyes widen. "You *knew?*"

"Wait, you *didn't?*" she asks, confused.

Cash chuckles as a deep voice yells my sister's name from across the grass. She immediately scans the area and grins when she sees who called for her. "I gotta go. Congrats. If you run into Mom and Dad, you didn't see me, okay?"

"Who is that?"

"I gotta go." She hugs us and then jogs away, meeting her friend. I take a mental snapshot of the dark-haired guy who pulls her into a hug.

Cash twirls my hair around his finger, wielding my attention. "Let's get out of here."

"Reading my mind?"

"That would be *too* convenient." He grabs my hand, and our bodies are close as he walks in a protective stance.

We stroll through the crowd and cross the back of the area where everyone is dancing. As we sneak away, my gaze focuses on London strumming her guitar, entirely in her element. She's singing a Dolly Parton song, and when she spots me and Cash together, she smiles wide.

"Finally," she says, holding the guitar pick between her fingers and pointing at us. Then she hits a high note, not missing a beat. Pro fucking level.

A few heads turn in our direction, but no one knows who or what she was referring to, except me and Cash. When I glance at him, he beams, and I pull him away. The music fades in the distance, and people sprinkle the sidewalks, moving between the Fourth of July celebration and the public parking area.

"You got your keys?" he asks.

"Yeah."

As he holds out his palm, I remove the fob from my pocket.

"You know I don't let anyone drive my baby," I mutter as I dangle it above his hand, then drop them.

"I'm not anyone, Valentine. I'm your future husband." He opens the door for me. "I think you know that, though."

"Yes, I do," I say. My heart flutters when I climb into my car. He pushes the passenger door shut, and as I buckle, he slides onto the leather seat, climbs inside, and cranks the engine.

A smile meets his lips. "Fuck, this car is almost as sexy as you." Cash pushes in the clutch, reversing out of the parking lot.

"Where are we going?" I ask.

"To relive old memories," he says, hauling ass down the main drag until we're zooming out of town.

Seeing him with that hat on, driving my car like he owns *me*, makes me want to do unimaginable things to him, but I can wait a little longer. I roll down the window. My hair flies around, and he smiles with soft eyes. He doesn't have to tell me where we're going. My heart knows.

We get out of the car when he parks on the side of my parents' garage. As soon as I'm on my feet, he lifts and carries me into their backyard, only setting me down when we're at the base of the tree house.

"Haven't been here since *us*," I admit.

"Your mom told me," he says.

"Suppose she *was* paying attention." I look up at the boards nailed to the tree, checking each before putting my total weight on them as I climb. When I poke my head up through the floor and climb in, I glance around. The ceiling isn't high enough to fully stand, so I stay hunched over.

The glow-in-the-dark stars Harrison tacked on the ceiling when we were teenagers are still in place, even after all this time. A few strings of fairy lights hang above, and I reach over to click the button, and they come on. The room glows in a warm orange.

Immediately, I'm transported back to when Cash and I would drink and share secrets in the dark until we became each other's, or at least he became mine.

"I remember it being bigger in here," he says, pushing himself up with his muscular arms. His biceps bulge, and I can't help staring at him; he's mine, after all. I'm brought back to the night when I slid his fingers inside my panties, and I nearly begged him to touch me.

That summer, I wanted to give him my virginity, but he wanted to give me forever.

We move across the small space and sit beside each other with our backs and heads rested against the wall.

"That's how you were in my memory," he says.

I deviously grin as I unbutton and unzip my shorts. When his fingers brush across my clit, my hips buck upward, and I'm catapulted back to that night.

SEVEN YEARS AGO

We'd drank for hours in the tree house, sitting on old couch cushions and listening to country music while fireworks echoed in the distance.

"Two truths and a lie," I said, staring at his mouth.

"You first."

I searched for courage as the fairy lights strung above perfectly lit his face.

"Okay." I contemplated how far I'd go with this, but as the whiskey floated through my system, I didn't care. "I've never had an orgasm."

Cash's Adam's apple bobbed in his throat.

"I've sent texts to Beckett that were supposed to go to you. I've kissed a girl."

His mouth slightly parted. "One is a lie?"

I nodded, smiling.

"Is it awful that I hope the Beckett one is the lie?"

I laughed. "It's not."

"Rem," he whispered.

"It was a swimsuit photo."

His eyes widened.

"So, which is the lie?"

"The orgasm one?" he whispered.

I shook my head. "Sadly, it's a truth."

He studied me under the warm lights, and words teetered on the tip of his tongue.

"Will you touch me?" I whispered, inexperienced but needing this as desire swirled between my legs.

I'd never been so honest with anyone about what I wanted, especially not sexually. No man had ever been inside my panties before, but I wanted Cash there. He made me feel safe and beautiful, and I longed for him in ways I'd never known possible.

"Valentine," he whispered cautiously.

"Do you not want me?" I asked, happy for the courage, even if the alcohol was to blame. "If you don't, please tell me."

After our kiss on my birthday, I thought it was clear. Maybe I was wrong. Perhaps I imagined it.

"You think I don't want you?" Cash chuckled. "I fucking crave you, Remi."

I unzipped and unbuttoned my shorts and shimmied them off before peeling off my shirt. His eyes raked over the lavender bra and panties set I wore just for him. Hoping and wishing on stars that I could show him.

My breasts rose and fell as his eyes raked over my body.

"I want it to be you," I told him.

He searched my face. "Remi... are you a virgin?"

"No," I say, lying because I don't know anyone my age still carrying around their V-Card. It's embarrassing. "Just inexperienced."

"Okay," he whispered, his eyes trailing down my body. Cash had no reason to question further. He'd asked, and I lied. One day, I promised myself I'd tell him the truth.

"Rem, if we do this, you're mine."

"Until you leave," I said, meeting his eyes. "I want this. I want you," I urged.

Cash laid me back on the couch cushions. When his hands brushed over my body and then slid inside my panties, I saw stars. His mouth was on my neck and my lips as I whimpered, not understanding the sensation but wanting more of it. I'd never touched myself before, wanting my first time to be with someone.

I whispered his name as he gently touched my clit. He was gentle. His fingers fluttered against me like butterfly wings. "That feels really good."

Something was happening. I felt it swarming through my body and pooling in my core, and I needed him to keep going.

"Mm," he said as he kissed me. "Tonight, you'll be a good girl and come for me."

I didn't know what to expect.

"What if I can't?" I asked him, desperate for more of what he gave me as his fingertips brushed across me.

"You will," he promised, not rushing as he glided his down to my arousal, barely dipping inside of me, but I wanted to be filled with him.

"Your panties are drenched for me," he whispered. "It's so fucking hot."

"I'm always wet for you," I said, slamming my eyes closed as a moan escaped the back of my throat. It's an admission he should know, something I've kept to myself.

"Your body is building up to release," he explains as my muscles tighten. "Enjoy it, Valentine."

Whatever this is, I need it so fucking bad. I couldn't explain the build that happened deep inside as my body waited on the edge.

I nodded, not knowing what would happen when I finally let go of whatever held me back.

And then it happened. My pussy clenched and pulsated as he continued touching me, just a little faster. I moaned out, and he covered my mouth with his hand. "Don't want your parents knowing I just made their little girl come for the first time."

A mischievous grin filled his face as he kissed me. I wrapped my arms around his neck. "Will you have sex with me?"

I glanced down at his cock that bulged in his shorts.

"There's no taking this back," he warned. "Once this line is crossed..."

"I know." I slid out of my panties, begging him with my eyes. With my thighs squeezed together, I knew I was drenched. I wanted him to discover me in ways no one ever had.

He didn't deny me. He was a passionate lover and was so fucking careful with me, almost as if I'd break. That night, Cash Johnson became mine, and I knew I'd found the man I'd marry.

THE SILENCE DRAGS ON, and we're lost in thought, our fingers interlocked. One glance and my mouth is on his.

"I'm still very sorry for not telling you," I say.

He shakes his head. "You said you were inexperienced. I assumed you'd only had sex once, and it was awful since you never talked about it. That's why I was careful with you. I'm glad I was. If it were anyone else and you'd lied..."

With my eyes shut tight, I shake my head. "I know. It was stupid, but I knew you wouldn't hurt me. And you didn't," I whisper.

My skin is between his teeth as we remove our clothes. He kisses me, then enters with one deep thrust. He lets out a grunt buried inside of me, and I sigh with satisfaction as we make love. There is no time limit, no rushing. It's just us and our pleasure as he plunges into the depths of my soul.

"I knew that night I'd marry you," I admit, wanting more of him, not having to explain further.

"I knew, too," he admits, his forehead pressed against mine. He slams against me, and I cry out his name, knowing no one is home. I don't care if the whole damn world knows Cash Johnson is mine, not when the orgasm takes over and pulls us under. After we're satisfied, we dress and return our backs to the wall. I glance at Cash with swollen lips and disheveled hair, knowing I'm responsible. He looks past me toward the window of my childhood bedroom.

"Harrison and Grace watched us from right here," he says as my heart thrums. "The night of their wedding, they saw everything."

That night, we kissed like our lives depended on it and nearly had sex on that bed. My dress was hiked, and he hovered above me, wanting to please me, but a text from Beckett stopped us. It was enough to bring me back to the false reality I was hiding in.

"You *never* gave up on me," I whisper gratefully. I'd given him more than enough opportunities to walk away from me, replace me, and find someone else.

"I never will," he says, his promise in a low tone. His words drift through the quiet night.

CHAPTER TWENTY-FIVE

CASH

TWO WEEKS LATER

After adjusting the stirrups, I adjust my baseball hat, watching the black Mustang GT cruise down the driveway. Gravel crunches under the tires, and dust kicks up in the distance.

The car parks, and I meet her at the barn's entryway as her door closes. I loop my arm around her waist, and she glances at Apollo, a red Quarter horse I ride in my free time. He's saddled and tied to a post, standing in the late evening shade. Golden hour is approaching, and soon, it will be dark.

I adjust my baseball hat, trying to hide my excitement as she approaches me. Knowing she left work and came straight to me puts a damn smile on my face. The past two weeks have been a dream come true, being with her and openly loving her. No one even bats an eye.

"Surprise," I say.

Her eyes slide over my T-shirt, jeans, and running shoes.

"It reminds me of old times, with the hat and all." Her tone is nostalgic as she meets my gaze. I'll never forget the time we spent together.

When she's close, I brush my thumb across her cheek, enjoying the closeness as I kiss her. She tastes like chocolate, coffee, and desire. "I missed you. How was your day?"

"Perfect now," she admits. "I missed you, too. So much."

Remi worked the morning shift at the B&B, and I asked her to meet me at my parent's barn after her shift. I've been mucking stalls and oiling saddles all afternoon, waiting for her. Now that Melody and I are rotating emergency calls on the weekends, I've had zero interruptions. It's been nice, something I haven't experienced in far too long, and I can't wait to spend more time with my girl.

"Thought we could go for a ride and watch the sunset at the outlook," I tell her. This is how we used to escape the noise of everyone. "Before we go, I wanted to show you something."

I wrap my arm around her shoulder and lead her through the barn. It's an ample space because my father is a horse breeder. Sometimes, when she looks at me, I wonder if I'm stuck in a perpetual dream where she's mine. I never want to fucking wake up.

As soon as her eyes land on the foal trotting in the pasture after a butterfly, she awws.

"What a *cutie*," she says, looking over his light brown coat and dark mane.

"This is Dakota." I laugh. He's a show-off asshole and has tried to kick me a few times. When I'm done, he'll be the best damn horse in the state. Remi holds out her hand, and he curiously approaches her. Eventually, her finger brushes the tip of his nose and then tries to nibble on her hand before backing away. He trots and bounces on his feet like a puppy but then moves closer to her.

"Dakota, you're perfect," she says as he paws the ground.

I lean against the fence, watching her. "He's yours, Rem. Same bloodline as Majesty."

Her mouth falls open, and I can see the emotions pooling in her eyes.

"I tracked down his lineage and found this little jerk. He's eight months old and rowdy. But he has the same spirit, ya know. From what I remember," I say, holding her tight and wiping tears away from her cheeks.

"Why are you so good to me?" she whispers.

I place my hand on her shoulder. "I thought we could start our farm early. And maybe I could train him for you so you can start riding again. I know you gave it up and loved it."

"I don't deserve you." Remi wraps her arms around me.

"And that's where you're wrong, Valentine." I brush my nose against hers, kissing her.

When he whinnies, she laughs. He trots away, bucking and even farts. She snorts. "I can't believe he's mine. Thank you so much."

"You're welcome." I hook her finger with mine, then check the time, knowing the sun will be setting soon. "Ready to go?"

"Hell, yes," she says, and we return to Apollo. My hand is on the small of her back as her ponytail swings with each step. When we walk up, I untie the lead rope and climb on, sitting behind the saddle on the pad.

I look down at her, holding out my hand as she places a foot in the stirrup and correctly mounts. I scoot forward until my chest is against her back, grab the reins, and place soft kisses on her neck with my opposite arm wrapped around her stomach. "There's gonna be a lot more of me and you time, Rem. Weekends just for us."

"You promise?" she whispers as my hand glides up to her breast. My thumb gently grazes her nipple over the thin material of her shirt. She didn't wear a bra, and I'd guess she's pantiless too.

"You've got my word."

I click my mouth, giving Apollo a slight nudge. The trail leads to a lookout on the property, with the perfect open field for stargazing. My opposite hand rests on her upper thigh.

"When you touch me like that," she whispers as we travel into the woods. "It does things to me. Always has."

"I know," I say, whispering against her ear as leaves crunch below Apollo's hooves. Sunlight reflects through the branches, and I want to lose control with her. I kiss her shoulder and taste the summer breeze on her skin.

"All I can think about is having you," she says, repositioning herself on the saddle, and I notice how she rocks against the leather.

Carefully, I wrap my arm around her waist, sliding my hands between her folds. "Always wet for me."

She gasps, gripping my arm as I tease her greedy little clit while we ride. With her feet in the stirrups, she rocks against me, and I whisper in her ear. "My filthy fucking girl."

"Yes," she says, leaning her back against my chest and her head against my shoulder, giving me access to her ear and neck. Thankfully, Apollo continues down the trail with zero guidance.

"I want your fingers. Make me come, cowboy," she whispers, and I give her what she needs. A hiss releases from her as I work her perfect little pussy how she likes with two digits and plenty of clit play. Right before she comes, I pull away.

"Don't make me finish myself," she warns.

"You're so fucking greedy," I say, but I love to see it.

Not wanting to play any longer, I give her what she wants. She holds the saddle's horn and spills over, coming so hard I think she might collapse. Her guttural moans echo through the trees as I laugh against her ear.

"Mm, I love that for you. Did it feel as good as it looked?"

"Sure fucking did," she whispers.

I hold my arm around her stomach as we ride to the trail's

end. It opens into a clearing, and she gasps when Remi notices the firepit and air mattress I set up for us.

Apollo walks straight to the small pond and drinks. Then, I pull the reins over to the holding post. I slide off his back as Remi dismounts. After I tie Apollo, I start the fire, and we sit on the mattress, holding one another as the sun sets. Neither of us speaks as the sky grows dark. The wood pops and cracks as the flame licks up the side.

Remi moves toward me, painting her mouth across mine. "I love you. Thank you for this. Needed it bad."

I study her. "Love you, babe. Anytime."

Her eyes darken with desire. "Make love to me under the stars," she says, noticing the bulge in my jeans. "*Please.*"

"You never have to beg." I lay her onto her back, and I grin, climbing between her legs, settling there, pressing my hardness between her. "Well, maybe just a *little*," I say, smirking.

We're still clothed, but she rocks against me, creating just enough friction to drive me wild. She digs her heels into my ass, wrapping my arms around his neck. "Then *fuck* me."

I kiss and lick up her neck to her ear. "How about both?"

"God yes," she says, tugging my hair and gasping. "Oh, shooting star!"

"Make a wish," I tell her.

She meets my eyes and grins. "I made a good one."

"How good?"

"The *best*," she whispers.

I push off of her and stand, holding out my hand to her.

As I pull her to her feet, fireflies dance in the distance.

She laughs, her hair messy and her lips swollen. "What are we doing?"

Then I dig into my pocket and drop to one knee.

"*Cash.*"

I grab her hand, staring into her bright blue eyes, admiring just how fucking pretty she is as the warm summer breeze surrounds us.

"I've had this ring for you for seven years, Rem, waiting for the perfect time to do this. It's only ever been you and will only ever be you. I'm so fucking in love with you. I would've never given up on you, on us, and the future we could have together. We'll have a big house, a picket fence, and a tree house for us to make love in during the summers. There will be plenty of horses and countless love letters, but most of all, we'll be together. And to be honest, you're all I've ever wanted. Please make me the happiest man alive and be my forever, Valentine. Be my wife."

"Yes, yes," she whispers, her arms wrapping around my neck, and she pulls me onto the air mattress with her, pouring herself into every kiss we exchange. "I choose you, Cash."

We laugh, kiss, and cry as I slide the ring on her finger.

"You told me to tell you when my wish came true," I whisper against her mouth. "It just did."

"My fiancé," she whispers against my mouth.

"And soon my wife," I confirm. She lies on my chest, and I run my fingers through her hair, elated.

I place my hand under her chin, tilting her head upward. "You were made for me, Valentine."

"I was."

EPILOGUE

CASH

ONE MONTH LATER

"Damn," I say as Remi stands in the doorway of the dressing room. She's wearing a white dress that perfectly hugs her body. "Lookin' gorgeous tonight, Valentine."

She shuts the door, then crosses the room toward me with hungry eyes. It's the first time I've seen her since yesterday. It's been a long as fuck twenty-four hours.

"You're not supposed to be in here," I whisper, walking toward her wearing a smile. "It's a rule. The bride shouldn't see the groom before the wedding."

"I wanted to see you without a hundred people staring," she whispers. "And I don't give a shit about rules."

"My deviant girl." I burst into laughter, pulling her into my arms and kissing her. "Was it worth it?"

"You better believe it. You're handsome as hell in that tuxedo." She takes a step back. "I look forward to removing it from you later."

"Funny, because I do, too," I admit, looking forward to undressing her, too.

"I love you, Cash."

I laugh against her mouth as she leads and pushes me into the chair I use to retie my shoe. Remi crawls onto my lap, thrusting her hands through my hair as she grinds against me. Her ass is in my hands, and I'm ready to take her right here, the last time before we say I do.

"You're *so* fucking bad," I desperately say as she kisses along my jaw.

"Cash," she whispers just as the door swings open.

"Ahem."

Remi creates space, meeting my gaze with wide eyes. "Please tell me that's not Beckett," she whispers.

"Remington! What the fuck?" he raises his voice, crossing the room, and she climbs off of me. "Everyone is looking for you! Do you know how many people think we have a runaway bride situation out there?"

A howl of laughter releases from her as she moves to her feet. "Seriously? Why would anyone think that?"

He glares at her. "Because you're unpredictable and secretive as fuck."

She shrugs. "Okay, that's true."

"I was told to tell Cash you were fucking missing! Where is your phone?"

"Aww," I say, standing and adjusting myself. "I wouldn't have believed you."

I glance at my girl as she eye fucks me.

"What will I do with you two?" He glances between us but lets out a relieved sigh.

"You're gonna marry us," I say with a shrug. Beckett filled out the paperwork to become an officiant. Not only is he my best man and my best friend, but he'll also be conducting the ceremony tonight. There was no other way.

"Well." He looks between us. "Are you ready?"

"Hell, yeah," I say. Remi pulls me in for a kiss. "Before I forget and get shooed out of here, I wanted to give this to you," she says, handing me a letter.

I pull one from my pocket. She looks down at it and takes it from my hand. "Great minds."

"Love you," I say, stealing a kiss. "Can't wait to do this."

"I'm so ready," she says, leaving the room.

Then it's just me and Beckett.

He shakes his head. "Got kinda worried."

"Nah, she's not going anywhere. Would bet my life on that." I place my hand on his shoulder and squeeze. He's more nervous than me.

I've dreamed about it for far too long, and my body buzzes with excitement. "Is it time to go?"

He checks his watch and nods.

"Yes, it is." My best friend pulls me into a tight hug. "I'm glad it's you, brother."

"Fuck, me too. Give me a minute," I say. "I'll be right there."

Beckett leaves me to myself, and I unfold the letter and read.

My Valentine,

I can't believe we're getting married tonight.

I think Grace is a magician with wedding planning, or maybe she's more like a fairy godmother.

Either way, I'm thankful. That summer we spent time together, I dreamed about marrying you and what it'd be like.

It was something I replayed, but it was more of a fantasy back then.

Kinsley would call it a manifestation.

Call it whatever you want, but my dreams are playing out like a movie as I live them with you.

Does that make any sense?

Sometimes, I find it hard to describe how you make me feel.

It's why I gave you all of those letters, so maybe you'd understand and see how much I desperately missed you.

It was always supposed to be you, Cash.

You're my protector, my lover, and my soon-to-be husband.

Can you pinch me when you see me, before you kiss me again?

I just want to make sure it's real.

My biggest fear is it isn't, and I will wake up living my miserable life without you.

It's why sometimes I hold you a little tighter or kiss you deeper, just to make sure.

Thinking about us and how you look at me and our future together makes my heart beat faster.

I look forward to all the adventures we're going on. Because the risk of getting caught with you is still alive and burning.

You're my fantasy, my thrill, and my biggest fucking temptation.

I was made to be your wife, and I've never been so sure about anything.

Thank you for loving me in unimaginable ways, waiting for me, believing in us, and never ever keeping me a secret.

You give me honest love, Cash Johnson.

I'm your Valentine with all the xoxo's and look forward to forever sitting on your face.

Mm.

I bet you're thinking about it right now, aren't you?

I love you with my entire self. I'm ready for our forever.

—Your Valentine

.

.

P.S. Keep this to yourself. I have a good girl reputation to keep up.

I SMIRK, holding my composure as I imagine her naked, hovering above me.

She did that on purpose. I might need to get even with that one.

My alarm goes off, and I silence it, going to where Beckett waits for me.

In less than an hour, his little sister, the love of my entire damn life, will be my wife.

I can't fucking wait.

EPILOGUE

REMI

"What the fuck?" Fenix says when she passes me in the hallway. "What happened to your makeup?"

"Whoops," I tell her with swollen lips as she grabs my hand, leading me back to the bridal suite. "Did everyone really think I ran away?"

"Yeah. But everyone else is fucking stupid," she explains. "I told everyone you were with Cash."

"How'd you know?"

She glares at me. "Because you march to the beat of your own drum, Rem."

I smile. I guess I do.

When we're in the bridal room, she sits me in the makeup chair and reapplies powder to my face. She cleans up my matte lipstick and reapplies another layer to look fresh.

As she works her magic on me, I open the letter Cash gave me, and my eyes fly over the pages.

MY VALENTINE,

Can you believe we made it this far?

Or that you'd be my wife this year?

In my heart, I knew you'd somehow be my wife before New Year.

Kinsley guaranteed it.

I know she's woo, but I asked her to pull my tarot cards in January.

She predicted it all. Or at least it's a fun thought, thinking she did. Apparently, the cards don't lie.

I can tell you're in love with me by how you look at me every fucking day. It makes me so damn happy.

I've missed you and have hated knowing I wouldn't see you until our wedding day.

Traditions that keep me away from you are fucking stupid.

The last night we were together, you must've been tired from moving all day.

As soon as your pretty face hit the pillow, you were asleep.

Twenty minutes later, you were moaning my name in a dead sleep, and I was almost jealous of the dream version of me.

Then I remembered you're mine, always have been mine, and always will be mine. And, it makes

ME SMILE KNOWING I GET YOU IN YOUR REAL AND DREAM WORLD.

HOW DAMN LUCKY AM I TO HAVE YOU AS MINE?

MM. MINE. I LOVE THE THOUGHT OF THAT. DON'T YOU?

LAST WEEK, ONCE IT SPREAD AROUND TOWN THAT WE WERE ENGAGED, I WAS CONGRATULATED AT LEAST A THOUSAND TIMES.

OVER AND OVER, I HEARD HOW KIND AND SWEET YOU ARE.

WHILE I AGREE, I FIND IT HILARIOUS HOW EVERYONE THINKS YOU'RE INNOCENT, LIKE A DELICATE LITTLE FLOWER. IT MAKES ME SMIRK.

I'LL KEEP YOUR DIRTY LITTLE SECRETS, KNOWING WHAT'S ON YOUR MIND EACH TIME YOU LOOK AT ME.

IF YOU'RE SMILING RIGHT NOW, <u>YOU'RE A BAD FUCKING GIRL</u>.

I KNEW IT.

I'LL SPEND THE REST OF MY LIFE TRYING TO SATISFY YOU, BABE.

WE'RE GONNA HAVE SO MUCH DAMN FUN, VALENTINE.

BUT I SHOULD PROBABLY WRAP THIS UP BECAUSE I'M SURE YOU WERE GIVEN THIS RIGHT BEFORE WE SAY I DO.

FUCK, I CAN'T WAIT TO CALL YOU MY WIFE. CAN'T WAIT TO SEE YOU. THIS IS JUST THE BEGINNING.

I'M IN LOVE WITH YOU, REM.

YOUR MIND, YOUR BODY, YOUR SOUL, AND YOUR NEED TO BREAK EVERY FUCKING RULE IN THE BOOK.

IT'S ONE THING I LOVE MOST ABOUT YOU.

LOGICAL, BUT ALSO DEFIANT. YOU'RE THE WOMAN OF MY DREAMS THAT I GET TO WAKE UP TO EVERY DAMN DAY.

I LOOK FORWARD TO GROWING OLD WITH YOU. I LOVE YOU NOW AND FOREVER. YOU HAVE MY WORD.

I WILL ALWAYS CHOOSE YOU. THANK YOU FOR CHOOSING ME.

—YOUR VALENTINE, YOUR HUSBAND

"No, no, no," Fenix says as my emotions bubble. "No crying. Not even if it's for happy reasons."

She wags her finger at me.

"Okay." I laugh, opening my eyes wide, trying to hold back tears as she grabs a tissue and presses it in the corners.

"Are you good?" she asks.

"Yes," I nod as my sister stands behind me.

Our eyes meet in the mirror. "You're so pretty," she says.

"We look the same," I tell her, turning to face her. "You deserve to be happy, too."

"Remi," she whispers. "Please don't do this right now. It's your big day."

I give her a sad smile. "Promise you'll tell me what happened when you're ready."

"I promise," she says, forcing a grin. "Dad is waiting for you at the top of the stairs."

"Okay," I whisper, pulling my sister into a tight hug. "I love you, Nix."

"I love you, sis. I'm so damn happy for you. This is how it was always supposed to be."

I smile. "True love always finds a way."

A minute later, we walk down the hallway to the top of the stairs. The wedding party stands against the wall in front of me. Colt walks over and hugs me right before the music starts.

Dad glances over at me as I loop my arm in his. "You look pretty, honey."

"Thank you, Dad," I say, grinning as my heart flutters with exhilaration.

It all happens so fast. Grace places her hand on my shoulder, smiling at me when it's time for me to walk down the stairs. As soon as I take the first step forward, I see Cash patiently waiting with his hands folded in front of him. Our eyes lock, and I imagine our entire life together, nearly choking up by how damn beautiful the thought is. Everyone's attention is on me, but I only see him. I've only ever seen him.

As soon as I'm close enough to touch him, I have to kiss him. He laughs against my lips. "You're supposed to wait," he whispers.

"I don't care," I say.

Then Beckett pulls out a note card, and the ceremony begins. No one in the room exists, just us, and it feels like it's just us as we say our I do's. Cash pulls me into a kiss, and when I hum against him, I realize we're actually not alone. The whole town just watched me twist my tongue against his.

"I love you," I whisper to him, and he says it back as we're introduced as Dr. and Mrs. Cash Johnson.

"Always my Valentine," he whispers in my ear, then I steal a kiss.

I ROLL over to an empty bed and smell bacon frying. When I open my eyes, I almost don't recognize the room. As I glance at the tall windows, I remember where we are: in the house we're renting from Colt.

Since we didn't want to be tied to a rental agreement, my brother offered to rent his house to us on a monthly basis. He only asked that we give him notice before we leave, which we agreed to.

I glance down at the rings on my fingers, still tangled in the sheets, and smile. "He loves me."

Then, my bladder forces me out of bed. After my morning routine, I slide on one of Cash's University of Texas T-shirts and some pajama pants, then meet him in the kitchen. He's standing over the stove with a spatula, shirtless and smiling.

"Damn, Valentine," he mutters, and I move to him with my arms out. "My wife sure is lookin' gorgeous this morning."

My hands trace up his abs, and I capture his lips. "Good morning, hubby."

"How'd you sleep?"

"Perfect next to you."

He kisses my forehead, breaks away, and pours me a mug of coffee. I blow on it, take a tiny sip, and smile. After our wedding reception, we came home and stayed up too late, rolling between the sheets.

"I needed this caffeine," I say, happy our honeymoon is next week. I can't imagine being on a plane right now.

"I know," he says with a wink.

A knock pulls me away from Cash as he grabs the carton of eggs from the fridge.

"Who is here?" I ask.

He shrugs. "I'm not expecting anyone."

I pass boxes full of our stuff as I walk toward the front door. It's barely past eight in the morning.

When I open the door, Colt stands on the porch, grinning. "Good morning, *sunshine*. Did you have fun last night?"

He's way too chipper for this early in the morning. I'm still in my pajamas and have barely sipped coffee. It's not officially autumn, but we got a cold front last night, and it's chilly, especially in this drafty house. I groan.

"Are you going to invite me in?" he asks.

"No," I tell him, and he kicks his foot forward before the knob can latch closed.

"I'm coming in," he says. "Sorry to bother the newlyweds, but Mom told me to tell you that dinner is at their house on Wednesday."

"You came here to tell me that?" I ask.

"Yep, and to share with you that I think I might've figured out what happened with Fenix."

I cross my arms and tilt my head at him. "Seriously?"

"Yeah, it had to do with—"

There's another knock at the door, and the three of us look at one another.

"Hello?"

I see someone press their face against the glass, but it's frosted, so they'll never see inside.

"Answer it," Colt says, helping himself into the kitchen. He grabs a mug as I move to the front door. It's too early for this.

I swing open the door, and a woman with dark hair and bright green eyes stands on my porch. She looks at me from head to toe. "Oh. I'm sorry."

"Hi, can I help you?"

She takes a step back, noticing I'm in my pajamas. "I saw this house was for rent. I'm searching for..."

LYRA PARISH

She pulls her phone from her pocket. "Colt Valentine."

"Oh. Um. One second."

I go inside and glare at my brother. "A gorgeous woman is searching for *you.*"

He laughs. "I'm not falling for that."

"I'm serious."

Cash glances at me with brows raised.

"I'm telling the truth." I sigh, then return to her. She gives me a small smile. "Would you like to come in?"

She looks around nervously. "Uh. Sure?"

I step to the side, letting her enter. "Now, who are you searching for?"

She scans the room, and her eyes lock on my brother. "Are you Colt Valentine?"

He drops the coffee mug, and it shatters across the floor. "Darlin', I'll be anyone you want me to be."

THE END

Want to know more about Colt Valentine
and the mystery woman who will *probably* steal his heart?
Continue their story in FIXING TO BE MINE:
https://bit.ly/fixingtobemine

Cash & Remi
Bonus Scene

R emi glances out the window of the Mustang as I drive to her parent's house. A mischievous smile plays on her lips, one I fucking love to see. We've officially been married for three days, and each morning, I can't believe she's my wife.

Actually, yes; yes, I fucking can.

I'd wished and daydreamed about having, protecting, and loving her just like this.

Remi bites the corner of her lip and rests her hand on my thigh as if she can read my mind.

"You've gotta stop looking at me like *that*," I say, glancing over.

Her eyes sparkle with anticipation.

"Hm?" she innocently asks with big doe-eyes. "Like what exactly? Explain it to me."

"You're *already* starting shit." I shake my head because she's purposefully playing dumb.

"I'm not starting *anything*. Technically, you started shit *before* we left," she says, licking her lips as she glances down at my mouth.

"It was one tiny kiss," I say with a laugh.

She scoffs.

"One kiss with your fingers in my panties," Remi murmurs as she slides the tiny skirt she's wearing up her thighs.

"You know we can't be late. Your mom gets pissed, and we'll have to do the dishes for fifteen people. That's a small army," I explain, but she already knows how this works. It's been a rule since Beckett moved out at age eighteen.

"I'm *not* arguing." She glides her hands over her white panties and continues, "You're right. We can't be the last ones there. If you pulled over and we fucked in the back seat, we'd be late. And we can't have that, can we?"

"Goddammit," I muttered, wanting to watch her but keeping my focus on the road's curves.

"Mm," she says, continuing to tease herself and me.

"*Remington,*" I growl her name.

"*Cash,*" she whispers with want and need, and it makes my dick grow thick. She knows what she does to me. This woman has had me wrapped around her finger for seven years, which will never change.

"Fuck it," I say, seeing the driveway to the old house Colt is remodeling.

I turn onto the gravel road, kicking up dust in my wake. The Mustang tires spin out, and I grip the wheel, taking complete control. When we're closer to the house with peeling paint, I glance around, searching for her twin brother's truck. No one is here.

To be safe, I park behind the house so no one can see her car from the highway.

Then the engine is off, her mouth is on mine, and she crawls closer to me. Our tongues twist together, and as she tries to climb on my lap, her ass presses against the horn. She jumps and laughs. "This ain't gonna work."

"You're right." I glance at the Mustang's back seat and then at her. I'm too tall, but we could make it work if we had to.

"Come on," she tells me, getting out of the car, then she walks across the grass to the back of the house and waves me on.

I can't say no. "You know, we always said this house was haunted."

"I guess the ghosts are getting a show." Remi grabs my hand and leads me up the back porch steps.

She wiggles the doorknob, and it's unlocked. Before stepping in, she glances back at me.

"We shouldn't do this," I say, trying to be the logical one.

"Which is why we absolutely should," she says, pushing open the door.

We enter, and I don't know what I expected to see, but it wasn't an almost remodeled first floor.

I'm shocked.

There's still a lot of work to be done, but Colt has worked hard over the last two months.

Remi's mouth falls open as we give ourselves a mini tour. Outside, it looks like it's falling apart; inside, it's like a brand-new house. He's removed several walls, creating an open concept between the living room and kitchen. The dry walls need paint, and there are no lighting fixtures, but he's accomplished a lot. This place will be beautiful when he's finished.

She pulls me into the primary bedroom and pushes me against the door.

"Are we really doing this here?" I ask with a brow raised as she rubs her hand over my cock..

A smile touches her lips as she unzips my jeans and falls to her knees. "You better believe it."

"We don't have much time," I tell her. Truthfully, I don't give a shit. We can arrive at her parent's house with swollen lips and messy hair, and I'd give zero fucks about it.

"I know," she says, dropping to her knees and placing me in her mouth. My head leans against the door, and my lips part as she cups my balls in her hand.

"Damn. That feels so good," I say, fisting my fingers through her hair. Once I'm rock fucking hard, she takes me in her hand and strokes while sucking.

Before I get too lost in the sensation, I hear footsteps walking through the house.

"Remi?" A deep voice says. It's Colt.

Her eyes widen, and she removes my cock from her hot mouth.

"Shit. Shit. Hide," she says, moving us both to the closet.

I grab her tight and try my best to hold back laughter. We're like teenagers afraid of getting caught.

"Sis?" Colt says louder, which means he's closer. "I'm about to go to our folk's place, and I know they're just waiting for me and you to arrive. Everyone else is already there. You know what that means, don't you?"

"*Bastard*," she whispers as footsteps move through the room.

The bathroom door creaks, and then his footsteps pick back up.

"You're going to have fun washing all those damn dishes," he whispers, and the bedroom door closes.

"We should leave and beat him to my parents just to make him eat his words."

I hold back a chuckle. "Let's do it," I say, sliding my lips against hers.

"I want a rain check first thing when we get home."

"Deal," I say. When we pull away, I adjust my cock.

Remi cracks open the door, and we sneak through the back door and jog around the house.

She slides into the driver's side and adjusts the seat.

"Hurry," she says as I buckle.

She cranks the car and steps on the gas. Gravel kicks up, and as we pass, Colt stands on the porch with both fingers in the air.

She laughs. "Had we not taken that damn tour."

"Sometimes it's good to wait for it, you know. The anticipation."

My girl chuckles. "I've had seven years of anticipation. That's long enough. You make me greedy."

"Mm. I fucking love to hear it," I say, and once we're on the main road, putting her car into 5th gear, she interlocks her fingers with mine. I lift her knuckles to my mouth and kiss her skin.

"I love you," she says.

"I love you, Valentine."

She smiles, and then her eyes flick to the rearview mirror. "Shit, he's behind us and is speeding up."

As I turn to look behind us, I see his headlights on, and he's hauling ass in his jacked-up RAM truck.

"I hope you're ready to run," she tells me, turning into her parent's driveway. "As soon as we park, we haul ass to the house. Got it?"

I chuckle. "I will never understand the Valentine's need to compete."

"My parents created this."

"See, this is why I told you we should arrive an hour early like Kinsley encouraged."

Remi puts the car in park, and we jump out, sprinting down the driveway. Colt gets out of his truck and runs at full speed.

"Fuck, he's fast," I say, pushing harder. We skip up the steps as he hops over the porch railing. I open the door and jog down the hallway with Remi behind me. When I step into the dining room, I stop. Remi slams into me.

"Cheater!" Colt yells from the doorway, snapping it shut.

We laugh as we catch our breaths. Beckett and Summer

wave at us. I smile at Hayden and Kinsley. Beside her are Fenix and Emmett, and on the other side are London, Vera, and Sterling. Harrison and Grace sit at the opposite end, talking close and kissing. I smile because I'm happy for them.

I'm happy for me, too. I squeeze Remi's hand a little tighter.

Fuck, I'm so happy to be here with *my wife*.

When they notice us, her brothers and sisters speak simultaneously, greeting us.

Mrs. Valentine enters carrying a pan of lasagna, and Mr. Valentine follows behind with another. Once a month, she requires the family to get together and break bread. A family who eats together stays together. It became a thing when Beckett first moved out and has continued throughout the years as everyone has grown up.

Their mom has always been a stickler for time, so she created a rule for those who no longer lived at home: whoever arrived last must do the dishes for the *entire* family. It's to encourage everyone to show up on time, and as more of them moved out, it turned into a competition. They'll even set someone up and arrive hours early. Glad it wasn't like that today.

We take seats by Grace and Harrison.

Colt enters and shakes his head. "I'm so gonna get you for that, Remi."

She smirks, grabs the pitcher of tea, and fills our glasses. "Lookin' forward to it."

"Are you excited about your honeymoon?" Summer asks, grinning between us.

"Yes. Can't wait," I say. Since we planned the wedding on a whim, it took some rearranging of my schedule to take off. Melody is covering the clinic from Friday to next Sunday. It will be the first vacation I've had in seven years, and I'll spend it with my Valentine.

Remi's smile widens. "Salem in September. I've been

watching tons of videos online about it. I'm so excited to try the clam chowder."

"I'm jealous!" Kinsley singsongs. "Salem is one of my bucket list places to visit."

"I'll get you a souvenir," Remi says.

"Better get me one, too," Fenix tells her.

Remi raises her hand. "Everyone will get something."

Laughter fills in, and their parents sit. "Alright. There's plenty of food, y'all. Let's dig in before it gets cold."

I glance around the table, being treated like the eleventh Valentine kid, just as I always have. They've been my second family for as long as I can remember, and knowing it's official warms my heart. Remi places her hand on my thigh and squeezes me, and we have a silent conversation.

I whisper I love you and she whispers it back.

"This is weird," Beckett says, shaking his head.

We laugh.

"You'll get used to it," I say.

"Nah, I don't think we will," Harrison adds.

"You will," Mr. Valentine states at the head of the table. He gives me a nod and a grin as we put large squares of homemade lasagna on our plates. A basket full of hot, garlic-twisted breadsticks is passed around the table. Remi snags us each one and then passes it to Colt.

London is telling everyone about all the performances her band has lined up for the rest of the year. She's excited, smiling wide.

"I need to talk to you," Colt says to Remi in a lowered voice as everyone listens to where she's traveling.

Remi squeezes my leg, and I can't help but smile. This woman is my wife, my forever partner, and I couldn't be happier being the man sitting next to her.

I'm living my dream.

BONUS CHAPTER 2

REMI

I meet my brother's eyes. "Is everything okay?"

"Yeah, I think so. I want to run some things by you. Can we meet for lunch?"

"Are you paying?"

Cash chuckles and shakes his head. My hand is still on his thigh, and he rests his hand on top of mine.

"Yes, I'll pay. And you can order cake to-go," Colt says.

"That's a deal," I tell him. "What day?"

"Are you free Thursday around eleven?" he asks, tearing a piece of bread from the stick and popping it into his mouth.

"Yeah, I can leave. I'll be there," I confirm. No one is paying attention to us except for Cash.

My mom asks Summer about the pregnancy, and they talk about babies. Then Kinsley chats about where she is with the wedding. Each of my siblings gives an update on their life, and I glance around, happy that everyone is doing well. When Fenix chats, she stays focused on her schoolwork. "I think I'm gonna start a body butter business," she says.

"Or you could work with us," Beckett tells her. "You'd be fantastic. We could use you, Nix."

"No," Fenix says, keeping her tone neutral. "I'm good. I finished my degree."

I meet Harrison's eyes, and he sighs. They've asked her hundreds of times, but she's consistently declined.

No one knows what happened, and when Colt was telling me a few days ago, we were interrupted by that woman at the door. I must remember to ask him when we eat lunch in a few days.

After eating, Cash and I take our dishes to the kitchen and rinse them off so he can wash them more easily. Then I meet his eyes. "Ready to leave?"

"You want to leave early?"

I smirk and let out a fake yawn. "I'm *exhausted.*"

He leans in and whispers in my ear. "You mean *horny.*"

When he pulls away, I grab his shirt and move him back toward me. "You know it, hubby."

He grins. "I love it when you claim me."

"Shit, me too." I take his hand and lead him into the living room, where almost everyone is. "Well, this was great. I'm super tired. I have to be up early because my boss likes to schedule me for the early morning shift."

Summer snickers.

Mom stands up and hugs me and then gives one to Cash. "Make sure y'all come see us before you leave on that honeymoon."

"We will," Cash says with a nod, and we wave at everyone as we head toward the door.

When we walk outside, I move forward, capturing his lips. His hands are fisted in my hair. "I'm so ready to be home," Cash whispers.

"Me too," I say, brushing my nose against his. "You're addicting. I need you right now."

"You are, too," he says. "You always have been. Let's get the hell outta here."

I hand him the keys, and we approach the car.

Cash gets us home in record time, hugging the curves.

"See, you're starting shit again," he says when we park at the house we're renting. I exit the car, and Cash lifts me into his arms.

"Was just admiring what's mine," I admit, wrapping my arms around his neck as he takes the steps up the porch. He sets me down as he unlocks the door, and as soon as we're inside, I take off my clothes as he removes his. By the time we make it to the bedroom, we're naked, our mouths connect, and we fall onto the bed.

"I can never get enough of you," he admits as I reach down and grab him. He's thick for me, and I don't want to wait to have him inside of me. I push him on his back, straddling him. His hands are on my hips as I slide onto him, falling over to kiss him and running my fingers through his hair.

We're pants, and desire, and moans. We're insatiable love. This man is my everything, the love of my life, the person I was meant to always be with. He growls out my name as I rock my hips, taking him from tip to base.

"You feel so good," I groan out.

"You do," he hisses as we greedily race to the cliff's edge. We're still base jumping together, but this time, we have parachutes. Our movements slow, and when his thumb grazes against my clit, I shudder.

"So close," I whisper, nearly collapsing on his chest as the build intensifies.

Cash takes my face between his hands, meeting my eyes, bucking his hips upward. "You gonna come for me like a good girl?"

"*Yes, yes,*" I mutter as he continues. And then it's like I was pushed off the top of a mountain, and I free fall, losing myself with his thick cock buried deep inside of me.

With his strength, he easily flips me onto my back, slamming into me until I see stars, allowing me to ride out my orgasm as he crumbles above me.

We're breathless, and as the scruff on his face grazes across my neck, I know I'll never get enough of him, my husband.

His soft lips kiss the softness of my skin, causing goose bumps to form. My ear lobe is in his mouth, and he whispers, "My Valentine."

"You're mine," I say with a sigh and a smile.

"Always have been, always will be," he confirms, and knowing that we're finally living our happily ever after fills me with joy. This is just the beginning of us. There is so much more to come.

After we clean up, he holds me in his arms. My head rests against his chest, and I hear his steady heartbeat.

"Colt wants me to meet him for lunch on Thursday," I say.

"I know," he tells me. "What do you think he wants to talk about?"

"I'm not sure," I say. "Maybe Fenix. Maybe that woman who showed up on Sunday."

I sit up and meet his eyes. "I think it was love at first sight."

Cash laughs. "I believe it. I felt the same way when we reconnected that day in Grinding Beans."

"Really?"

He nods. "Love at first sight."

I smile and kiss him. "Cupid had my back."

"Or maybe he had mine."

THE END

KEEP IN TOUCH

Want to stay up to date with all things Lyra Parish? Join her newsletter! You'll get special access to cover reveals, teasers, and giveaways.

lyraparish.com/newsletter

Let's be friends on social media:
🤍https://tiktok.com/@lyraparish
🤍 https://www.instagram.com/lyraparish
🤍 https://facebook.com/lyraparishauthor

ACKNOWLEDGMENTS

Here we are again! Here we effin' go! I wanted to start this off by saying **THANK YOU**.

Thank you for giving my words a chance and choosing me. I have THE best readers in the world. I'm honored that you picked up Smooth as Whiskey when you have so many other incredible books to choose from. I know I say that a lot, but I mean it from the bottom of my heart. As long as you keep showing up for me, I will show up for you. I respect you and your time, and I can never thank you enough. I don't take for granted that I get to do this because of you.

A super huge thank you to my advanced readers. Your excitement ALWAYS pumps me up! Thank you, thank you!

Thank you to my literary team who constantly shows up for me. Big thank you to Bookinit! Designs for creating a cover that I'm so obsessed with that I can barely handle it!

Thanks to Beth Hudson and Crystal Burnette for squeezing me into your editing and proofing schedule. Special thanks to The Author Agency PR for continuing to tell me YES and being so incredibly happy to help me. Your communication skills are what dreams are made from. Big shout out to my executive assistant and friend, Meg Latorre, for helping me juggle all these balls. (LOL, that's what she said!) I might write all the words, but it takes a village to publish them, and I'm so appreciative!

Thank you to Thorunn Kristjansdottir (@thehappilyev-erafter_blog) for reading this book early and giving me invaluable feedback that I needed. The book is stronger because of you. I appreciate your insight so much!

Big thank you to Rachel Brookes (read her books!) and Kelsey Uhlik (@Midnight.Reads.With.Kels) for also reading early and being so excited for Cash and Remi. You're both the best cheerleaders and I'm so lucky to have you!

Thank you to JS Cooper for the endless encouragement and excitement! I'm honored to call you a friend and to have someone so incredibly prolific by my side. Magic is happening!

Big thanks to my 4thewords friends and everyone who has joined me in the Night Owl Writing Lounge, especially Jackie, Alexis, KJ, and Red. Without you, I wouldn't be able to write all these words after midnight.

As always, I'll end this with a thank you to my hubby, Will Young (@deepskydude). He's the only one who really knows the struggles I go through when I write and believes in me when I don't. You're *my* Valentine.

ABOUT LYRA PARISH

Lyra Parish is a hopeless romantic obsessed with writing spicy Hallmark-like romances. When she isn't immersed in fictional worlds, you can find her pretending to be a Vanlifer with her hubby. Lyra's a Virgo who loves coffee, the great outdoors, authentic people, and living her best life.

Made in USA - Kendallville, IN
30089_9781961229587
12.10.2024 2107